# MAGGIE CHRISTENSEN

# Waves of Change in Pelican Crossing

# Dedication

To Jim, my soulmate of over forty years

**Also by Maggie Christensen**


*Oregon Coast Series*
The Sand Dollar
The Dreamcatcher
Madeline House


*Sunshine Coast books*
A Brahminy Sunrise
Champagne for Breakfast


*Sydney Collection*
Band of Gold
Broken Threads
Isobel's Promise
A Model Wife


*Scottish Collection*
The Good Sister
Isobel's Promise
A Single Woman


*Granite Springs*
The Life She Deserves
The Life She Chooses
The Life She Wants
The Life She Finds

The Life She Imagines
A Granite Springs Christmas
The Life She Creates
The Life She Regrets
The Life She Dreams


A Mother's Story


*Bellbird Bay*
Summer in Bellbird Bay
Coming Home to Bellbird Bay
Starting Over in Bellbird Bay
Christmas in Bellbird Bay
Finding Refuge in Bellbird Bay
Escape to Bellbird Bay
Second Chances in Bellbird Bay
Celebrations in Bellbird Bay
Happy Ever After in Bellbird Bay


*Pelican Crossing*
The Restaurant in Pelican Crossing
Secrets in Pelican Crossing
A New Dawn in Pelican Crossing
A Christmas Surprise in Pelican Crossing
Safe Harbour in Pelican Crossing

# One

Olivia Grace gazed down at the familiar landscape, her lips curling into a smile. She would soon be home, home to Pelican Crossing, back in the small coastal town where she'd grown up and where her two children had been born.

She'd been in England, staying with her daughter, Nancy, her planned visit of a few months for the birth of her third grandchild extending to almost a year. But while it had been special to be with her daughter for Shannon's birth, and she loved Nancy and her granddaughters so much, her life wasn't there in the busy town in the south of England where the narrow streets and tall buildings made her feel claustrophobic and long for the clear skies, the scent of the ocean and the sand between her toes.

Now Christmas was over, she couldn't wait to be back home, back in her little cottage, to resume her position as counsellor in the local medical centre, to see all her friends again, and her son, Dylan.

When she'd left, Dylan had been based in North Queensland, picking up work on various yachts as positions became available, seemingly unable to settle to anything permanent. It was only a few months earlier he'd called to say he was back in Pelican Crossing. Rory, a good mate of his, had been attacked by a shark when, coincidentally, the yacht Dylan had been working on was docked in Cairns. He'd rushed back to see him and decided to stay, taking on his mate's job at *Pelican Marine*. It would be good to see him again. Dylan had always been a sensitive soul, and Livvy suspected he and Rory had been more than friends before he'd left home several years earlier.

The seat belt sign came on, and the aircraft began its descent. Livvy peered out the window, her sense of excitement building. Dylan had promised to meet her, to drive her home, and her best friend, Erica, had promised to buy in enough basic food to keep her going for a few days. She couldn't wait to see Erica again too. While Livvy had been gone, her friend's life had undergone a huge change, and she was now living with her childhood sweetheart a few doors along from Livvy's own cottage. She'd heard all about it on calls and emails, but there was nothing quite like hearing the news firsthand over a cup of tea or a glass of wine.

With a slight bump, the plane landed and taxied along the runway, then everyone was getting to their feet to collect their belongings from the overhead lockers. They were here!

As soon as she stepped into the terminal, Livvy saw a grinning Dylan walking towards her. He'd changed since she last saw him, his face more tanned, his shoulders broader, his manner more confident. But he was still the little boy who used to run after her, pulling on her skirts and demanding her attention, always would be.

'Mum!' He pulled Livvy into a warm hug, almost lifting her off her feet, and she inhaled the scent of the sea that had always been part of him since he first set foot on a boat. She'd known then that Pelican Crossing would never hold him back, but always hoped he'd finally decide to settle down and come home to live.

'It's so good to see you, honey. Let me get a good look at you.' Livvy pulled away to peer at her son. His face, in addition to being tanned, had developed a web of lines around the eyes and there was the hint of a beard on his cheeks and chin. But the blond hair she remembered was just the same, albeit a tad longer and a few shades lighter due to his outdoor lifestyle, and it still fell over his forehead the way it always had.

In a habitual gesture, Dylan raised a hand to push it back. 'We should get going. Your luggage?'

'Oh!' Livvy realised that while she had been staring at her son, the other passengers had disappeared to the luggage carousel. She and Dylan followed and were soon on their way out to the parking lot.

'This is yours?' she asked, when Dylan stopped beside a bright red Landcruiser. *Had he bought himself a car?* He'd always refused to engage in what he called the trappings of consumerism, which included owning a car. *If he'd bought one now, did it mean he intended to stay?* Livvy's heart leapt at the prospect of having him back home for good.

'It's Rory's. He's still in rehab so he asked me to keep it running for him. It's a good car. Might think of getting one myself if things work out.'

'Mmm.' Livvy knew better than to ask what he meant, but presumed he meant things between him and Rory. *So, she'd been right*. She hoped they did. Rory was a nice boy, not such a boy now, though. Both he and Dylan were close to thirty. It was time they settled down. The boys had grown up together, spent their teenage years messing about in boats, encouraged by Rory's dad, Jamie, who came from fishing stock and now owned a fishing charter and boat hire business. It was Jamie Whittaker who Livvy's friend, Erica, was now living with. Livvy could remember when they were all teenagers together – her, Erica Harris and Rhana Black who now bred spaniels on her property outside town.

'How's Nancy?' Dylan asked when they were driving up the coast. 'She has three now, doesn't she?'

Livvy gave her son a sceptical look. *Did he really not know?* 'Three lovely girls. She's well, and busy, but she seems to cope. You should keep in touch more. She *is* your sister.'

'Yeah, but you can keep me up to date on her news.' Dylan threw her the lopsided grin which always won her over.

'And what about you? What are your plans? You said you're working Rory's job while he's recovering.'

'Yeah. *Pelican Marine*. It's not bad. A lot of paperwork, but I do get to work on the boats from time to time. Cam's a good boss,' he said, referring to Cam Mitchell who owned *Pelican Marine* and managed the Pelican Crossing marina.

Although tempted to ask more about what Dylan intended to do once Rory had recovered, Livvy knew her son too well to probe, so satisfied herself with enjoying the rest of the trip and making plans for picking up her own life again.

To Livvy's disappointment, Dylan carried her bags inside, hugged her then left, claiming he had to get back to work. Erica had promised to call round, but she was working today too. Livvy wandered around the cottage, her eyes feasting on all the familiar objects, noting a few differences, sniffing an unfamiliar scent. It was only natural a few things would have changed. Erica had stayed here for a few months while Livvy was gone. Of course she would have left her mark.

It didn't take Livvy long to get everything back the way she liked it. She made herself a cup of the herbal tea she preferred and took it out to the courtyard to soak in the pleasure of being back home. But the sense of delight and relaxation she'd anticipated didn't happen. She had forgotten what it was like to be alone, had become accustomed to the noise and bustle of her daughter's house. Here, there was only her and the birds with their familiar cackling and squawking.

Livvy had never felt this way before. She had always enjoyed the company of others, whether it be the wild swimmers she met each morning at dawn, the members of her book club, her neighbours or the other friends she met for coffee. Now, for the first time, she took stock of her life and didn't like what she saw. It occurred to her that, while Rhana was still single and likely to remain so, three of her other good friends had found partners and were making new lives for themselves. Now it looked as if Dylan might be about to do the same with Rory. A chill ran down her spine at the realisation she was alone and facing the prospect of growing old by herself.

For her entire career, Livvy had counselled others on how to overcome their challenges. Now it might be time to work on herself. Was it too late for her to find her happy ever after like her friends?

# Two

Dan loved the beach in Pelican Crossing at this time of day, the morning sun glistening on the waves. Although it was early, there were already several people in the water, despite the fact the dog beach wasn't patrolled. As he strolled along the edge of the ocean, his grey-muzzled labrador at his heel, he congratulated himself on his decision to move to this small Queensland coastal town four years earlier. Now, instead of the hum of traffic, there was the roar of the waves and the squawk of the seagulls, and, instead of the stench of car fumes, the salty scent of the ocean.

It suited Kim too, though at first his daughter had rebelled against the move, wanting to stay in the house where she'd grown up, in the suburb where all her friends lived. But the house in the busy Sydney suburb held too many memories for Dan. He needed to get away, hence his choice of a sea change, something as far removed from his old life as possible.

To his enormous relief, his daughter had settled in well, making new friends and discovering the delights of living so close to the beach. But now she was in her final year at school she'd be off to university soon, and while Dan didn't want to stand in her way, he knew he'd miss her dreadfully, only hoping she'd choose one close to home. For the past four years it had just been the two of them and they'd become closer than most daughters and their dads.

Picking up a stick, Dan threw it into the water, laughing as the old dog swam after it. Cooper had been with him since Kim was in primary school and was suffering from old age. He enjoyed living in Pelican Crossing too, even if he was never going to catch one of the pelicans they often came across on their walks.

Back home, Dan fixed breakfast for himself – it being school holidays, Kim was still asleep – and took the bowl of muesli topped with strawberries and yoghurt out into the sunny yard. Even at this time in the morning, the Queensland sun had a bite to it. It was going to be another scorcher.

An hour later, Dan was driving to the outskirts of town to where the old red sandstone building was glistening in the sun. Parking in his usual spot, he got out of the car and stopped for a moment in front of the large sign which read, *Pelican Crossing Wellness Centre*. He'd done it! Here, in this small coastal Queensland town he'd fulfilled his long-held dream. A wellness centre, a place where like-minded advocates of natural therapies could come together to practice.

It had taken him four years to establish, and there were still a few empty suites, but it was well on its way and was proving popular. Purchasing the building from the Catholic Church had been the first step and not without its challenges. Then there had been the two years of renovation turning what had been a school into premises suitable for the range of therapists he hoped to attract. Meanwhile, he'd managed to establish his own physiotherapy practice, setting up a clinic in his garage, not ideal but it had been a start, and he'd gained some loyal clients. It was a far cry from the busy four-man practice he'd belonged to back in Sydney.

Sometimes those days in the southern city seemed like another lifetime, others like a bad dream. When he and Cheryl had married, he'd thought he'd won the lottery, amazed that out of all the men she could have chosen, this beautiful woman picked him. At first, things were good as they built a life together, first in a tiny apartment in the inner city, then a house north of the harbour.

Cheryl was already pregnant with Kim when she'd started cheating on him, tearfully promising each time that it was the last. After Kim's birth she did seem to change, spending more time with him and their daughter. Then it all began again, the lies, the secret phone calls, the evenings out with *friends*. He should have left her then, would have if it hadn't been for the auburn-haired little bundle who'd stolen his heart. He stayed because of Kim, and because he knew it was unlikely a court would give him custody, but promised himself that one day...

But that day never came. By the time Kim started high school, he and Cheryl had stopped pretending to have a happy marriage. They stayed together for their daughter, sleeping in separate bedrooms and living separate lives. It was time. Kim was old enough to understand that the fact her parents no longer loved each other didn't mean they didn't love her. Dan planned to leave. Then Cheryl became sick, and it was too late.

The next few years were a nightmare as Dan cared for his terminally ill wife, only leaving the house to go to the clinic where he was working reduced hours. Cheryl needed him as she never had before, and he supposed they became closer as he tended to her needs. He and Kim became closer too, united in their concern for Cheryl's welfare.

When she died, Dan was saddened, but the loss he felt was of a close friend, not of the woman he loved. That love had gone much earlier. Kim was devastated. She had loved her mother dearly and took the loss hard. He guessed that was one of the reasons she'd been so loath to leave Sydney. It was not only leaving her home, school and friends but leaving the last link with her mother. Dan, on the other hand, couldn't wait to get away from the memories in the house he and Cheryl had shared.

He didn't often think of the past, preferring to concentrate on the present and the future. It was Kim's birthday tomorrow. His little girl was turning eighteen and he planned to take her out to dinner to celebrate, then she intended to have a beach party with her friends the following evening. She was growing up too quickly. She would soon be heading off to university, making her own way in life. She wasn't his little girl anymore.

Dan sighed and pushed open the door, ready for whatever the day had in store.

# Three

Livvy stretched luxuriously. It was lovely to wake up in her own bed again, a pair of kookaburras cackling outside confirming she was back in Australia. It had been wonderful to catch up with Erica last night and to see her looking so happy. After what she'd been through, it was amazing how her friend had managed to make a fresh start, and she seemed happy with Jamie, filled with excitement about how they planned to renovate his cottage.

It had been late when the pair finally hugged goodnight, but to her surprise, Livvy felt wide awake. She jumped out of bed and into the shower, delighted to be able to pull on a sundress instead of the layers of woollens she'd been forced to wear at her daughter's. January in Queensland was much more to her taste than the one she'd left in England.

Taking a cup of lemon and ginger tea and her breakfast of toast spread with mashed banana out to the courtyard, Livvy mentally listed what she wanted to do that day. First, and most importantly, she needed to visit the medical centre where she'd been a counsellor for the past twenty years. She'd informed them of her return but wanted to check everything was in place for her to pick up her clients.

Livvy had never meant to stay in England for so long, but it had been so lovely to spend time with Nancy and the girls... then it was summer, and summer in Wiltshire was a delight, so different from what she was used to. It was only when the weather turned cold again that she began to hanker for home, to miss the hot days and warm nights, the smell of the sea and the scent of the gum trees in her backyard, even the loud squawking of the cockatoos which liked to destroy her banksia.

But she'd agreed when Nancy begged her to stay till after Christmas, and the sight of her granddaughters' faces on Christmas morning had made it all worthwhile. If only Nancy and her husband would move to Australia. He and Nancy had met when he was on a working holiday in Australia, spending several months on a sugar cane farm outside Pelican Crossing. They'd met and fallen in love, and she'd followed him back to England. Livvy sighed, wishing she could wave a magic wand and bring them out here. At least they'd promised to think about it. She could only hope.

The ringing of her phone brought Livvy back to the present and the realisation of how much time had passed while she was thinking about her daughter. Seeing Rhana's number, she answered the call. 'How are you? I saw Erica last night and she tells me she's bought one of your pups.'

'She wanted company, but I think she found that anyway,' Rhana chuckled. 'I'm good. What about you? If you're not too jetlagged, am I going to see you out here? I won't be able to get into town for a bit as I have another bitch due to give birth any day now.'

Livvy laughed. Rhana would never change. She'd always loved animals, so it had been no surprise when she'd bought an acreage and set up her kennels, seeming to prefer the company of her dogs to humans. But she always had time for Livvy, and now Erica was back, for her too. The three had been inseparable at school, until Erica left to study nursing and never returned, choosing instead to marry and move to Perth in Western Australia. But now the three could get together again.

After a short chat and promising to visit as soon as she was able, Livvy ended the call and went inside. A few minutes later she was on her way to town, excited at the prospect of getting back to work.

*

'What?' Livvy stared at the dark-haired woman sitting opposite. Her friend, Liz, was the practice manager in the medical centre and looked as devastated as Livvy felt. 'She can't do that… can she?' she asked, her heart sinking. How could her partner, the woman she'd trusted, have acted in such an underhand manner?

'It seems she has. I'm so sorry. None of us knew what was going on. I knew your practice was behind with the rent but… I'm so sorry, Livvy.' She put a hand on Livvy's arm to comfort her.

'It's not your fault, Liz. You weren't to know. I should have realised Ingrid wasn't to be trusted. What about Cath?' She'd counted herself lucky that the retired counsellor who'd acted as a locum while she was away had been happy to remain in the position for such a long time.

'She's gone. To be honest I think she was glad to leave. Ingrid made things uncomfortable for her.'

Livvy took a deep breath. She was still trying to come to terms with what Liz had told her. Her counselling practice, the one she'd built up over the past twenty years, no longer belonged to her. Somehow, while she'd been gone, Ingrid, the woman she'd trusted, had allowed it to get into debt, closed it, set up her own practice with the client list she and Livvy had shared, then paid off the debts of the old practice. Livvy's immediate instinct was to confront her former partner, tell her what she thought of her, but common sense prevailed. She needed to speak to a lawyer.

*

Livvy's head was reeling as she made her way out of the medical centre. She felt completely disorientated, as if the ground had been swept from under her. Her whole life's work was gone. Blinking to keep away the tears, she made it along the street till she came to *Books and Coffee*. The combined bookshop and café had proven a solace to her on many occasions in the past and right now it looked like a familiar sanctuary when everything else had turned to ashes.

'Welcome back!' The cheerful voice stopped Livvy in her tracks. Lou, who owned the business and ran the bookshop was a good friend, also a neighbour.

'Thanks, Lou.' Livvy's stress must have been obvious in her voice, because Lou's eyes filled with concern. She walked over to her.

'Everything all right?'

Her kind words brought forth the tears Livvy had been trying to staunch. 'Oh, Lou!'

'Let's get you a cup of coffee,' Lou said. 'Zoe, can you take over here?' she called to her assistant before guiding Livvy to the café section of the shop and to a small round table. Then she went to order their coffee from one of the young men who ran the café. Ron and Denny were known for their delicious coffee and cakes as well as their amusing repartee. Livvy was glad Lou was placing the order. She wasn't sure how she'd have coped with one of Ron's quips today.

'Thanks, Lou,' Livvy said, taking her first sip of the delicious coffee she remembered. 'Oh, this tastes so good. I've missed Ron's coffee.'

'Now, what's up? It's not like you to give way to tears.'

'It's my practice. It's gone!'

'How can it be gone? Your counselling service is still running in the medical centre. Ingrid was in only last week talking about how busy she was.'

Livvy felt a spurt of anger. 'She might well be, but not with our practice. While I was gone, it appears Ingrid closed the business we shared and set one up in her own name.'

Lou's eyes widened. 'The conniving bitch! How could she do that?'

'I'm not sure. I still have to discover exactly how she managed it. I need to talk to a lawyer. I plan to go to see Gill, but I needed a coffee first. I didn't want to turn up in her office like this.' She gestured to her red eyes.

'You're friends, aren't you? Can't you see her out of office hours?'

'I suppose.' Livvy knew she wasn't thinking straight. Gill practiced family, not commercial, law. But it would be a start and maybe she would have some ideas of what Livvy could do, or could recommend someone who could help.

She looked across at Lou, seeing the concern on her face. She wasn't alone. She had friends, friends who would stand by her. But this wasn't how she'd expected her first day home to turn out.

*

Gill's office was in a building close to the medical centre, bringing back the hurt of Ingrid's treachery. Livvy averted her eyes from what was now her former workplace and pushed open the thick wooden door beside which was an impressive metal plate listing the four solicitors who shared the premises.

'Can I help you?' a gentle voice asked.

'I wondered if I could see Gill Dickson. I don't have an appointment. I'm a friend.' Livvy held her breath. Perhaps Lou had been right, and she should have tried to see Gill outside business hours. But she couldn't wait.

'She has a pretty full schedule. Let me check with her. Your name?'

'Livvy, Livvy Grace.' Livvy stood waiting impatiently, drumming her fingers on the reception desk.

'If you'd like to take a seat?'

'Sure.' Livvy sat down, her left foot tapping on the floor. It seemed to take for ever but was only a few minutes before a smart young woman appeared.

'I'm Josie, Gill's PA. She can give you a few minutes.'

'Thanks.' Heaving a sigh of relief, Livvy followed the young woman into an office where Gill was seated behind a desk. She rose when she saw Livvy and came round to give her a hug.

'I heard you were back,' she said. 'Something the matter?'

'Oh, Gill! I don't know what to do.' Livvy broke down, the tears running down her cheeks. 'Sorry.' She sniffed as Gill handed her a tissue. 'Thanks.'

'What on earth's the matter?' Gill asked.

'I know you don't do commercial law, but I hope you can at least tell me my rights. It's like this…' Livvy proceeded to describe to Gill what Ingrid had done, finishing with, 'Is what she's done even legal?' She was hoping Gill might say it wasn't and that she could sue her former partner, though she couldn't bear the thought of protracted legal proceedings.

Gill's forehead creased. 'I'd have to check with one of my colleagues, but from what you've described, I suspect she's acted within the law.'

'But…'

'She certainly hasn't acted ethically, but that's not against the law. You had no inkling she might try to oust you?'

'Not a whisper. It was my practice to begin with. Then, as it became too much for one person, I took Ingrid on to assist, made her a partner, added her name to the business. I thought we had a good relationship.' She grimaced.

'I see people every day who thought exactly that,' Gill said, 'and they are married to the other party.'

'Hmm.' At least Livvy wasn't in that position. She and her ex-husband had split amicably over fifteen years earlier. Chris had remarried and had a new family. They exchanged cards at Christmas, and he kept in touch with Nancy and Dylan, but they all led their own lives.

Gill checked her watch. 'I'm sorry I can't be more helpful, and I have another appointment now, but let me check it out for you and why don't you come to dinner with Joe and me tomorrow evening. You do know we've moved into the cottage at the end of your row?'

'I didn't. You'll like it there. It's a lovely place to live.' *But how long would Livvy be able to keep her cottage? With no clients, she had no income. Her small savings wouldn't last for ever.* Her eyes filled with tears.

# Four

It had been a busy day for Dan, many locals having tried to do too much over the festive season were now feeling the result of their over exertion and presenting with back pain. This was in addition to his regular set of clients.

The day had started well. Kim had arrived at the breakfast table bleary-eyed to receive his birthday hug and traditional rendering of an off-key version of *Happy Birthday*. She'd curled her legs under her on one of the kitchen chairs and proceeded to scroll through the birthday greetings on her phone, smiling and chuckling from time to time. *Whatever happened to birthday cards?* Then she'd shot up and dashed off saying she had to shower and dress as she was meeting friends for breakfast.

'Don't forget dinner tonight,' Dan had called after her.

'As if…' she shot back with a grin. 'I'm looking forward to drinking champagne.'

In honour of the event, Dan had booked a table at *Crossings*, Pelican Crossing's premier restaurant. It had started life as a fish shop and, after various reincarnations, had now developed a reputation which brought tourists from all over Australia. Poppy Taylor, the owner, was well-known in the town. It had been she and her late husband who had completed the last renovation, but sadly he had died in a tragic accident just as it was about to open. Dan had heard the story soon after he arrived in town and had enjoyed the delicious food there on several occasions, the last being on Melbourne Cup Day the previous year when the restaurant put on a special luncheon.

Dan hummed to himself as he stepped out of the shower, scarcely able to believe his little girl was eighteen. Wrapping a towel around himself, he rifled through his wardrobe, finally settling on a pair of beige chinos and a short-sleeved pale green shirt emblazoned with a hibiscus pattern. It was one he knew Kim loved, telling him the shade of green matched his eyes. Back in the bathroom, he pulled a brush through his thick hair. He wasn't a vain man, but was pleased the dark blond showed no sign of grey. He still looked younger than his fifty-four years.

'Wow, Dad. Looking sharp!'

'Thanks, sweetie. You're looking lovely as usual.' Kim was wearing an off-the-shoulder turquoise dress he hadn't seen before, which set off her auburn hair to perfection, and a pair of white high-heeled sandals. Around her neck, a pearl drop which had belonged to her mother hung on a silver chain which matched her earrings. Unlike him, she looked older than her years.

'Thanks, Dad.' She gave him a hug, taking care not to spoil her makeup. 'I just wish Mum was here.' Her eyes moistened.

Dan felt a pang of guilt that he wasn't able to feel the same. 'She'd have been proud of you,' he said, his voice breaking despite himself, 'and she wouldn't want you to be sad on your birthday. Ready to go?'

'Sure.' Kim nodded and slung her bag over her shoulder.

The restaurant looked as inviting as Dan remembered. The door and windows of the hundred-year-old, two-storey building were painted in a shade of blue that gleamed in the light from the moon and stars which were particularly bright that night, and twists of bougainvillea adorned the wrought iron balconies on the upper level. Inside, they were greeted by a hum of conversation and a welcoming smile from a smart young woman dressed in black who led them to their table and handed them menus.

Scanning the menu, Dan immediately ordered the champagne Kim had requested and continued to peruse the meals on offer. Kim did too, finally deciding on the Hervey Bay half-shell scallops followed by char-grilled eye fillet with fat rosemary chips and asparagus. Dan chose the same.

When the champagne was served, Dan raised his glass. 'Happy birthday, sweetie,' he said.

'Thanks, Dad.' Kim took a sip from her glass, giggling as the bubbles went up her nose. 'This is really special, makes me feel so grown up.'

'You are... both special and grown up.' Dan still couldn't believe his baby girl was eighteen, even though she looked more like twenty-one in the outfit she'd chosen to wear. Although she was only now of a legal age to drink, he was sure this wasn't her first taste of alcohol. He remembered his own teenage years, how he and his mates had started sneaking cans of beer when they were only fifteen, thinking their parents didn't know what they were up to.

During the meal, which lived up to his expectations, Dan and his daughter reminisced about past birthdays, with Kim becoming melancholy and saying, 'It would be perfect if Mum was here,' before cheering up again at the sight of her dessert, a warm, dark chocolate brownie with white chocolate mousse and vanilla bean ice cream.

Dan waited till she had finished, and they'd been served coffee before saying, 'This is for you.' He handed her a package wrapped in gold paper and tied with a ribbon – he'd asked the receptionist at the clinic to help him with this.

'Oh, thanks, Dad.' Kim's eyes glowed.

'You didn't think I'd forgotten?'

'No... but when you didn't give me anything at breakfast...' She grinned and tore the wrapping apart to reveal a small white box. Glancing up at him, she opened the box, her eyes widening at the sight of a keyring bearing her name and attached to a black fob key. She stared up at him. 'Is this...?'

Dan had been watching her carefully, anticipating this moment. It was his turn to grin.

'Oh, Dad!' Kim leapt up and hugged him, while other diners looked on in amusement. 'Is it...?' Ever since she'd gained her licence, Kim had been pestering him for a car of her own, leaving pictures of her favourite Kia where he couldn't fail to miss them. Until now, he'd been adamant that in a town the size of Pelican Crossing she had no need for one and could get around perfectly well on her bike. But he'd had a good year, and now she was eighteen, Dan had decided the time had come. The little, white, second-hand Kia Cerato was waiting for her outside the restaurant where he'd parked it earlier in the day. 'Where is it?' She gazed around as if the car was suddenly going to appear in the restaurant, her eyes filled with excitement. She might look and act grown up, but at times like this she reminded him of the four-year-old Kim gazing at the doll's house she'd received for Christmas.

'Finish your coffee first.' Dan chuckled at her excitement, pleased he'd bought the car. Even though it was second-hand, it was in good condition and should last her for some time, maybe until she was able to buy one for herself.

Once outside the restaurant, Kim stared at the white car in amazement. 'This is for me? Truly? It's exactly what I wanted. Thanks, Dad,' she said again and threw her arms around Dan, hugging him tightly. 'Can I drive it home?'

Dan hesitated. They'd been drinking champagne, and they'd walked to the restaurant, so he didn't have to drive home. It should have occurred to him Kim would want to drive it right away. 'Best not to,' he said with a frown. 'You can come back for it tomorrow,' he added, seeing the light disappear from Kim's eyes. 'It'll be quite safe here overnight.'

'Okay, Dad,' Kim said after a long pause during which he thought she was going to insist. But she gave the bonnet an affectionate pat, then took his arm and started prattling on about all the things she could do now she had her own wheels.

Once Kim had gone to bed, Dan went into the kitchen and poured himself a glass of the whisky he kept there for special occasions, sad the day was over. He had been stating the truth when he told Kim she was grown up. At eighteen, he had already left school and entered university. At least she had one more year to go. But Dan knew in his heart that he'd already lost the little girl who had hung on his every word, and now she had her own car she was going to be even more independent. He was going to have to get used to being alone.

# Five

Livvy had barely slept, the thought of what Ingrid had done, and what her future looked like keeping her awake most of the night. It was still dark when she slipped into her old one-piece swimsuit, pulled on a pair of shorts and a tee-shirt and headed out to join the group of wild swimmers who greeted the dawn in the ocean.

Livvy was back in her element as she swam out across the bay. *How I've missed this*, she thought as she turned on her back to float and watch the sky change from pink to gold as the sun rose above the horizon. It was such a beautiful sight, the wide expanse of sky reminding her how small her life was in comparison to everything else in the world. It was hard to feel sad or upset in the face of such wonder. But despite trying to put her fears aside, Livvy couldn't stem the dread of what might lie ahead.

'Good to see you made it this morning,' Gill said, as Livvy picked up her towel. She was glad Erica wasn't there this morning too. She wasn't ready to share her news with her.

'I didn't get much sleep,' she said, 'and I thought this might make me feel better.'

'And did it?' Gill asked, rubbing her hair with a towel.

'Not really, though I'm glad I came. I missed my early morning swims when I was at Nancy's.' She wasn't looking forward to telling Nancy what had happened, knowing her daughter would worry. Dylan was different. He didn't have a single ounce of worry in his makeup. Things had always just fallen into place for him. No doubt he'd be full of positive sayings and suggestions for what she could do. But counselling was all she knew. She was good at it, and she loved the work and her clients.

As they walked up to their cars together, Gill said, 'I spoke to one of my colleagues and he promised to look into what Ingrid has done, but, like me, he suspects she stayed within the law. I'm sorry.'

'Thanks.' It would have been too much to hope for, to learn that she'd acted illegally, and Livvy could have her practice back.

'Don't forget dinner tonight. Seven?' she said as they parted.

'I'll be there,' Livvy said. Even though she'd prefer to curl up in bed and feel sorry for herself, Livvy knew she had to face people.

Back home, after showering and dressing in another of her sundresses, she scrambled a couple of eggs, popped them onto a slice of toast and took them along with a cup of her favourite lemon and ginger tea out to the courtyard. Sitting there in the familiar setting, Livvy began to feel better. Nothing had changed but she was home in Pelican Crossing and, despite the sense of loneliness she'd felt when she first arrived, she knew she wasn't alone. She'd drive out to see Rhana, she decided, remembering how her friend's down-to-earth manner had always been able to cheer her up in the past when she was feeling low.

*

Arriving at the gate and seeing the metal sign with a picture of a spaniel and the words *Spaniels Live Here,* Livvy felt a familiar sense of coming home. She'd visited here so often in the past, the dirt driveway and the house nestled among a mixture of palms and pandanus was a welcome sight.

When Livvy parked in front of the steps leading up to the veranda, a volley of barking greeted her, and a pack of dogs swarmed around her car. Then Rhana appeared, shooing away the dogs with a laugh and a wave of her hand. The tall, heavily built woman, her dark hair now threaded with grey, had never really changed from the untidy teenager who had bossed them around, often abrupt, but always kindly and a loyal friend. Today her face was creased into a welcoming smile.

'Welcome back.' Rhana pulled Livvy into a warm hug, sending a wave of affection through her. It was good to see her old friend again.

'Thanks. It's good to be back... I think.'

Rhana peered at her for a moment, then said, 'You don't look very happy to be back. You'd better come in and tell me what's worrying you.'

An hour and two cups of coffee later, Livvy finished telling Rhana about Ingrid's treachery, ending with, '... and I don't know what I'm going to do, Rhana. I've never done anything other than counselling and I love being able to help people. Maybe I'm the one who needs a counsellor now.' She unsuccessfully attempted a laugh.

'Oh, Livvy. I'm so sorry. What a despicable thing for her to have done. And it's legal?'

'That's what Gill's checking out, but it appears so.'

Rhana was silent for a few moments, then smiled. 'I'm sure something will turn up. You know what they say about one door closing and another...'

'Don't!' Livvy interrupted. She wasn't in the mood for one of Rhana's adages.

'Sorry, but do try to look on the positive side, Liv. It's not the end of the world, even if it seems like it right now. You're still a counsellor, right?'

'Ye...es.' Livvy wasn't sure where Rhana was going.

'Well, you can set up your practice again, can't you?'

'I... I suppose. But with no resources, no clients.' It seemed impossible.

'It probably won't be easy to start again from scratch, but you did it before.'

'But...' Livvy's head began to ache. She'd come here for comfort, hoping Rhana would find a way for her to regain her practice in the medical centre, not this. How could she possibly start over? A counselling practice needed premises where clients would be happy to visit, a professional space. It wasn't something she could set up in her little cottage... or was it? She visualised the small rooms, the tall windows, the view. Could she expect clients to come to her there? And where would she find them? No doubt the doctors at the medical centre were referring their patients to Ingrid, just as they had to her when she had been located there.

'What's happened to all your stuff?' Rhana asked, her voice breaking into Livvy's thoughts. 'Didn't you have a desk, computer, filing cabinets?'

'They all belonged to the practice,' Livvy said with a grimace. 'Ingrid has them now. I still can't get my head around it, how she deliberately and systematically set out to ruin me and take over.' She shook her head in disbelief.

'Well, it's done now. What you need to do is work out what *you're* going to do next. What would you counsel one of your clients to do if they came to you in the same blue funk you seem to be in right now?'

Livvy stared at her friend. Rhana had always tended to be blunt, but this was rough, even for her. She thought for a moment. 'I'd tell her to look at her options, that there was always a solution.'

'There you go. So, what's your solution?'

'It's not that simple, Rhana. You don't understand.'

'Try me.'

'Well, I'd need a new business name, to register it as a business, find a way of attracting clients, invest in office furniture, a computer…' All things which would eat into her small bank of savings, but without which she couldn't contemplate setting up a practice. The prospect of having to do all that was overwhelming, but for the first time since she walked out of the medical centre, Livvy felt the stirrings of anticipation. *Could she do this? Would it work?*

*

Livvy was still puzzling over possibilities when she made her way to have dinner with Gill and Joe. She hadn't known the previous occupant of the cottage at the far end of the row, an elderly man who kept himself to himself, so was keen to see inside and to discover how her friends planned to renovate it.

'Come in,' Gill said, meeting her at the door and giving her a hug, while Joe's dog, Coco, sniffed at her ankles. 'How has your day been?'

'Surprising,' Livvy said, thinking over her conversation with Rhana. 'I'll tell you all about it later.'

'Well, you're looking a bit better than you were this morning,' Gill said, giving Livvy a piercing look.

'Wouldn't be difficult.' Livvy managed a grim smile. At the beach, she'd been feeling very low, her lack of sleep contributing to her mood and the news about her practice making her fear for the future. At least now there was a glimmer of hope.

'Hey, Livvy, welcome back.' Joe pulled her into a hug too, making Livvy envy her friend. After Gill's ex led her on a merry dance throughout a protracted divorce, she'd vowed never to become involved with a man again. Then she'd met Joe Harris. The Pelican Crossing mayor had managed to break through the hard shell with which she'd protected herself, and she'd fallen in love with him.

To Livvy's relief, there was no more talk about her or her future while Gill and Joe proudly showed her around the cottage and described their plans for it, or while they were enjoying the chicken salad Gill had prepared for dinner. It was only when the meal was over and Joe had refilled their wine glasses that Gill said, 'What did you mean when you said your day had been surprising?'

'Oh!' Livvy took a sip of wine before replying, 'I went to see Rhana today.'

'I'm sure she had lots of suggestions for you,' Joe said. 'She never was one to beat about the bush.'

Livvy smiled. As Erica's brother, he had known how close the three girls were as teenagers. 'She suggested I set up in practice again, but...'

'What a good idea,' Gill said before Livvy had time to finish. 'Show Ingrid she has some competition.'

'I'm not sure...' Livvy let her words trail off. Although she'd thought of little else since leaving Rhana, she had still to come to a decision. 'It's not that simple,' she said, repeating what she'd said to Rhana. 'There's registration, premises, setting things up, marketing... I'm not sure I can face starting all over again. I'm not as young as I used to be.' She knew it was a weak excuse but the prospect of starting from scratch at fifty didn't thrill her.

'Rubbish!' Gill said. 'You're not old. I've met many women older than you who've made a fresh start. I know it'll probably take time to get everything sorted out but look on it as a challenge.'

*A challenge? It would certainly be that, and Livvy wasn't sure she was up for it. But what else could she do? She wasn't qualified to do anything else.*

'If it's premises you're looking for,' Joe said, 'you might want to check out the new wellness centre.'

Livvy stared at him. *What was he talking about?*

Seeing her puzzlement, Gill broke in, 'Oh, you wouldn't know. It opened while you were gone. It's been set up by a team of natural health practitioners who focus on holistic health and offer services in physiotherapy, remedial massage, acupuncture, naturopathy, osteopathy, chiropractic. You'd fit right in.'

'You seem to know a lot about it.'

Gill reddened. 'I strained my back last winter and needed to see a physio. I was impressed by their professionalism.'

'And you should know Gill isn't easily impressed,' Joe said with a grin, while Coco gave a grunt of agreement. They all laughed.

'If they're well-established, they probably don't have space for another practitioner,' Livvy said, her heart sinking at the thought of trying to establish herself within an existing team, even if they all offered different services. But it might be better than trying to set up her practice in her cottage.

'So, you're interested?' Gill asked, seeming to have grasped what Livvy was only coming to realise.

'Maybe,' Livvy said slowly. 'Who's running it?'

It was Joe who replied. 'A guy called Dan Parker. You may not have come across him. He's the physio, been in town for a few years now and has become well-respected. He's planning to stand for the council.'

'And that demonstrates how respectable he is,' Gill said laughing. 'But, really, Livvy. It surely won't do any harm to check them out, see if they have space, if you could work with them, if…'

'Okay, okay, no need for the sales pitch. Where is this wellness centre located?' Livvy didn't recall seeing it when she went to the medical centre or to Gill's office.

'That's part of the beauty of it. It's nowhere near your old clinic. Remember the old Catholic school on the edge of town, the one that's stood empty ever since they built the new college? Dan's kept the original façade and converted the interior into a series of offices and clinics. You wouldn't recognise it.'

'Hmm.' Livvy did remember it. She'd always admired the old, red sandstone building and thought it was such a pity it had become derelict.

No more was said on the subject as Gill asked about Dylan and they speculated on a relationship between him and Rory. But, walking home, Livvy couldn't stop thinking about this wellness centre and wondering…

# Six

'How do I look, Dad?' Kim twirled in front of Dan, the short skirt of her dress billowing around her.

Dan swallowed, biting back the first words which came into his head. Kim wouldn't thank him if he told her she looked like a tramp in the skimpy black dress, its neckline so low it almost reached her waist. 'You look lovely, darling,' he lied. 'Where did you say you were off to?'

'The new wine bar. It's where all the action is. Clover says…'

Dan didn't want to hear what Clover said. She was the wildest of his daughter's friends, the one who was sure to get herself into trouble before she was much older. He could only hope she didn't take Kim with her. 'Who else will be there?'

As Kim listed the group of friends who'd be included in the party, he felt a sense of relief. The others were more sensible than Clover. Surely they'd manage to restrain any of her wilder impulses? He'd never forget the time he had to pick Kim up at the police station after she and Clover were caught trying to climb over the railings at the marina after it had been locked up for the night.

'Have a good time and don't…'

But Kim was already on her way out the door. Dan sighed. The challenges of having a teenage daughter were never-ending.

'Just you and me, Cooper,' he said to the dog, who had settled down in front of the sofa, anticipating a night in. Cooper raised his head and grunted, then dropped it back onto his paws. If only he could speak, Dan wondered what he would say. Sighing again, he made his way to the fridge, returning with a can of beer and a slice of leftover pizza to flick through the channels on the television, hoping to find something to take his mind off what Kim and her friends might be getting up to. *At least she wasn't driving tonight.*

Dan was almost asleep, watching a rerun of Morse, when he heard a disturbance at the door, and Cooper gave a low growl. He checked his watch. One-thirty. He'd been sitting here for hours, unable to go to bed till he knew Kim was safely home.

'Dad, what are you doing still up?' Kim tumbled through the living room door, her hair dishevelled, her voice slurred.

*How much had she had to drink?* 'I must have fallen asleep,' Dan lied, swallowing the harsh words which he knew would anger her, and switching off the television, while Cooper stretched at his feet. 'Did you have a nice time?'

'It was awesome,' Kim said, collapsing onto the sofa.

'You can't have been at the wine bar all this time.'

'No, we met some guys and when the wine bar closed, they bought some wine, and we all went down to the beach.'

Dan's antennae went up. 'Guys?'

'Just some guys from school. You'd approve.' Kim grinned.

She knew him so well.

'Anyway,' she said, using the sofa arm to lever herself to her feet, 'I'm off to bed now. See you in the morning.'

Walking unsteadily, she wandered off, leaving Dan gazing after her, unsure how he was feeling. He wondered how Cheryl would have reacted to seeing their daughter in this state. She'd most likely have laughed. He'd always been the one to worry about Kim, to set boundaries and to pick up the pieces when things went wrong.

*

Next morning, Dan was the one who was bleary-eyed, Kim seemingly none the worse for her late night and the amount of wine she'd drunk. To his surprise she was already up and dressed when he walked into the kitchen to the enticing aroma of freshly made coffee.

'You're very bright this morning,' he said, dropping a kiss on her head before pouring himself a much-needed mug of coffee and filling a bowl with the homemade muesli he preferred for breakfast, topped with fruit and yoghurt.

'We're going sailing,' Kim said. 'We arranged it last night. Clover's brother has access to a boat and offered to take us to a bay where we can scuba dive. Should be a perfect way to spend the day.'

*Sailing? Scuba diving? After a night of drinking?* Dan had forgotten what it was like to be eighteen, to have boundless energy and the ability to bounce back after a late night. He knew Kim was an experienced diver, having taken lessons at the local dive school – that had been her last year's birthday present from him – and gone diving several times since, including one trip to the Great Barrier Reef with a school group. 'That should be fun,' he said. But Kim was no longer paying attention to him. She was completely focussed on her phone, between taking bites of toast liberally spread with Nutella, a taste she'd developed as a child and had never lost, though he insisted on her eating a healthy breakfast in term time.

'See you later, Dad.' With a kiss on his cheek, she was off, leaving Dan alone with Cooper again. He supposed that, now she was of age and had a car of her own, he'd have to get used to this.

It was Sunday, so no need to go to work, work which was always his solace. 'How about a walk, Cooper?' he asked the dog, when he had finished breakfast and packed his and Kim's dishes into the dishwasher. At the sound of the word *walk*, the dog's ears pricked up and he rose from where he'd been lying at the kitchen door. A few minutes later he and Dan were on their way to the beach.

It was a glorious morning, and Pelican Crossing was looking its best, the sun beaming down on the pair as they made their way past the harbour and the marina, avoiding a trio of pelicans who strutted across in front of them as if they owned the walkway. Dan never tired of seeing the beautiful, if ungainly birds with the large pouches under their bills which helped them hunt for food. He'd read that they could hold thirteen litres of water. They were such a feature of the town; he was sure it was where it had got its name.

Pelican Crossing boasted several beaches, and this morning Dan bypassed the busy surf beach and headed straight for the dog beach where he'd be able to let Cooper run free. As he unfastened the dog's leash, he noticed a figure he recognised at the edge of the ocean. He'd come across the woman everyone called old Agnes soon after he arrived in Pelican Crossing, quickly learning about her strange ways and her habit of imparting wisdom and advice whether it was welcome or not. So far, he'd not been the recipient of either.

'Good morning,' she said as he caught up with Cooper who was cavorting in the shallow water with Agnes's spaniel.

'Morning. It's going to be another hot one.'

'A typical January day,' the old woman replied, pushing a strand of her long, white hair out of her eyes and peering up at Dan. 'Saw that daughter of yours heading out of the marina with a group of youngsters. She's growing up.'

'Eighteen now.' Dan rubbed his chin. It was still difficult to believe.

'You look like you've got the whole world on your shoulders. Time moves on. People change. You must trust that your daughter will prosper, and you should make changes yourself. Don't stand still or time will move on without you.' Agnes nodded to herself, before calling to her dog and walking off, her long, white hair flying out behind her, her skirt trailing in the water.

Puzzled, Dan stared after her, as the waves flowed over his bare feet and Cooper continued to dive into the ocean. *What did she mean? What sort of changes? Was she suggesting he should find someone to share his life with?* Dan had dated a few women when he first arrived in Pelican Crossing but had soon discovered how little he had in common with them, and he was wary of forming another relationship, aware of how it could easily go so terribly wrong. Also, he had Kim to consider. After four years, she was still grieving for her mother.

# Seven

Livvy was feeling a ripple of excitement. She'd registered her new business online and applied for an ABN. Now she needed to design a logo, order business cards and set up her new website. *Grace Counselling* was on the way to becoming a reality.

She still hadn't made up her mind about the location, but this morning she planned to check out the wellness centre Gill and Joe had recommended. After her previous experience, she was a bit dubious about joining with a group of other practitioners, but if she was the only counsellor, it might be safe.

Dressing in a pair of cut-off jeans and a loose, flowered shirt, Livvy drove out of town to where the wellness centre was located and parked outside. The old building she remembered looked different, as if it had been given a new lease of life, the red sandstone appeared to have been cleaned and outside was a sign proclaiming it to be *Pelican Crossing Wellness Centre*, with a list of the services offered. The number of cars in the car park were testament to its popularity.

On impulse, Livvy pushed open the door to find herself in a smart reception area, the desk manned by a young woman wearing a black tee-shirt with the wellness centre logo.

'Can I help you?' she asked.

Livvy only hesitated for a moment. 'I'd like to make an appointment for a massage,' she said, deciding this was one way to check the place out.

'Certainly. Let me check when Katrina is free.'

While she was checking the computer, Livvy looked around, impressed by how the entrance to the old school had been remodelled into what was now a bright office area painted in a pale pastel colour with several pot plants scattered around. She wondered what had been done to the rest of the building.

'Katrina has a free spot later this morning, at eleven. Would that suit you?'

'It would be perfect, thanks.'

'Your name?'

'Livvy, Livvy Grace.' As she spoke, Livvy wondered if the girl would know her name, would know what had happened to her practice, but she gave no indication she recognised her, merely typing her name into the computer, smiling and saying, 'We'll see you again soon then.'

Livvy left with a feeling of anticipation. She wouldn't be able to grill the masseuse about the centre but surely she'd be able to get some idea of what it might be like to work there. It was only nine-thirty now. She had time for a coffee before her appointment. She drove back to town and headed for *Books and Coffee*, eager to share her plans with Lou.

'You're looking more cheerful today,' Lou greeted her when she walked in through the bookshop entrance – although all one business, the bookshop and café was located on a corner and had separate entrances.

'I'm feeling better.' It always felt better to have taken some action. 'Do you have time for a coffee?'

Lou glanced around and, seeing only a couple of people browsing the shelves, nodded to her assistant and gestured towards the café.

Once they were seated with coffee and a slice of carrot cake to share, Livvy told Lou what Gill and Joe had suggested, listing what she had been doing, and finishing with, 'I'm not sure about the wellness centre but I've booked a massage to check it out.'

'Oh, why didn't I think of that? It's perfect for you. And you'll love your massage. Katrina is a marvel.'

Livvy stared at her friend in surprise. It seemed that everyone knew about the wellness centre, had even used its services while she'd been gone.

Seeing Livvy's surprise, Lou reddened. 'I like to pamper myself from time to time,' she said. 'And I'm sure you'll be impressed by what's been done to the old building. It's a miracle. It had been lying empty for so long before Dan saw its potential. He's been an injection of fresh blood to the town. I'm sure when you see how it's all been modernised and refurbished into therapy rooms, you'll decide you want to be part of it.'

'Hmm.' Livvy wasn't so sure. The centre had now received a strong recommendation from two of her friends, both of whose opinions she valued. But would she want to work there?

Livvy checked her watch. It was almost ten-thirty, time to leave if she was to make her appointment. 'Thanks, Lou,' she said, rising.

'Let me know how you go,' Lou said.

'Sure.' Livvy smiled. One more person who wanted to see her settled into the wellness centre. She was beginning to think fate was pushing her towards it, but it was an important decision, and she intended to check it out thoroughly before making up her mind.

*

Arriving back at the wellness centre, Livvy was shown into one of the therapy rooms, impressed again by how what must have started out as a classroom had been refurbished to form a professional treatment room and what appeared to be an adjacent office.

'Hi, you must be Livvy. I'm Katrina,' a tall, auburn-haired woman wearing pale green pants and matching tunic greeted her with a smile. 'Welcome. Is this your first visit to the centre?'

'Hello Katrina. Yes, it is. I've been away and a friend recommended it… and you.'

'Always good to hear. Do you have a specific area you need me to focus on today?'

'No, just a general massage, thanks.'

'You can undress behind the screen,' Katrina said, pointing to a screen in one corner. 'You'll find a robe to wear. Just come out when you're ready and lie down on the massage bed.'

'Thanks.'

When Livvy re-emerged, wearing the white cotton robe, she

discovered Katrina had dimmed the lights and a delicate aroma of lavender, geranium and bergamot filled the air. Some soft music was playing. Feeling relaxed already, Livvy disrobed, climbed onto the narrow bed face down and pulled a towel over her.

Lou had been right. Katrina was a marvel. Livvy felt the tension of the past few weeks leave her body under Katrina's firm but gentle hands. She almost forgot her reason for coming here.

'Thanks. I feel so much better now,' she said, sitting up and drinking the glass of water Katrina handed her. 'That was wonderful. How long have you been here?'

'The centre opened last year, and I was one of the original therapists,' Katrina replied. 'Dan has been amazing, arranging the refurbishment of the building and attracting us to join him.'

*Another champion of the man*, Livvy thought. He certainly seemed to have attracted a sense of loyalty from his colleagues, if the masseuse's attitude was anything to go by. 'There seem to be a few of you,' she said. 'How does it all work?' She smiled, pretending only a casual curiosity.

Katrina was happy to tell her. 'Dan – he's the physio – owns the building, and the rest of us rent our suites from him. It's worked well so far. Everyone gets on well. We all do our own thing and rarely see each other on a daily basis, but a few of the group do get together for drinks from time to time.' She chatted on a bit more, but Livvy barely paid attention, her mind going round in circles trying to work out if this was somewhere she'd enjoy working, if she'd fit into this group of therapists or if it would be better to set up independently.

As she paid and turned to leave the centre, an attractive man who looked to be in his fifties came rushing through the reception area and ran out the door. He was wearing a similar outfit to Katrina. Livvy wondered who he was and why he was in such a hurry, before shrugging. It was none of her business and, if she decided to set up her practice here, she would no doubt meet him.

# Eight

Dan only caught a glimpse of the tall, blonde woman standing at the reception desk as he flew out of the centre, propelled by the call he'd just received from Kim. It wasn't like his daughter to call him at work, to call him at any time. She usually preferred to communicate by text, if at all. Her jumbled message was to the effect that Cooper was being sick, it was gross, and she didn't know what to do. Luckily, he'd been between clients and his next one wasn't due for another hour, so he had time to pop home to check up on his pet – his suggestion that Kim take him to the vet fell on deaf ears.

When he arrived home, Dan found Cooper alone. Kim had already left to meet her friends. The dog was very agitated when Dan walked in, and there were chocolate wrappers lying on the floor.

'What's the matter, boy?' he asked, crouching down beside him. 'Okay,' he said, when Cooper didn't lick his hand as he usually did, but moved around restlessly, 'let's see what the vet has to say.' He picked the animal up and carried him out to the car, settling him comfortably in the back seat where he could be protected by a restraint.

Dan had already met Luke, the local vet, when Cooper had his annual shots and trusted him to know how to treat Cooper. But when he walked into the vet surgery, it wasn't Luke who greeted him.

Seeing his surprised expression, the man held out his hand. 'I'm guessing you expected to see Luke. He's been acting as my locum while I was in the States. I'm Bob Reed.'

'Dan Parker.' Dan shook the outstretched hand, recalling Luke telling him he was filling in for someone. 'This is Cooper. He seems to have eaten something that disagreed with him. I suspect it was chocolate.'

'Well, let's have a look at you, Cooper,' Bob said, lifting the dog up onto the examination table.

Dan waited patiently while Bob conducted several tests before asking, 'Do you know when he might have ingested it, and what type of chocolate?'

'No, I don't, probably some time this morning, and…' Dan thought for a moment, remembering the boxes of chocolates Kim had received for Christmas, and the wrappers he'd seen on the floor, 'they were milk chocolates. My daughter… She knows not to let Cooper near chocolate but might have let her guard slip.'

'Don't have any children myself,' Bob said with a grin. 'But we'll soon have Cooper fixed up. Did the chocolates contain anything else, like raisins?'

Dan tried to remember the wrappers he'd seen. 'I don't think so.'

'I'll need to keep him here in the vet hospital for a few days, till we can flush the toxins from his system and his heart rate and blood tests are all normal. Give me a call in a couple of days.'

'Thanks.' While he hated to leave Cooper there, Dan was glad it was no worse. He'd heard of dogs having seizures from eating chocolate, and Cooper was an old dog and his loyal companion.

Dan checked his watch. 'I should be getting back. Cooper… he'll be right?'

'He should make a good recovery. Just remember… no more chocolate.'

'No. Thanks.' He'd have words with Kim next time he saw her, he vowed. But he knew she'd be devastated to think she might have been the cause of Cooper getting sick. She loved the dog as much as he did.

'Looks like you came here in a rush.' Bob nodded at the green pants and tunic Dan was wearing with the wellness centre logo on the pocket.

'Oh, yeah. I was at work when my daughter called me. At the *Pelican Crossing Wellness Centre*,' he added seeing Bob's puzzled expression.

'Ah yes. It was just getting going when I left. May have to pay you a visit there sometime. My back often lets me down. All this bending over sick animals.' He chuckled. 'I did a bit of hiking when I was in the States, then sitting in a plane for hours… I'm not as young as I used to be.' He chuckled again. 'You're the physio, aren't you? I saw the article in *The Echo*.'

Dan grimaced. He hadn't wanted to be interviewed, but it was good publicity and Finn, the editor, had done a good job promoting the centre. It had brought in more clients. 'That's me,' he said.

'You've done well. It's an asset to the town, and it was time someone did something with that old building. It was becoming an eyesore.'

After leaving Cooper in Bob's capable hands, Dan headed back to the clinic, to his next appointment. 'Sorry, Alf,' he said to the octogenarian who was waiting patiently for him. 'Had to make a trip to the vet with a sick dog.'

'Hope he's okay.'

'He will be. How are you today?'

'Mustn't grumble.' Alf gave a tight grin that belied his pain. A former rugby player, he had retired to Pelican Crossing when he finally gave up the game, but the years of punishing his body had taken its toll and he was now one of Dan's regular clients coming in for what he called his *monthly tune-up*.

The rest of the day passed uneventfully, and Dan was glad to get home. The conversation with the vet, and his mention of the article in *The Echo* had reminded him of his promise to meet Finn and his partner at the yacht club for dinner that evening. There was no sign of Kim having returned, and no text to let him know her movements, so he showered and changed before heading into town. School would be starting next week, and he presumed Kim was making the most of her freedom before the stress of her final year kicked in. She was a good kid, most of the time, but he worried when he didn't know where she was or who she was with. He supposed he'd have to get used to that.

*

When Dan entered the yacht club, Finn and Liz were already there, seated in a prime spot overlooking the marina. 'Hey,' he said when he joined them, shaking Finn's hand and giving Liz a peck on the cheek.

He'd become friends with the couple soon after arriving in Pelican Crossing, when Kim and Tilly, Liz's granddaughter, met at school. At first, Liz had tried to match him up with several women she knew, but she'd finally given up and declared him a lost cause.

They were halfway through their meal when Dan said, 'Thanks for that article, Finn. I know I was hesitant, but it's brought in a few new clients.'

'No problem. Any time. I'm happy to promote the wellness centre. It fills a need in the town. Even Liz agrees.' He glanced at his partner, who as practice manager at the medical centre was more familiar with traditional medicine.

'There's always a place for alternative medicine,' she said with a smile. 'And Mum raves about the masseuse there.'

'Katrina. She's very popular.'

'So, you're happy with the therapists you've managed to attract?'

'Very. They're a good crew. Only a few spaces left, and I'm hopeful of filling those soon.'

'I…' Liz began just as the waiter came to remove their plates and in the discussion about choosing dessert, what she was about to say was forgotten as Finn began to talk about an article he was planning on electric scooters and bikes in conjunction with a council crackdown on them.

Dan never found out what Liz intended to say earlier, as she recounted some horror stories a nursing friend had told her about teenagers – and younger – presenting at Emergency. Then Finn shared several near-miss experiences caused by teenagers ignoring the road rules on these bikes which seemed to have proliferated after Christmas. He hoped Liz hadn't been going to suggest he meet another of her friends.

Though when he arrived home to find Kim was still out, a small part of him wished he had someone there to talk to, to share things with, maybe even to cuddle up to in front of the television. Sometimes a dog wasn't enough company.

# Nine

Despite her positive experience there, by Saturday Livvy still hadn't made up her mind about the wellness centre. Even though she'd been impressed by what she'd seen and by Katrina's professionalism, she wasn't sure if it was right for her.

Putting it all to the back of her mind, she headed for the beach and her morning swim, the fresh smell of the sea and the invigorating effect of the salt water on her skin managing to banish all thoughts of setting up her practice again.

But when she emerged from the water, it all came back to her. She thought about the logo she'd designed, the new website, just waiting for a location before it could go live. She'd have to make a decision soon.

'Fancy meeting for breakfast at *The Blue Dolphin?*'

Livvy looked up to see Erica standing beside her, wrapped in a towel. She'd been so engrossed in her thoughts, she hadn't noticed her friend arriving.

'I guess so. Jamie not around this morning?'

'He has a fishing charter, a group from Melbourne. He'll be gone by the time I get back, so I'm a free agent today. How about I call in for you on the way? Okay if I bring Bandit along?'

'No problem.' Livvy had already met Erica's spaniel and fallen for the charms of the cute black puppy, and *The Blue Dolphin Café* had always been a favourite of hers, one she hadn't been to since she got back. Her mouth watered at the thought of one of their special breakfasts. There had been nothing like them in the town where Nancy lived.

Livvy was feeling more positive when she reached home, the prospect of breakfast with Erica brightening her mood. By the time she heard Bandit's bark at the door, she was ready to leave.

She and Erica had just settled at one of the café's outdoor tables with Bandit lying at their feet when a familiar voice greeted them.

'I hoped I'd find someone I knew here this morning,' Liz said. 'May I join you? Finn's spending the day with his grandson, and I wanted company.'

'Of course,' Livvy said. 'You know Erica, don't you?'

'Of course.' The two women smiled at each other.

When they'd ordered breakfast, all choosing the smashed avocado with poached egg on rye with skimmed milk cappuccinos, and Livvy commenting on how much she had missed this sort of breakfast when she was in England, Liz asked, 'Have you decided what to do, Livvy?'

Livvy reddened under Erica's puzzled gaze. 'Sorry, I didn't tell you,' she said. 'I thought the fewer people who knew the better.'

'Didn't tell me what?'

'Her partner stole her practice while she was gone,' Liz said, before Livvy could reply.

'Ingrid?' Erica's eyes widened, and Livvy remembered how Ingrid had been the one to counsel Erica when she had fled her marriage.

'Who else?' Livvy said, unable to keep the bitterness out of her voice.

'Oh, I'm so sorry. What will you do?' she asked, almost repeating Liz's words.

'I'll have to start again. I've already registered my new name, designed a logo and set up my website, but...'

'I had a thought last night,' Liz said. 'Finn and I had dinner with Dan Parker. I'm not sure if you're aware but he's set up this wellness centre in the building where the old Catholic school used to be. It would be a perfect location for you. What?' she asked, as Livvy rolled her eyes.

'Not you too? You're the third person to suggest it to me.'

'Well? He still has some vacant suites. Why don't you check it out?'

'I have done. Checked it out. I had a massage there. It's impressive, but I don't know...'

'And Dan's single and attractive... though...' Liz creased her forehead, '...I haven't had any luck in trying to set him up.'

'Don't you dare!' Livvy was having enough problems working out if she wanted to join the group in the wellness centre without Liz trying to set her up with the owner of the place.

'Okay, I won't.' Liz held her hands up defensively. 'But it would be a good solution for you… businesswise.' She winked.

Livvy sighed. Liz was incorrigible, but she did have a point. And the only other option was to set up in her cottage. 'What do you think, Erica?' she asked, knowing Erica could be counted on to give her an honest opinion.

'Well, I don't know much about the wellness centre, but from what I do know, in the short time it's been going, it's developed a good reputation. Anyone I've heard speak about it has been full of praise, and there was that article in *The Echo* recently. It might have been before you got back.'

'I can let you have a copy,' Liz said eagerly.

'There's no need. I can read it online.' Despite initially refusing to countenance the idea, Finn had given into the pressure to provide an online version of the local paper, though Livvy knew most locals still preferred to buy the paper copy. But it was useful for checking out old editions.

'Be sure you do.' Liz grinned.

'How is Dylan?' Erica asked, changing the subject, much to Livvy's relief.

'Good, though I haven't seen much of him since I got back. He's either at work or visiting Rory.'

'It's nice they have each other. Jamie says his presence is helping Rory's recovery. He should be getting home soon, though will still have to take things easy. He has a long road ahead of him.'

'He was lucky,' Liz said. 'Did you see that news item last week – the surfer lost off the coast of Western Australia? His friends saw the shark take him.'

Livvy shivered. 'It doesn't bear thinking about, but Rory's encounter with the shark brought Dylan and him together again. It's an ill wind…'

Liz nodded.

'So, Dylan. Is he planning to stay around?' Erica asked. 'I know Jamie is hoping he will.'

'I am too, but he hasn't told me his plans. I really need to make an effort to catch up with him again.' Maybe she could arrange to have dinner with him, or breakfast tomorrow. Livvy made a mental note to text him when she got home. Unlike Nancy, who loved to chat on Facetime, Dylan responded better to texts than phone calls or emails.

Once home, and before she forgot, Livvy sent a text to Dylan suggesting a catch up. To her surprise, he replied immediately, agreeing to meet for breakfast next day at *The Blue Dolphin*. Sending back a thumbs up emoji, Livvy smiled in anticipation of not only seeing Dylan but of another breakfast in her favourite café.

Then she fired up the computer. She wasn't sure why she hadn't checked out the wellness centre website before her massage, but it was time.

The home page looked good with its logo of a series of waves, then she scrolled down the *about* page which listed the services offered. She'd already seen these on their sign. Next, she clicked on the list of staff and there, at the top, wearing the pale green outfit she was already familiar with, and smiling at the camera, was the man she'd seen rushing out of the centre. He was Dan Parker, the man everyone had told her about, the man who had set it all up.

Reading through his list of qualifications and experience, Livvy couldn't help but be impressed and begin to feel more positive about joining the group – if they'd have her. She scrolled down through the other practitioners in the centre, noting that they all wore the same pale green tunics with the wellness centre logo. She'd never worn a uniform, preferring her clients to see her in her everyday clothes, though she supposed she had always tended to wear similar outfits. She wondered if the uniform was compulsory, if she'd feel comfortable with it. There was only one way to find out.

There was an email address for each of the practitioners. Going back to Dan's, she composed an email stating her qualifications and background and suggesting a meeting to discuss the possibility of adding a counselling service to the centre's offerings. After a moment's hesitation, she pressed *send*. Now all she could do was wait.

# Ten

Dan was pleased to read the email when he arrived at work on Monday morning. It would be good to fill another of the suites, and a counsellor would balance the group nicely, as long as she was able to get on with the others. They were a happy group and, although each of the therapists ran their own practice, any sort of conflict would spoil it for everyone. There was only one part of her background that concerned him. Olivia Grace wrote that she'd originally set up her practice in the Pelican Crossing Medical Centre and had only recently returned from overseas. He wondered what had happened to her practice and why she was looking to base herself in another location. He had an idea who might be able to tell him.

A few hours later Dan was seated in *The Grand* with the editor of the local paper, enjoying pie and chips and picking his brain. 'So, you know this Olivia Grace?' he asked, taking a sip of the sparkling water which was all he allowed himself when he was working.

'Livvy. She used to work at the medical centre, and Liz is practice manager there. They are friends.'

'Of course. So, what's the story? Why is she looking to join us at the wellness centre? Her email was pretty cagey about her reason for moving. There wasn't anything dodgy, was there?'

'Not on her part. Actually…' Finn pulled on one ear, '… I believe Liz might have suggested to Livvy that she contact you. I'm surprised she didn't mention her when we had dinner.'

Dan remembered Liz starting to say something before she was

interrupted. Had she been about to mention her friend? 'So, what happened?'

'She took leave to visit her daughter in England and while she was gone, her partner did the dirty on her. Managed to take over the practice and cut her out.'

'What?' Dan's eyes widened. 'How could that happen?'

'I don't know the details, but it seems it was all done within the law… just. Anyway, you'd have no problems with Livvy. She's an excellent counsellor, was with the medical centre for years before…'

'That's something, I suppose.' Dan still wasn't sure, but with Finn's recommendation… 'I'll arrange to meet her, see if I think she'd fit in. It would be a good service to add to what we already offer, but…' He frowned. He wanted to find out more about what had happened to her previous practice, what had prompted the partner to oust her. Had it been some sort of sheer maliciousness, a desire to have the practice all to herself, or had there been another reason?

When he got back to the centre, he sent off an email in reply to hers, arranging to meet with her in two days' time, two days in which he intended to delve into her background. It wasn't that he didn't trust Finn's opinion. He did, but he wanted to check her out for himself, and the internet was always a good source of information.

His mind went back to the bombshell Kim had dropped on him at breakfast, the one he'd been trying to forget.

'Haley has invited me to her twenty-first,' she'd said, between mouthfuls of muesli.

'In Sydney?'

'Where else?' Haley was Cheryl's niece, Kim's cousin. All the family lived in Sydney. It was one of the reasons he'd been so keen to leave.

'But you won't go. You have school.'

'It's during the Easter holidays. I can fly down and stay with Aunt Sharon.'

Dan had felt his stomach clench. Kim and her older cousin had been close growing up. There were only three years between them, and the younger girl had always looked up to Hayley. Their friendship had stalled when Dan and Kim moved to Pelican Crossing. It was only natural for Kim to be invited to the other's twenty-first party and for her to want to attend. But the thought of her spending any time with the family which had always maligned him as not being good enough for Cheryl made his blood boil.

Still, Easter was over two months away. A lot could happen before then. Checking the time, he saw there was still an hour before his next appointment. He opened his computer and entered Olivia Grace's name, curious to see what he could discover.

*

Two days later, Dan was no further forward. Everything he'd read about Olivia Grace was positive. It seemed she'd grown up here in Pelican Crossing, married, divorced, had two children, one of whom was living in England. That tallied with what Finn had told him. It was when he looked up the practice in the medical centre that he came to a brick wall. There was no mention of her or her practice. It was as if it had never existed. He supposed it might support Finn's account of what the partner had done, but it still didn't explain why. He'd have to ask her for himself, and hope she gave an honest answer. He considered himself pretty good at working out if someone was lying to him or telling the truth.

When his phone rang, he expected it to be Jacinta, the receptionist, calling to tell him she had arrived. Instead, it was a voice he'd hoped never to hear again.

'How dare you!' Sharon said, her voice so loud Dan had to hold the phone away from his ear.

'Sorry?'

'How dare you try to alienate my niece from her mother's family, tell her she can't attend Haley's twenty-first. What would Cheryl think if she knew what you were doing? You'd never try it if she was alive, if...'

'Steady on, Sharon. Who said I was trying to alienate Kim?' He tried to remember what he'd said to his daughter, realising he could have been more tactful. He hadn't actually said she couldn't attend, had he? But he had certainly been less than enthusiastic, pointing out how it was a long way to go for a party and the fact she'd miss the Easter celebrations here in Pelican Crossing. He knew her group of friends were in the habit of organising activities on the beach on the holiday weekend.

'Haley told me. She was in tears at the thought Kim might not be here to share her birthday. It's not every day she turns twenty-one, and Darryl and I are planning a special celebration. If it's a case of money, we're perfectly willing to pay for her air fare, and of course she'll stay with us.'

'I can afford to pay for my own daughter's fare, Sharon.' Dan felt a burst of anger at the suggestion he was too impoverished or too mean to do so. Darryl had always tried to lord it over him, suggesting his physiotherapy income was paltry compared to what he earned as a company lawyer. 'It's up to Kim to decide. I admit I'm not keen for her to make the trip, but if she does want to attend Haley's party, I'm perfectly willing to pay for it.' *Even if it means her spending time with you and Darryl.*

*

When the slim, blonde woman was shown into his office Dan was aware she'd caught him at a bad time, the call with Sharon still fresh in his mind, the way she'd managed to rile him as she always had. Cheryl's older sister and he had never seen eye to eye and with Cheryl's death there had been no reason to keep in touch, not till now when it seemed Kim was determined to keep the relationship alive.

'Welcome,' he said, aware he sounded less than welcoming. He drew a hand through his hair and tried to focus on the woman standing in front of him, and to remember what he wanted to find out about her. 'Please take a seat.'

'Thanks.'

Once she was seated, her hands in her lap, her ankles crossed, Dan could see Olivia Grace looked younger than he'd expected. He knew, from reading her CV, that she was close to fifty, but with her ash blonde hair curling around her face, she could pass for ten years younger. She was attractive too. He suddenly realised he was staring. 'So, Olivia,' he said, 'What makes you want to join us at the wellness centre?' He leant his elbows on the desk and steepled his hands as he waited for her response.

'Livvy, please. I prefer to be called Livvy.' She smiled, twisting her hands together. 'As I said in my email, I've recently returned from overseas to discover my partner has taken over my practice. As you can imagine, it came as a shock. I find myself forced to start again from scratch. I've set up my new business and all I need to make it work is a suitable location. The wellness centre didn't exist when I left, and several friends recommended it, suggested it would be a good fit for me. I understand you currently don't offer counselling services?'

'That's correct. Can you tell me more about your previous practice and why your partner acted as she did? Was there some conflict?'

Livvy reddened. 'Not that I'm aware of. I really have no idea why Ingrid did what she did. I trusted her, left her in sole charge while I visited my daughter in England for the birth of my granddaughter. I stayed longer than I intended.' She cleared her throat and her eyes moistened before she continued. 'It appears she allowed the practice to go into debt before closing it, setting up her own practice and paying off all the debts. When I returned there was nothing left for me. I've taken legal advice, but I have no recourse. She acted within the law.'

'Hmm.' It was much as Finn had told him, and she seemed to be speaking the truth. But could he be sure? 'I'm sorry you had such a dreadful experience. You do understand I have to be careful who I allow to join us here.'

She nodded, twisting her hands again.

'Is there anyone I could contact who'd be familiar with your service – other than your former partner, of course.'

She seemed to think for a moment, then, 'As a health professional yourself you'd realise I have to respect the confidentiality of my former clients, but I can give you a few names – people who have referred clients to me.'

'That would be excellent.'

'I received most of my referrals from the doctors at the medical centre, but also from Gill Dickson, a local family law solicitor, and there's Finn Hunter, he's familiar with a couple of my former clients. I'm sure he'd speak for me.'

Dan hid a smile. Finn hadn't mentioned any professional connection with her. The sly dog. He wondered who the clients had been. 'Good. You're happy for me to contact them?'

'Of course.'

'Well, your qualifications are impressive, and you appear to have extensive experience. Why don't I show you around, then I can answer any questions you might have.'

'Thanks, I'd like that.'

They rose together and left the office, Dan leading the way. She sounded very plausible, but Dan wondered if allowing her to join the team would work out or if he would come to regret it. He intended to check her out thoroughly, make sure she wasn't hiding anything.

# Eleven

Livvy followed Dan out of his office, wondering if she could bear to work with this arrogant guy. She could understand his concern about her background, but did he have to sound so dubious about her? She wouldn't be surprised if he contacted Ingrid, and she had no idea what her former partner might say. She could only hope the referees she'd named would give her a good rap.

As they walked through the building, past the room where Livvy had had her massage, Dan named the various suites, most of which appeared to be occupied. It was cleverly designed, with each opening off a central hallway giving them privacy and easy access. At the far end, Dan threw open a door. 'This is one of our vacant suites. If we decide we suit each other, I believe it may meet your needs.'

Livvy walked in and gazed around, stifling a gasp. It was perfect. What had once been a classroom had been painted in pastel colours, carpeted in a soft shade of grey and divided into several smaller spaces. There was a window between two of them which could easily be converted into the one-way mirror she liked to use to allow the parent to watch when she was counselling a child. The areas were empty at the moment, but she could visualise them with the comfortable chairs and low table she'd furnish them with, along with the box of toys for her younger clients, clients she still had to source or have referred to her.

She turned to her companion with a wide smile, 'It's perfect,' she said. 'It's almost as if you were expecting me… or someone like me.'

Dan reddened. 'When we did the renovation, it did cross my mind we might attract someone with your capabilities, a psychologist or counsellor. I'm glad you like it. Shall we go back to my office, and I'll have Jacinta fetch us some tea while we continue to chat.'

*Chat, is that what he called it? It had felt more like an interrogation.* But now it would be her turn, and she had some questions for him.

Once back in Dan's office with a cup of peppermint tea, Livvy felt more relaxed as she enquired about the financial arrangements and the other members of the team.

Dan seemed to be more at ease too, answering all her questions to her satisfaction. It seemed there were still three spots available, but Dan had done well to find those therapists who had already joined him. He had even grinned when she admitted she'd booked a massage with Katrina to check the centre out before contacting him.

'Well, I think that's it,' he said when they had covered all her questions. 'With your permission, I'll contact those people you mentioned, then perhaps we can talk again… if you decide you do want to join us.' He raised an eyebrow.

'Of course.' Livvy already knew she'd love to work here, even if Dan proved to be difficult. The location and set up was even better than the one she'd had at the medical centre, and she'd be working alongside likeminded people who she was looking forward to meeting. 'Oh, one more thing,' she said. 'I notice that both Katrina and you wear a similar outfit. Is it a uniform? Do you require all the therapists to wear it?'

'It's not compulsory, but we all do.' He glanced down at his own outfit. They're comfortable and practical to wear, and we have them made up locally. To date, no one's had a problem with it, and the clients seem to like it. Would it make you feel uncomfortable?'

'I'm not sure. It's not something I'm accustomed to.'

'Something for you to consider then.'

'Yes. Well, thanks so much for your time, and for showing me around. What you've established here is very impressive. It's given me a lot to think about.'

Dan smiled, a more genuine smile than before. 'It seems we both have things to think about. I'll be in touch when I've contacted those people you mentioned and don't hesitate to contact me if you have any further questions.'

'Thank you, I will.'

*

Once outside the building, Livvy found herself thinking about Dan Parker. He hadn't been what she'd expected, though she didn't know what she'd expected from the man who had bought the old school building, renovated it and set up a wellness centre, attracting a number of alternative health professionals to join him. He appeared younger than she'd anticipated and… Liz had been right, he was attractive, though it was spoilt by his arrogant manner.

What she'd expected to be a discussion between two health professionals had turned out to be more like a job interview, and she had no idea how she'd fared. But now it was over, she needed to talk to someone, to debrief… and she'd have to let the various people know Dan would be contacting them. She mentally went through their names. Gill and Finn would be busy at work. She could call Finn and drop in on Gill once she was home. That left the doctors at the medical centre, and Livvy couldn't face going there and risking running into Ingrid. She didn't know what she'd do if she ever got sick, but she'd deal with that eventuality when it happened.

But there was Liz. She worked with the doctors and might be willing to act as a go-between for Livvy. She checked her watch – almost lunchtime. She picked up her phone and pressed the speed dial for Liz's number.

Fifteen minutes later, Livvy was sitting across from her friend in *Books and Coffee*. Both had ordered open sandwiches of roast beef and salad on rye with cups of lemon and ginger tea.

'So,' Liz began, 'you talked to Dan.'

'I decided to check it out, but it felt more as if he was checking me out instead.'

Liz chuckled. 'Wish I'd been a fly on the wall. I've only met him a few times, but Finn knows him well and his daughter's a friend of Tilly's.'

'He knows Finn?' Of course he must. There was the article in *The Echo*. 'He didn't say. I gave his name as a referee as I counselled both his daughter and grandson.'

'So, what did you think?' Liz gazed at her eagerly.

'The centre's perfect. He's done well with remodelling it, turning what was a dark old school building into a bright centre with light, airy suites. But the man himself…' Livvy shook her head. 'Maybe I caught him on a bad day, but he acted as if I had something to prove, as if he was judging me, blaming me for the fact that Ingrid stole the practice, as if it was my fault.' Livvy was still smarting from Dan's inuendo. 'He says he'll need to check me out.'

Liz frowned. 'Doesn't sound like Dan. Maybe he was having a bad day. But you are going to join him?'

'We'll see, but I must admit the place ticks all my boxes. I guess I could put up with him. It's not as if we'd actually be working together. I'd only be leasing space from him.' *And the space was perfect for* Grace Counselling *to set up business.* 'It'll all depend on my referees. Honestly, Liz, it was like being interviewed for a job. Which reminds me. I also gave him the names of the doctors who were in the habit of referring patients to me at the medical centre, but I don't want to go there right now and risk…'

'I understand. Why don't I speak to Mary,' she said, referring to the senior medical practitioner at the medical centre. 'I'm sure she'll speak to the others, and I can't imagine there will be any problem. I'll let Finn know too.'

'Thanks. I gave him Gill's name too. I plan to catch up with her tonight.'

'Good idea. Now, I should be getting back, but…' she bit her lip, '… don't let your first impression of Dan affect your decision. I feel this is right for you, and he's a good guy, really.'

Livvy had to smile. Liz was incorrigible. But she was wrong about Dan Parker. True, he had seemed easier to talk to when they returned to his office after walking around the centre, but his hesitation was still there, and Livvy wasn't sure he'd agree to her joining his team of therapists, regardless of what her referees told him. It was only thinking about this that she realised just how much she hoped she was wrong. She really wanted to be part of the *Pelican Crossing Wellness Centre*.

# Twelve

Dan managed to put Livvy Grace out of his mind and concentrate on his patients for the rest of the day. But when he arrived home to be welcomed joyfully by Cooper, now thankfully fully recovered from the chocolate debacle, the blonde woman's face swam before him. He wasn't sure why, but the memory of her expression when he questioned her about her former practice had stuck in his mind. She hadn't looked like someone who had something to hide. He needed to speak to Finn again… and Gill Dickson. She'd been a patient of his, the go-to divorce lawyer who was living with the town mayor. Livvy Grace certainly knew some prominent people in Pelican Crossing.

'What's up, Dad?' Kim asked, appearing in the kitchen just as he was taking a beer from the fridge – he'd already filled Cooper's bowl, and the dog was munching happily. 'Oh, can I have one?' She gestured to the can he was holding.

'I don't think so.' Now Kim was legally able to drink alcohol, was he going to have to curtail his drinking? It would probably be a good idea. He'd got into the habit of having a few beers when he came home each evening and it was beginning to show on the scales.

'Worth a shot.' She grinned. 'So, why are you looking so glum?'

*Glum?* 'I was thinking about a woman I met today, a counsellor who might take one of the vacant suites in the wellness centre.'

'And why does that make you frown?'

'I'm not sure about her.'

'Why not?' Kim opened the fridge and took out a can of Coke. 'Can we have takeaway for dinner?' She leant her back against the sink and took a swig of the drink.

'Sure.' It would save him wondering what to cook, although he had become pretty adept in the kitchen when Cheryl became sick. Kim often cooked too. He thought about Kim's question. He wasn't clear in his own mind how he felt about Livvy Grace and didn't want to say too much to his daughter. 'Nothing really. I guess I need to check out the references she gave me.'

'Hmm.' Kim had lost interest already. 'Can we have Thai?' she asked, opening her phone.

'Sure,' he said again, deciding to call Finn after dinner and set up a meeting with him. Even though his friend had already mentioned the counsellor to him, he wanted to check with him again. Then he'd need to contact Gill Dickson. He had her personal number on his database, but it might be more appropriate to contact her at her office. The doctors were easy. He could call the medical centre. He already knew several of the doctors who had referred patients to him.

Dan and Kim were enjoying sharing the pork belly with greens and the khao soi talay which were Kim's favourite dishes from the local Thai restaurant, when she asked, 'Did Aunt Sharon call you?'

Dan almost choked, remembering the call from his sister-in-law which he had still been reeling from when Livvy Grace walked into his office. *Had that coloured his impression of her? Had he still been thinking about Sharon?* 'How did you know about that?'

Kim shifted uncomfortably in her seat, causing Cooper who was lying at her feet to emit a low growl of annoyance. 'Haley texted me. She said her mum was going to call you. I may have suggested…' she glanced down at her bowl, '… I may have said you didn't want me to go.' She reddened. 'I'm sorry, Dad. I know you and Aunt Sharon don't always see eye-to-eye, but she is Mum's sister.'

'I know, sweetheart. And I'd never stop you from seeing your mum's family, but to go all the way to Sydney for one night…' He shook his head and took another mouthful of food.

'It's not one night.' Kim played with a strand of hair. 'Haley wants me to stay for a week.' She glanced up at Dan from lowered eyes. 'Can I?'

Dan sighed. It was what he'd been afraid of, though not sure why.

There was nothing wrong with Kim spending time with Cheryl's family, but... 'Let's wait and see, sweetie. Easter is still some time away.'

'Okay but...' Her words trailed off at Dan's expression. He couldn't deal with this now, not with the issue of Livvy Grace to deal with. He didn't know why the woman bothered him so much. He'd never worried about any of the others who leased suites in the wellness centre.

As soon as they'd finished eating, Kim had disappeared into her room, and Cooper had settled down in his bed in the kitchen, Dan picked up his phone to call Finn.

By the time the call ended, Dan had agreed to have dinner with Finn and Liz the following evening where he was to meet Gill and her partner, Joe, too. It wasn't how he'd envisaged checking out the references for the next tenant of the wellness centre, but would kill two birds with the one stone, and would enable him to meet the local mayor who he'd heard so much about.

*

Livvy was glad she had arranged to have dinner with Dylan. Otherwise, she knew she'd spend the time worrying about Dan Parker and the wellness centre, wondering if there was anything she could have said or done to help her application. She smiled to herself as she cooked the spaghetti Bolognese which had always been her son's favourite meal. He had always been such an easy child, unlike his sister who had been prone to tantrums. How she hoped he planned to stay around.

She had just poured herself a glass of wine when there was a knock at the door. She answered to find herself picked up and swung around in her son's arms. 'Put me down!' she protested weakly, though enjoying the switch in roles from when she had been the one to pick *him* up and swing *him* around.

'What have you been up to?' he asked, when she'd poured him a beer and they were sitting in the back courtyard. 'Any news on the wellness centre thing?'

'I met with the owner today. He...' Livvy wasn't sure how to describe Dan or their meeting.

'I hear he's well thought of. Rory's physio at rehab has recommended he see him when he gets home.'

'Yes.' Livvy knew of his reputation as a healthcare professional, and she'd now read Finn's article in *The Echo*. It was the man himself she wasn't so sure about. 'Anyway, don't let's talk about me. What about you and Rory? Any plans?'

A tinge of red appeared on Dylan's cheeks. He took a gulp of beer. 'The docs say he can go home soon, as long as he has someone to help him shower and stuff like that. We thought it might work out if I stay for a bit, well, for good, actually. When I left…' he drew a finger down the condensation on his glass, '… I wasn't sure if he and I… if…'

'But you are now?' Livvy covered her son's hand with hers. 'If you and Rory are happy together, I'm glad for you.'

'Thanks, Mum.' Dylan grew redder. 'I love it here in Pelican Crossing. I think I'm ready to settle down. And Rory's the one I want to be with. We know it may be difficult for a time, until he's properly back on his feet, but… we want to make a go of it.'

Livvy felt her eyes moisten. It was what she wanted too. Now, if only Nancy would decide to come home too, her heart would be full.

But she needed to focus on getting her new practice up and running, and that depended on Dan Parker.

# Thirteen

Livvy was a bag of nerves. Gill had called to let her know that she and Joe were having dinner with Liz and Finn… and Dan Parker. It seemed as if two of the people she'd named as referees were ganging up on him to persuade him of her suitability. She should be pleased, but wondered if their united approach might have the opposite effect from what they intended. It was good of Finn to have arranged it, and she must be grateful to him. But she knew she wouldn't have any peace of mind until she heard from Dan again.

She'd spent the day with Rory, having promised Dylan to visit him, and had been impressed by how the young man was coping with the trauma he'd experienced. It was something she'd seen often in her counselling work, but Rory was her son's partner and there was no way she could offer to counsel him. At any other time, she'd have recommended he see Ingrid, as she had with Erica, but now…

When she left the rehab centre, she found herself at a loss. Maybe she needed counselling herself. She laughed at the idea, then thought how she would deal with a client who presented to her with her situation. First, she'd suggest she find ways to take her mind off her problem, then ask her what her preferred outcome would be.

Well, she knew the answer to the latter. It would be for Dan Parker to accept her into the wellness centre and to act in a more professional manner towards her. As for the first? She was on her way home when her eyes fell on the deserted beach opposite her cottage. She used to walk there a lot but hadn't spent much time there since she got back, confining her beach time to her early morning swims. Slipping off her sandals, she stepped down onto the sand.

As soon as she felt the sand between her toes, Livvy felt better. She should have done this before now. It was hard to feel down on this expanse of white sand, the white-flecked waves pounding on the shore and the salty tang of the sea filling her nostrils. She took a deep breath. This is what she loved about this place, what she'd missed while she was away. She had a sudden notion that everything was going to work out, that she was worrying for nothing. Even if Dan Parker refused her application to lease one of his suites in the wellness centre, she'd find somewhere to set up her practice. She wasn't dependent on *his* goodwill.

Having decided that to her satisfaction, Livvy made her way back up the beach to her cottage, determined not to think about the dinner at Liz's that evening. Instead, she'd invite Erica and Jamie for drinks and make sure there was no mention of Dan Parker or the wellness centre.

*

Dan had mixed feelings as he made his way to Finn's for dinner. He wondered if he was going to be steamrollered into allowing Livvy to become one of what he liked to think of as *his therapists*, even though they were all sole traders, owning their own businesses.

'Welcome!' Finn greeted him at the door with a handshake. 'Glad you could make it. I hope you don't mind that we invited Gill and Joe along. Liz thought it would be a good idea, kill two birds with the one stone,' he said, repeating what had already gone through Dan's mind.

Once inside, Dan was greeted by Liz with a peck on the cheek, before being introduced to Gill, who he remembered, and Joe, who gave him a firm handshake and said, 'Glad to meet you at last. I've been very impressed by everything I've heard about you.'

'Good to meet you too.' Dan had seen Joe's photo in the paper, heard him speak at a public meeting, but this was the first time he'd met him.

'I hear you intend to stand for the council?' Joe raised one eyebrow.

'I'm considering it.' Dan wondered how Joe knew but he supposed that, as mayor, he was privy to most things happening around town.

He was soon seated on a wide deck overlooking the ocean with a glass of beer.

'No business talk until after dinner,' Liz announced before Dan could say anything. The others laughed, clearly accustomed to her manner which Dan found to be somewhat abrasive. It was something he'd noticed when they'd met previously.

The company was excellent and during the meal, Dan learned more about his companions. All four had been married before and while Finn, Gill and Liz had been divorced, like him, Joe had been widowed. He was surprised when Joe said, 'You must get lonely at times. I know I did, though I never thought I'd fall in love again.' He glanced at Gill with such affection that Dan was forced to look away.

'I have my daughter,' he said, though he was well aware Kim would soon be gone too. Even if she chose to study close to home, she'd have to leave Pelican Crossing. It was something he often thought about, but he wasn't sure he could trust himself to fall in love again as these four had.

'She won't be there for ever,' Liz said, as if she'd read his mind. 'My two couldn't wait to get away once they left school even though they stayed in Pelican Crossing. And...' she said with a grin, '... we can all recommend love a second time around.'

'Liz!' Finn remonstrated, but the other two only laughed, clearly accustomed to hearing this sort of comment from her.

But Liz was undeterred. 'Isn't there a song about it?'

'Frank Sinatra,' Joe said, singing a few chords of the old melody, much to Dan's surprise.

'I wonder...' Liz began.

'Liz!' It was Gill who stopped her this time. 'How about I help you make coffee, then we can discuss the reason Dan is here tonight?'

Apparently suitably chastened, Liz agreed, and the two women disappeared into the kitchen.

'Don't mind Liz,' Finn said. 'She means well but sometimes...' He shook his head.

'And she's not wrong,' Joe said chuckling. 'After I lost Barb, I never thought I'd fall in love again. It wasn't something I was looking for. Then I met Gill and... the rest is history.'

'Hmm.' Dan didn't know why the image of Livvy Grace suddenly floated behind his eyes as vividly as if she was right there with them.

'Here we are.' Liz and Gill reappeared carrying cups of coffee.

'Now,' Finn said, 'Down to business, Dan. You're here to check out Livvy as a possible addition to the wellness centre.'

'That's right.' Dan was beginning to feel uncomfortable. He'd just enjoyed a delicious dinner with these folks and now he wanted them to give him the lowdown on a woman who was a friend.

'I'll go first, as I've already recommended her to you,' Finn said. 'While I don't have any personal experience of Livvy's counselling skills, she counselled both my daughter and grandson, and the results were amazing. You probably aren't aware, Dan, but my son-in-law drowned tragically trying to save young Sandy. The little fellow saw his dad go under and, in addition to his grief, he was terrified to go near the water. Now he'd be happy to spend all his time there. Old Agnes might have had something to do with it too, but I put it down to his sessions with Livvy. As for Adele, she has now recovered sufficiently to have formed a new relationship. It's all good.'

'Thanks for sharing that.' Dan was impressed. He turned to Gill.

'As you know, I handle divorce and family law cases,' Gill said. 'I've often referred my clients to Livvy both for marriage counselling and for the trauma caused by ex-partners. I've never had any complaints. I can definitely recommend her.'

'I can too,' Liz piped up. 'As I'm sure you're aware, she used to work out of the medical centre. As practice manager there, I see a lot of what goes on and I've seen how the doctors repeatedly referred their patients to Livvy. I can help you contact the doctors if you wish, but perhaps it would be sufficient for you to speak with Mary – Dr Spencer – who is the senior medico. She's known Livvy since she first set up her practice.'

'Thanks, that would be good.' Dan cleared his throat. 'My main concern is why her former partner acted as she did. It seems odd.'

'Because she's an evil bitch,' Liz said. 'She wanted it all to herself. But I suspect, once Livvy sets up again, Ingrid will lose those clients she's stolen from her. There's such a thing as loyalty, something Ingrid doesn't understand.'

'Wow!' Dan couldn't help himself. Liz certainly didn't mince words.

But he was glad to hear what she – and Finn and Gill – had to say. It had helped resolve his doubts. Though he would accept Liz's offer and speak to the senior doctor at the medical centre, just to ensure there was no bias in present company. But it looked as if he'd found an occupant for one of his empty suites.

# Fourteen

True to his word, Dan Parker had contacted Livvy the Monday after they'd first met, inviting her to another meeting. Her heart had been in her mouth as she walked into the wellness centre again, despite the fact both Liz and Gill had told her not to worry.

But they'd been right. The Dan who greeted her this time was smiling. 'You appear to have loyal friends,' he said. 'Both Finn and Gill were full of your praises, and when I spoke with Dr Spencer, she seemed delighted you were planning to set up again in the wellness centre. So… given what they all said, I'd be happy to offer to lease you one of our suites.'

'Thank you.' Livvy was so surprised, it was all she managed to say. Now she could launch her website and set up her new practice.

Over the next week, she and Dan had met again to finalise the financial arrangements, and she'd ordered the furniture she required to set the suite up to suit her needs. She'd also placed an advertisement in *The Echo*, surprised and delighted to hear from several of her old clients who were thrilled to be able to work with her again. And Gill and several of the doctors at the medical centre had promised to refer clients to her. It seemed Ingrid was going to find her client base sadly depleted, and Livvy couldn't help but take pleasure in the prospect.

Livvy dressed in the pale green pants and tunic and scrutinised herself in the mirror, surprised to discover she liked herself in what could only be described as a uniform. Although Dan had said it wasn't compulsory, she was aware it was how all of the other therapists dressed and had decided to give it a try. She could always change her mind later, but it certainly saved time not having to decide what to wear each morning, and Erica had told her how smart she looked in it. Even Dylan had been impressed when she showed the outfit to him. 'It looks really professional, Mum,' he said with a grin.

It was still a tad nerve-racking to push open the door to the centre and fit her key into the door to her suite. It all smelled so fresh and new. Livvy placed the flowers she'd picked from her garden that morning into a vase which she set on the low coffee table in the room where she'd be meeting with her clients and then went into the office area. It was a tiny space, just big enough for a desk and chair. She took a deep breath and opened her new laptop to check her diary for the day. She still had an hour before her first client was due to arrive, time for a herbal tea to settle her nerves.

The centre had a small kitchen which was shared by all the therapists. Placing a camomile teabag into the mug she'd brought along, she made her way there.

'Good morning. Welcome. I heard you were joining us,' Katrina greeted her. 'Did you really need a massage or were you just checking us out?' She chuckled.

'A bit of both, and I loved the massage.'

'I'm glad. And I'm glad you're joining us. I've heard lots of good things about you. I have a friend who was one of your clients during her marriage break-up. She said you helped her enormously.'

'Thanks.' It was always good to get positive feedback and did much to settle Livvy's nerves. She didn't know why she felt nervous. She'd been a counsellor for over twenty years, but she felt she had something to prove to Dan Parker, to show him

she deserved to be here. She was just thinking this when the man himself appeared.

'Welcome aboard, Livvy,' he said with the warmest smile she'd seen him give. 'I see you've met Katrina. If you can hang around at the end of the day, you'll be able to meet some of the others. Not everyone works every day, but there will be a few of us here.'

'Thanks.' Livvy felt flustered. She hadn't expected to be greeted so warmly. But it was a good start to the day.

'See you later,' Katrina said, heading off, followed by Dan.

With a sigh of relief, Livvy took her tea back to her office, thinking about what had just happened. Maybe Dan wasn't such an ogre after all.

*

The day passed quickly for Livvy. She found it easy to get back into her counsellor role after her break. Several of her clients had come from her old practice and it was good to see them again, though she was sad to know they still needed her help. She wondered how Ingrid was faring, but didn't waste time over it. All that was in the past. *Grace Counselling*, based in *Pelican Crossing Wellness Centre* was the future.

However, Livvy was glad when she farewelled her final client for the day. She had got out of the habit of working, and dealing with clients was draining. She'd be glad to get home, take a cool shower and sit down with a glass of wine. She wished Dan hadn't mentioned the get-together after work. Even though Dan had appeared warmer towards her that morning, she wasn't looking forward to being in his company again. But she couldn't dodge it, and it would be good to meet some of the others.

There was a hum of chatter which ceased when Livvy walked into the kitchen area, recommencing almost immediately.

'Welcome.' Katrina said again, drawing Livvy into the group and handing her a glass of wine. 'Come and be introduced. Everyone, this is Livvy, the new addition to the centre. She's a counsellor.'

Livvy smiled as one after another, the other members of the group were introduced to her. There was no sign of Dan. She hadn't been looking forward to seeing him, so why did she feel a hint of disappointment?

After the introductions, conversations resumed, and Livvy found herself talking to a tall, dark-haired man called Patrick, who'd been introduced as the naturopath.

'I've heard of you,' he said. 'You worked out of the medical centre, didn't you? What happened?'

Livvy had been afraid of this, aware her former practice had been well known in the town. 'I was away for a time and decided on a change,' she said. She had no intention of revealing what had happened or of bad-mouthing Ingrid. People would find out soon enough if they did enough digging.

'Oh,' Patrick said, as if this was a common occurrence. 'Well, you couldn't have chosen a better location to set up again. Dan has done marvels with this place,' he gestured around him, 'and has collected a good group of therapists. We all complement each other. It's something Pelican Crossing has needed for some time.'

'He's certainly done well in renovating this old building. I remember it when it was a school.'

'Before my time,' Patrick said with a grimace. 'You lived here long?'

'All my life. I've seen a lot of changes in that time, but the heart of Pelican Crossing has remained the same. I love it and wouldn't live anywhere else.'

'You have family here?'

'My son. He's recently returned. My daughter lives in England. That's where I spent the last year. You?'

'Just me.' His eyes clouded. 'My two children live with their mother in Brisbane. I don't see them as often as I'd like, but… You know how it is.'

Livvy didn't, and didn't want to enquire. Patrick must be at least ten years younger than her, so his children might still be in school.

'Not like Dan,' he continued. 'He lost his wife, so his teenage daughter moved here with him. I think there was some problem with her today which is why he's not here. He usually likes to introduce new therapists himself.'

'Oh!' Livvy didn't want to engage in gossip about Dan but was interested to learn more about him. So, he was a widower with a teenage daughter. Perhaps it was grief which was causing him to act as he had. She remembered what it had been like when Nancy and Dylan had been teenagers, and Dan was dealing with it on his own. For the first time, she felt a sliver of sympathy for him.

# Fifteen

'I'm okay, Dad. Really.' Kim struggled to get up from the bed in the emergency department of the local hospital, before falling back against the pillow and wincing with pain. 'It's my car I'm worried about. I'm sorry, I've messed up again. First, Cooper, then this. But this time it wasn't my fault. I promise you. The other car came out of nowhere and the airbag deployed.' A tear slid down her cheek.

'I'm not angry with you, sweetheart.' Dan was relieved to see his daughter apparently unharmed though clearly in pain. The call from the hospital to say his daughter had been brought into emergency after an accident in her car had sent him rushing to see her, cursing the fact he'd given in and bought it for her. He saw the results of so many of these accidents on a daily basis, people who'd damaged their limbs, neck or spine and required his services. They could even suffer severe brain injury.

He was pleased to see a doctor he knew walk in.

'Tell my dad it's nothing to worry about,' Kim said to him.

'Your daughter's right, Dan. She was lucky. She's broken a couple of ribs, but it could have been much worse. We checked, and there's no internal damage.'

'See?' Kim said. 'But the car. My lovely car. It must still be sitting there.'

'We'll worry about that later. A car can be fixed, but I only have one daughter.' Dan felt a wave of relief.

'If it's too badly damaged, could I get a new one?' she asked, tongue in cheek.

'Don't try me.' But Dan chuckled. Kim was right. There wasn't much wrong with her.

'As you'd be aware, the most important thing for Kim is rest and pain relief. You should also apply an ice pack – a frozen gel pack or even a bag of peas from the freezer would do – on the injury for about twenty minutes every hour while Kim's awake for the first two days, then reduce it to ten to twenty minutes three times daily as needed to reduce pain and swelling. I can trust you to make sure she adheres to instructions and doesn't try to do too much – no strenuous exercise, gentle walking only. She should stay off school and see her GP in a couple of weeks. Otherwise, she should be fine.'

'Hello? I'm here,' Kim said, narrowing her eyes. 'Can't I go to school? It's...'

'Best not,' Dan and the doctor said together.

'But it's the beginning of the year and they're trying out for the swim team.'

'No swimming for you until your ribs heal,' Dan said. 'You can use the time for extra study. This is an important year for you.'

'I know,' Kim said, sounding more subdued.

'And we'll drive by and check the car on the way home. Maybe stop off at McDonald's,' he suggested.

'Thanks, Dad.' Kim smiled. The fast-food restaurant was a rare treat Kim had never grown out of, normally reserved for special occasions.

'Thanks,' he said to the doctor, then helped Kim hobble out of the cubicle and to the car which he'd parked as close to the hospital entrance as he could manage.

There was no sign of Kim's car when they reached the scene of the accident, but a couple of workmen nearby were able to tell them the police had had it towed away, along with the other car involved. They'd no doubt want to check out who was at fault and to determine the damage.

They made a quick stop at McDonald's, then Kim lapsed into silence for the rest of the trip home. *Maybe she was in more pain than she was willing to admit.*

Once back home, Cooper hovered around Kim, sensing she'd been hurt, but she brushed him off. 'I think I need to lie down,' she said. 'Can you help me...?' She was biting her lip.

Dan helped her to bed and propped her up on a pillow with an icepack, handing her a couple of painkillers with a glass of water. 'Would you like anything else?' he asked, feeling helpless. Although he dealt with injured patients every day, it was different when it was his own daughter.

'Just my phone and iPad,' she said. 'I want to let Clover know. We were supposed to be meeting tonight.'

*On a school night?* But Dan said nothing, merely fetching the phone and iPad. 'I'll look in again in a little while,' he said, as Cooper slipped past him to jump up on Kim's bed. 'Do you want me to take him out?'

'No, Cooper and I will be fine,' she said, her attention already on her phone.

Dan sighed as he left and closed the door behind him.

As he stepped into the kitchen, Dan found he was shaking. What if it had been worse, if he'd lost Kim too? Had he been wrong to buy her a car? She was only eighteen, after all. But a sensible eighteen, he reminded himself, and this could just as easily have happened when she was driving his car. He poured himself a glass of whisky and, remembering the police officer who was one of his clients, picked up his phone.

A few minutes later, Dan was feeling better. Luckily, Gavin had been one of the officers called to the accident. He was able to reassure Dan that Kim had been correct when she stated she wasn't driving fast, and the accident wasn't her fault. It appeared that the other driver was driving over the limit. If Kim hadn't been going so slowly, it could all have been a lot worse. The car itself had suffered damage to the bonnet and passenger door, but that could all be fixed. Kim wouldn't be driving for a few weeks anyway.

Relieved, Dan took a second glass of whisky out to the patio where he was soon joined by Cooper who Kim must have shooed out of the bedroom. He'd check on her later and suggest she try to get some sleep but knew it would be difficult for her.

Now the worry about Kim was over, Dan had time to think about how he'd had to leave the centre early and missed out on introducing Livvy Grace to the team. It was something he always liked to do with new members of the group. It gave him the opportunity to see how they'd fit in, identify any possible conflicts before they became a problem. Not that he expected any conflicts with Livvy. She was a counsellor after all, someone who dealt with other people's challenges every day. But he still wasn't convinced that nothing had happened between her and her former business partner, something that either no one knew about or which they weren't willing to share. And there was the fact that Livvy Grace had managed to get under his skin in a way no other woman had since Cheryl all those years ago.

# Sixteen

Livvy had been working in the wellness centre for two weeks now and had developed a routine, not dissimilar to the one she'd had when she worked at the medical centre. She'd rise before dawn and head to the beach for her early morning swim. It was such a wonderful way to start the day, to swim out across the bay, then float on her back gazing up at the changing hues of the sky as the sun rose above the horizon. Then she'd drive home to shower, change and have breakfast before going in to work.

She was enjoying working at the wellness centre, the bright surroundings, the camaraderie of the other therapists when they met in the kitchen. Even Dan didn't seem so bad when you got to know him. The news his daughter had been in an accident had triggered her sympathy for him. She knew what it was like to worry over children, even though both Nancy and Dylan were grown and had their own lives. Dan's daughter was still in her teens.

Livvy smiled to herself as she sipped her morning cup of lemon and ginger tea, the cackling of the local kookaburras filling her ears. Tonight, she was having dinner with Dylan and Rory, who was now home from rehab and in Dylan's care. Her son was surprising her with the concern he showed for the man who was now his partner. Rory was confined to a wheelchair, would be until he was walking again. Tonight would be the first time the two men had entertained and had invited not only her, but Rory's dad, Jamie, and his partner, Livvy's friend, Erica. She was looking forward to it.

The day passed in a flash as Livvy dealt with one client after another. She had been surprised how quickly her new practice had grown as the news of it had spread, helped by a feature article in *The Echo* in which Finn focussed not only on Livvy's return to Pelican Crossing, but on the success of the wellness centre. According to what Liz had told her, Ingrid was not at all happy and was losing clients to Livvy. It gave Livvy a touch of satisfaction to hear that things weren't going so well for her former partner, but she decided not to dwell on it. All of that was in the past.

She was on her way out of the building when she almost bumped into Dan who was walking in the opposite direction.

'Sorry,' she muttered.

'No, my fault. I wasn't looking where I was going.' He stopped and peered at Livvy. 'You've been with us two weeks now, haven't you? I'm sorry I haven't seen much of you. I've been…'

'I heard about your daughter. I'm sorry. I hope she's recovering.'

'Thanks.' Dan gave a sigh. 'She's on the mend. We'll be seeing her GP tomorrow, then hopefully she'll be going back to school on Monday. She's been a difficult patient.' He dragged a hand through his hair. 'How are things going for you? I hope you're not regretting your decision to join us.'

'Not at all. I've been busy… especially after the article in *The Echo*.' She smiled.

Dan smiled too, suddenly seeming more relaxed. 'I think we all have. It pays to have good friends. Well, I'll let you get on. Maybe we can have coffee together some time.' Then he was off without giving Livvy time to reply.

Livvy stared as Dan disappeared through a doorway. What was that about? Did he mean in the wellness centre kitchen, with the others, or did he mean…? She shook her head trying to dismiss the tingle of anticipation that had sprung up at his words. It was nothing, just the sort of thing he'd say to any of the therapists, but… what if it wasn't?

*

*Now why had he said that?* Dan forced himself not to look back to see Livvy's reaction. He didn't normally offer to have coffee with any of the therapists. Sure, they sometimes bumped into each other in the kitchen, but he preferred to stay in his office rather than mix with them, believing that it was what they preferred too. There was something about this latest addition to the group, about Livvy Grace, that made him act out of character, and he wasn't sure he liked it.

He forced his mind back to the reason he was going back to his office. He'd been about to drive off when he realised he'd left his phone on his desk. Picking it up, he set off again. This time, to his relief, there was no sign of Livvy.

As soon as he opened the door to his house, Cooper raced to greet him. 'Good boy,' Dan said, crouching down to fondle the dog. Although Kim had become bored with being at home, at least she'd had Cooper for company and, in the past week, had been able to take him for walks. The dog would miss her when she went back to school.

As he straightened up, Dan heard the sound of voices and laughter coming from upstairs, from Kim's room. Pleased some of her friends had come round, he made his way upstairs to say hello. But when he pushed open the door to Kim's room, there was only one friend there. 'Hey,' he said to the boy who leapt up from where he had been seated on the bed. Dan had never seen him before.

'Dad!' Kim pushed herself up from where she had been lying against a bank of pillows. 'This is Jay… Jayden. He dropped round with my maths homework.' The blush staining her cheeks belied her words. Dan doubted that whatever they'd been up to when he walked in, it wasn't maths homework.

'Hi, Jay,' he said. 'You're in Kim's class?'

'Yeah, I mean yes, Mr Parker. We were just…'

If it had been with anyone else but Kim, Dan would have smiled, but this was his daughter… her bedroom, and he could remember his own hot blood at their age. He swallowed, trying to hide his emotion, aware it would be pointless to be angry. Kim was eighteen, would be at university next year, and once she left home he'd have no say in what she did or who she did it with. But for now… 'I was about to make tea,' he said. 'Why don't you both come down and join me?'

Kim and Jay looked at each other, then Kim nodded. 'We'll be right down, Dad.'

Dan made his way downstairs, his mind in a whirl. He knew there were boys among the group of friends Kim hung out with, but he knew most of them, had met their parents. Jay was a stranger to him… but clearly not to Kim. He wondered how long this had been going on, what…? *Stop there*, he told himself as he filled the electric jug and took a box of teabags out of the pantry, Cooper at his feet as if he knew something was bothering him. 'It's okay Cooper,' he said, but was it?

He heard footsteps coming down the stairs, then the front door closing. When Kim appeared in the kitchen there were two red spots on her cheeks. 'How could you, Dad?' she asked, her voice trembling with annoyance. 'Bursting in like that, making Jay feel guilty, as if… We were only chatting. We weren't…' She reddened again, and Cooper padded over to comfort her. She put one hand on the dog's head.

'I only came up to say "Hi", honey. I didn't know who your guest was. Is this something new, is Jay…?'

'I don't need an interrogation. He's a friend, or he was until you barged in and played the heavy father. Now…' Her eyes moistened. 'I don't want tea. I'm going for a walk.'

Dan rolled his eyes at a sympathetic Cooper as the front door closed for a second time, this time with a loud bang. He sighed and drew a hand through his hair before pouring boiling water on the peppermint teabag and taking it out to the patio, Cooper following. It was at times like these that he missed Cheryl. Surely a woman would have a better idea of how to handle the situation? His mind went to the latest addition to the wellness centre, to Livvy Grace. She was a woman. He'd heard she had children of her own. She was a counsellor. Maybe she could help. But was he game to ask her?

# Seventeen

Livvy was glad to get home and put the encounter with Dan behind her, deciding she was making a mountain out of a molehill, and he hadn't meant anything by his comment about coffee. But she needed to do something to help her focus, and the beach was calling her. Changing out of the green work outfit she'd now become accustomed to wearing, Livvy pulled on a pair of capris and a tee-shirt and slipping her feet into a pair of sandals and popping on a hat, made her way across the road and down on to the beach. She had the long stretch of sand to herself at this time of day and removing her sandals, headed straight for the edge of the water. As she stood there, the waves flowing over her feet, her toes sinking into the soft wet sand, she breathed in the salty air and felt the tensions of the day disappear.

It was beautiful here, peaceful, the only sounds the waves lapping on the shore and the cries of the seabirds flying overhead. The town with its wellness centre along with its owner seemed to belong in another world. As she wandered along the edge of the ocean, her sandals in her hand, Livvy's mind drifted back to the thoughts she'd had when she returned from England, to her envy of those friends who were in happy relationships. Even Dylan seemed to have found his happy ever after. When was it going to be her turn?

In spite of herself, Livvy conjured up the image of Dan Parker and his suggestion they have coffee together. Surely she wasn't so desperate she was imagining things with the first available man who'd crossed her path? Although not her boss, Dan was the closest thing to one. Shaking her head in disbelief, she turned and headed back home.

Erica and Jamie had offered to pick Livvy up and give her a lift to Rory's apartment, but she'd refused, needing time to think… about what, she wasn't sure. She only knew she didn't want to be stuck in a car with her friends. There would be enough opportunity to talk over dinner.

Livvy was glad she was the first to arrive. It gave her time to meet Rory again. Apart from her visit when he was in rehab, she hadn't seen him since he and Dylan were teenagers together. She'd been away when he had his accident, the encounter with the shark which meant he might never be able to walk unaided again. Looking at him now, at his cheerful expression, it was difficult to believe what he'd suffered, the multiple surgeries, the weeks and months in hospital. The wheelchair was the only reminder of what he'd gone through, was still going through. She was thrilled he and Dylan had found each other again, and her son was happy with him.

She was enjoying a glass of wine and laughing at an anecdote Dylan was relating when there was a knock at the door. 'That'll be Dad and Erica,' Rory said. 'I'll get it.' He spun his wheelchair and headed for the door, reminding Livvy of when he and Dylan had raced around on rollerblades.

'He hasn't changed,' Dylan said, his voice affectionate. 'Still the same old Rory, though it has slowed him down a tad.'

'Hello.' Livvy waited till Jamie and Erica had greeted Rory, before hugging Erica and giving Jamie a peck on the cheek. She noticed both of them hugged Dylan too.

'How are you?' Erica asked, when the three men were exchanging news, and she was seated next to Livvy. 'We haven't seen you since you started at the wellness centre. How are you liking it? It's a bit different from the medical centre. I hear Ingrid's not over-pleased to be losing clients to you.'

'Where did you hear that?'

Erica tapped the side of her nose. 'You'd be surprised how much gossip we hear in Emergency.' She was on the nursing staff there at Pelican Crossing hospital.

Livvy chuckled. It was good to see Erica looking and sounding so happy. 'Well, you're right. It is different, in a good way. I'm enjoying it, even…' She buttoned her lip. She wasn't going to mention Dan.

But Erica did. 'What about Dan Parker? From what I hear he's attractive and available. Liz says…'

Livvy didn't want to know what Liz had said. Their mutual friend had already made her opinion of him clear. 'Liz says a lot of things,' she said, cutting Erica off.

'But…' Erica began, then seemed to recognise Livvy's expression, the way her lips had tightened. 'Okay, I won't say any more, but you know we only want you to be happy, and now we've both found someone special, we'd love it if you did too.'

'Thanks, Erica. I appreciate your concern, and I can't deny I'd like to find someone, but I don't need your help – or Liz's – and I won't be looking in Dan Parker's direction.'

'Okay.' Erica put her hands up defensively.

'What are you two whispering about?' Dylan asked, making Livvy realise the men's conversation had ceased.

'Nothing,' Livvy replied, feeling herself redden. This was the last thing she wanted Dylan to hear. She had no idea how he and Nancy would react if there was another man in her life. But that wasn't going to happen any time soon, though it would be nice to have a companion, someone to relax with at the end of the day, someone to cuddle up with in front of the television, someone to… *Don't go there*, she told herself.

Soon, they were all seated at the dining table enjoying the chicken casserole which Dylan claimed to have cooked, much to Livvy's surprise. She hadn't realised he was a competent cook.

'I had to turn my hand to everything on the yachts I crewed,' he said chuckling. 'Maybe I can earn a living as a chef when Rory goes back to work.'

They all laughed, and his comments led to a discussion of Rory's recovery and how soon he could expect to be able to walk again.

'Now I'm home, I'll be having private physio,' Rory said. 'I've been referred to the guy at the wellness centre. It's where you're located now, isn't it?' he asked Livvy.

'It is, and I believe he has a good reputation.' She might not like Dan very much but she couldn't deny his skills as a physio.

'I can vouch for that,' Erica said. 'He's well thought of at the hospital.' She sent Livvy a meaningful look which Livvy ignored.

'What's the centre like, Mum?' Dylan asked. 'I remember the old school building. We used to play footie against the kids there, before it closed.'

'The facade is the same, but you wouldn't recognise the inside,' Livvy said, glad to be able to contribute something to the conversation that didn't revolve around Dan. 'The classrooms have been converted into suites which form treatment rooms and offices, and everything has been painted in pale colours. It's a delightful place to work. I feel very lucky.' As she spoke, Livvy realised that was how she did feel, lucky to have been accepted into the team at the wellness centre. For the first time it occurred to her that perhaps Ingrid had done her a favour in forcing her to start again.

# Eighteen

Dan was hoping the GP would give Kim a clean bill of health. She was desperate to get back to school, and he didn't know how much longer he could put up with her moods. Then there was the boy, Jayden, or Jay as she called him. He didn't want him coming around when Kim was home alone. It wasn't that he didn't trust his daughter, but Jay was an unknown quantity, and Kim bridled each time Dan mentioned him.

There were the nightmares too. After Cheryl died, Kim had found it difficult to sleep, waking him with her cries almost every night. Things had improved when they moved to Pelican Crossing – one more benefit of their relocation. But her accident had revived them, and he'd been awoken again by her crying in the night, only to have her tell him it was nothing when he enquired about them next morning.

'Ready?' he asked when Kim appeared in the kitchen looking nervous.

'I don't need you to come with me. I can drive myself,' she said. The damage to her car had been repaired, but it still sat, unused, in the garage.

'Soon, I hope, but not today. I'm your dad, Kim. I care about you. I want to hear what the doctor has to say.'

'I… if Mum was here, she wouldn't…' Her eyes moistened.

Dan experienced the helpless feeling he always did when Cheryl was mentioned. He was sure Kim had no idea how bad things had been between them. They'd hidden it well. In her mind, they'd been a happy family.

'Mum would have wanted to be with you too, sweetheart.'

'Maybe. Anyway, I'll be glad when my life can go back to normal.'

At the medical centre, they didn't have long to wait before they were ushered in to see Mary Spencer, coincidentally one of the doctors who'd been a referee for Livvy Grace. After a short examination and discussion of how she was coping, the doctor pronounced Kim fit enough to return to school but advised her to avoid any strenuous exercise. Kim's face brightened, but when Mary asked her how well she was sleeping, she hesitated and looked at Dan.

'Is there a problem?' Mary asked.

'Dad will tell you that I wake in the night like I did after Mum died. The accident brought it all back, made me remember…'

The doctor frowned, her face etched with concern. 'I'm sorry. I hadn't realised.' She glanced across at Dan. 'I think perhaps… I can recommend someone you could talk to, who could help you come to terms with your grief and the shock of the accident which seems to have brought it back to the surface.'

Dan flinched. He had an inkling of what she was going to say.

'Livvy Grace used to work out of here, but I believe she's now part of *your* group,' she said, nodding to Dan.

'Who is she?' Kim asked.

'She's a counsellor, helps people deal with issues that are troubling them. I think she could help you, but only if you agree to see her.'

'I don't know.' Kim's forehead creased. 'I'm not sick, I… What do you think, Dad?' she turned to Dan.

'It's worth a try, honey, if the doctor thinks it would help.'

'Hmm. Can I think about it?'

'Of course.'

'Is that it, then? Can we go now?'

Mary nodded, smiling, and Dan and Kim left. It was only when they were outside that Kim asked, 'What's she like, this counsellor woman?'

'Why don't we have a coffee?' Dan wasn't prepared to discuss Livvy with his daughter, not yet, perhaps not ever. But he knew he had to say something, and he agreed with Mary that a few sessions with her might help Kim who, it seemed, still hadn't fully come to terms with her mother's death.

'Can we go to *Books and Coffee*? I love their caramel salted brownies.'

'Of course we can.' Dan was partial to their sweet concoctions too, and the coffee was the best in town.

The café seemed unusually busy, even for a Saturday, and there was a loud buzz of conversation coming from the bookshop end of the business.

'What's happening in the bookshop?' Dan asked Ron when he was ordering two coffees, one white, one macchiato, and two of the special brownies.

'Lou has a book signing going on this morning. Adam Holland, the thriller writer, is practically a local. Lives in Bellbird Bay. He's attracted quite a crowd.'

'Don't you like his books, Dad?' Kim asked.

'I do.' Dan hadn't known one of his favourite authors lived down the coast from Pelican Crossing. He'd love to meet him.

'Why don't you go through while I snag a table,' Kim said with a grin, in a much better mood now she had the go-ahead to return to school. If only she would agree to speak with Livvy…

Dan walked through to the bookshop where a queue had formed in front of a table, behind which sat a man with a thatch of thick white hair looking a tad older than the photo on the jackets of his books. But there was no mistaking the face of Adam Holland, author of both the series of political thrillers which had introduced Dan to the author, and which was now a popular television series, and the current series featuring murders in a small coastal town not unlike Pelican Crossing or Bellbird Bay. Picking up a copy of his latest release – one he had yet to read – and the latest one in the *Queenmakers Saga* by Bernadette Rowley which he knew Kim loved, Dan paid for them before joining the queue.

It was a pleasure for Dan to actually meet the author whose books he loved and to be able to tell him how much they meant to him. He was thrilled to have his copy signed, but, unlike many of the other fans, didn't ask for a photo with the author.

'Thanks, Dad.' Kim smiled when Dan handed her the book. 'How did you know?'

Dan laughed. 'It's not difficult. I see you hunched over your kindle often enough, and I know you have a paperback of this series on your bedside table.

Their coffees arrived along with the brownies.

Her attention diverted from the book, Kim fiddled with her coffee spoon, then took a bite of the brownie. 'This counsellor, Dad. Do you really think she could help me… stop the nightmares? I wake up in the night remembering Mum, how she looked when…' She swallowed.

Dan winced. He wished he knew, but… 'I only know that Livvy's good at what she does,' he said, taking a sip of coffee, and hoping he was right. But he'd had good reports about her. Finn had vouched for her, and if the number of clients she'd managed to attract in such a short time had anything to do with it…

'Hmm. And I'd see her in the wellness centre? Would you be there?'

'Not with you in your sessions. They'd be private, just you and her.' Although Dan was aware of the two-way mirror Livvy had arranged to have installed, he knew it was for younger clients. He had no intention of eavesdropping on Kim's sessions, if she decided to go ahead.

'Hmm,' Kim said again, finishing her coffee and swallowing the last morsel of her brownie. 'What's she like?' she asked again.

'She…' Dan visualised the tall, slender, blonde woman. He hadn't seen her since the time he suggested they have coffee together and wondered if she'd been avoiding him. He still didn't know what had prompted the suggestion, but there was something about her that…

'Dad?'

'Sorry, sweetie. You were asking about Livvy Grace. She's tall, blonde, attractive…' he remembered their conversations, '…has a mind of her own. Unlike us, she grew up in Pelican Crossing and I seem to remember hearing that her son lives here… with Rory Whittaker.'

'Gary's brother?'

'I guess so.' Dan had forgotten Kim had taken diving lessons from Gary Whittaker.

'So, she's old?'

Dan almost choked on his coffee. 'She'd be a few years younger than me but, yes, I guess you might consider her old.'

'What does a counsellor do? Is she like a psychologist?'

'Not exactly. A psychologist might want to conduct various tests, whereas a counsellor will focus on helping you cope with what's troubling you.'

'You mean Mum's death, and how the accident brought it all back?'

'That's right.'

'And she wouldn't think I was crazy?'

'Not at all. She'll probably encourage you to talk about your feelings, help you work through what you can do to move forward.'

'Mmm.' Kim picked up her empty cup and put it down again. 'What do I need to do if I decide to see her?'

'We… you need to let Doctor Spencer know, then make an appointment with Livvy.'

'Okay, then. I'll do it… if she can stop my nightmares.'

'I'm sure she can.' Dan wasn't sure at all, but he realised he had every faith in Livvy, and if anyone could help Kim, she was the one.

'Thanks, Dad.' Kim slipped her arm through his as they left the café.

Dan felt a warm glow. For once, he and his daughter were on the same page. But he wasn't sure how he felt about Livvy learning about his family history.

# Nineteen

The call from Mary Spencer had come as a surprise. Normally, referrals from the medical centre, like those from Gill, came by email.

'I wanted to speak to you about this one,' Mary said. 'She's Dan Parker's daughter, and I know you work closely with him.'

*Not too closely*, Livvy thought, but she could understand Mary's concern. She and Dan did both work in the wellness centre and, in Mary's opinion they were colleagues. She supposed they were, even though she tried to keep out of his way. There had been no further mention of coffee, and she'd tried to make sure she was never in the kitchen at the same time he was. She didn't know why she felt the need to avoid him. She just did.

'There's no conflict of interest, if that's what you're worried about. We all operate separate businesses in the wellness centre. I don't see a problem.'

'Good. I just wanted to check. I'll send through the details in the usual way.' Mary ended the call, leaving Livvy staring at her phone. *What had that been about?* Surely Mary knew her well enough to understand she'd treat Dan's daughter as she would any other client and would maintain confidentiality.

It wasn't till the end of the day that Livvy had time to open the email from Mary, along with several other referrals which had come in that day, two from one of the other doctors in the medical centre and one from Gill. There was certainly no lack of clients. She frowned as she scanned Kim Parker's referral. Mary referred to the girl's nightmares as a result of her grief at her mother's death four years earlier which had been exacerbated by a recent accident. She knew about the accident. Everyone in the wellness centre did. It had happened on Livvy's first day at work and been the reason Dan hadn't been there to introduce her to everyone.

Livvy knew very little about Dan's late wife. All she'd been able to glean was that he and his daughter had moved to Pelican Crossing soon after her death. She could understand that, the need to move away from all the memories. She'd had several clients who'd done the same, and Pelican Crossing was a good place to heal. But four years… Perhaps it explained Dan's manner. Maybe it was Dan she should be counselling, not his daughter.

Smiling to herself, Livvy filed the referral, then read the remainder of her emails.

She was on her way out of the building, when Dan approached her. 'Can I have a word?'

'Of course.' Livvy smiled politely.

'Coffee?' He led the way to the kitchen which was deserted. Everyone else had left for the day.

'Thanks.' Livvy took a seat. It had to be about Kim's referral, and she wasn't prepared to discuss her clients with him. As a health professional, he should know that.

She took a sip from the mug he handed her. It was good coffee. Whatever else she might think about him, she couldn't fault his choice of coffee maker, or coffee beans.

'It's awkward,' he began. 'It's about my daughter.'

Livvy tensed. She couldn't believe he wanted to discuss her client. 'I can't…'

'No, not about her referral which I presume Mary sent through. It's…' He drew a hand through his hair. 'I need advice. I want to talk to you as a woman, as a mother. I… The other day, I arrived home to find Kim in her room with a boy. She promised they weren't doing anything, but he was sitting on her bed and… Oh, hell, I'm putting this badly. It's not that I don't trust her, but…'

Livvy pinched the skin between her finger and thumb to stop herself from smiling. 'How old is your daughter?'

'She's just turned eighteen. It's at times like this I wish her mother…' He sighed. 'I just remember what I was like at eighteen.' He grimaced.

This time, Livvy did smile. 'I know times are different to what they were when my two were that age. But some things don't change. Not every young boy is out to ravish your daughter,' she said. 'I'm sure you and your late wife gave her a sound upbringing. You need to trust her, believe her when she says nothing happened, even if everything points to the contrary. I know it can be hard, especially when you're a single parent.'

'You too?'

'My ex and I parted when Nancy and Dylan were in their teens, around the same age your daughter was when she lost her mother. It's a difficult age. I can understand how tough it must be.' Livvy had no idea why she was telling Dan all this. She wasn't in the habit of talking about herself, especially to someone like Dan.

'I'm sorry.'

'No, *I'm* sorry. A divorce isn't like a death. You and your daughter must have been devastated.'

'Kim was, but…' Dan gazed into space, 'Cheryl and I hadn't been getting on for years. If she hadn't fallen ill, we'd have divorced too. We managed to keep it from Kim, so she thinks everything was fine. It makes it all more difficult.'

'Oh!'

'I'm sorry. I didn't intend to burden you with my problems. I only wanted some advice on how to handle… I guess I hate the idea my daughter has grown up, is old enough to have a boyfriend, to be…'

'She does know about safe sex?'

Dan's eyes widened. 'You don't think…? You said… And, yes, they handled it at school. I don't… I couldn't…' He dropped his head.

Livvy almost laughed again, but it would have been cruel. 'Probably not, but it's always a good idea to be prepared.'

'Thanks… I think.' Dan gave a wry grin. 'Sorry to have taken up your time. I'm sure you have things to do, places to be.'

'Not really,' Livvy found herself saying. *Where had that come from?*

'In that case, will you let me buy you dinner as a thank you for taking up your valuable time?'

'Oh, I…' *But why not? She had only an empty cottage to go home to.* Suddenly, the prospect of being treated to dinner, even by Dan Parker, sounded attractive. 'Thanks, that's very kind of you.'

# Twenty

Being mid-week, the yacht club was almost deserted when Livvy and Dan walked in. Glancing around rapidly, Livvy was glad to see no one there she knew. A waiter showed them to a table overlooking the marina and handed them menus.

'It's nice here.' Dan looked around. 'Sorry, I was about to ask if you came here often, but that would be too corny for words.'

'It would.' Livvy laughed, surprised to see this other side of Dan. 'But I do, or did, before I went to England. I haven't been here since I got back.' She sighed, thinking of how Liz would crow if she could see them. She could just hear her friend saying, '*I told you so.*'

'Right. You were staying with your daughter?'

'Nancy. Yes. I went over to be with her for the birth of her daughter – my third granddaughter. Gosh, that makes me feel old. Anyway, I stayed there longer than I intended, too long as it turned out.' She grimaced at the memory of how Ingrid had used her absence to steal her business.

'But it's turned out well. You are happy at the wellness centre, aren't you?'

Livvy thought for a moment. 'Yes, I am. As I think I already said, I'm impressed with the set up there, what you've managed to achieve. I just wish I… that it hadn't happened the way it did.'

Dan nodded. 'Of course. I can understand that.'

Livvy stared at him. How could he possibly understand how it felt to have everything you'd worked for taken away from you by the very person you'd trusted? She shook her head. Perhaps this had been a mistake. What was she doing having dinner with this man who until today she'd vowed to ignore?

She was considering finding an excuse to leave when the waiter approached the table with a bottle of wine, filled their glasses and asked if they were ready to order. Knowing it would be rude to go now, and she still had to work with the man, she settled back into the chair and picked up the menu.

Livvy ordered the beer battered fish with salad, while Dan chose the chicken burger with fries. She picked up her glass and took a sip of the chilled Yarra Valley chardonnay, willing the time to pass quickly. Suddenly her lonely cottage was looking very attractive.

'What was it like to grow up here in Pelican Crossing?' Dan asked, once their meals had arrived and they'd exhausted the usual small talk.

'It was brilliant. I love the sea, swimming, surfing. I never wanted to live anywhere else. I was shocked my daughter chose to leave, but she met an Englishman and followed him back there. I don't know how she can stand the weather. Too cold for me.' Livvy shivered.

'But your son lives here?'

'Dylan. Yes.' Livvy smiled. 'He was a bit of a wanderer for a while but seems to have settled down now he and Rory are together. As long as he can work with boats, Dylan will be happy. I'm just sorry it took Rory's accident for them to get together. What about you?' Livvy asked, deciding she'd revealed enough about herself.

'City boy, born and bred. School. Uni. Physio practice. But after Cheryl died, I needed to get away. It was tough for Kim, but she's settled in well, made friends, enjoys the beach lifestyle.'

'Mmm.' Livvy wondered if the move to Pelican Crossing was part of Kim's problem. It must have been a wrench to be torn away from her school, her friends, everything familiar when she'd just lost her mother. Maybe she could persuade her to talk about it.

The meal over, Livvy and Dan stood outside the yacht club. She was glad they'd come separately so there would be no awkward moment in the car. 'Thanks for dinner,' she said. 'It was lovely.'

'Perhaps we could do it again?'

The very words she did not want to hear. Livvy steeled herself. 'Oh, I don't think so. It's best to keep things on a professional footing, especially if I'm to be your daughter's counsellor.'

Dan's face fell. 'If you say so,' he said. He seemed about to add something, but Livvy spoke first.

'See you at work tomorrow,' she said before walking smartly to her car, realising she was shaking a little.

Once home, Livvy made herself a cup of camomile tea. It had been a mistake to agree to have dinner with Dan, one she wouldn't make again. Even though he'd been better company than she'd expected, there had been that moment… She was looking forward to meeting his daughter. It would be interesting to see what she was like, to help her overcome the challenges she was experiencing. She could remember her own jumble of emotions at that age, and Kim had the grief over her mother's death and the relocation to cope with. It wasn't surprising the girl was experiencing nightmares.

But, despite the company, Livvy had enjoyed her meal at the yacht club. It had been a long time since she had dinner out with a male companion. Her mind went back to her thoughts when she first returned, to her envy of her friends' new relationships. Maybe she'd been too quick to dismiss Erica and Liz when they suggested she should find someone too. As long as it wasn't Dan Parker.

*

Dan watched Livvy hurry back to her car. *What had gone wrong?* It had seemed like the perfect opportunity when he'd caught Livvy before she left for home. Although he did want advice about Kim, it had really been an excuse to get her alone, to speak with her about something, anything, to get to know her better. Her advice had surprised him. The very idea of his daughter having sex was anathema to him, but he supposed he couldn't keep her wrapped up in a cocoon for ever. Kim was eighteen, as she kept reminding him. If only Cheryl… But there was no sense going there.

His invitation to dinner at the yacht club had been an inspiration. He hadn't expected Livvy to agree, but when she did, he felt as if all his Christmases had come at once. But things didn't turn out as he expected, and at one point he thought she was going to get up and leave. Thankfully she didn't. They had a nice meal together. He even learned a little more about her. Then, just as he was thinking everything was going well, that this could be the beginning of something between them, she'd insisted *they keep things on a professional footing* – these were her very words.

Dan sighed and started the car, his mind in a turmoil as he drove home.

# Twenty-one

It had been over a week since Livvy's dinner with Dan, and she had managed to avoid him at work, but today was his daughter's first appointment with her and she wasn't sure what to expect. When the tall young woman with shoulder-length auburn hair walked in, Livvy could see the resemblance. Kim was a female version of Dan, or what he'd have looked like at her age. She paused in the doorway.

'Kim?' Livvy smiled. 'It's okay, I won't bite. I realise this may feel a bit strange to you, but I promise to do my best to help you.'

'Thanks.' Kim walked in and took the seat Livvy indicated. 'Dad said you were good, that you could cure my nightmares.'

*Dan had more faith in her than she had in herself.*

'Well, let's see, shall we?'

The hour went quickly as Livvy listened while Kim shared her grief about her mother's death, her fear about the future and her worry about how her dad seemed to dislike her mother's family. 'They're my family too,' she said, sniffling into the tissue Livvy had given her, 'and my last link with Mum.'

'I think that's enough for today,' Livvy said, seeing how close to tears Kim was. 'Remember what I told you about giving in to your emotions. Try to talk with your dad about how you feel… about your mum and her family. It'll help if he understands. And try to focus on your good memories of her. We'll talk again next week.'

'Thanks, Livvy. I'll do what you said. I'll get out some of the old photos… of when Mum was still well, when we did things together as a family. And I'll talk with Dad… if he'll listen. He doesn't like to talk about Mum.'

When Kim left, Livvy heaved a sigh of relief. Perhaps it had been a mistake to accept her referral. Maybe she should have suggested Mary refer Kim to Ingrid. Livvy was too close to her situation, one of her dad's therapists, having had dinner with him. Feeling the need for something to drink, she made her way to the kitchen but had barely reached it when Dan appeared behind her.

'How did it go?' he asked, his forehead creased.

Livvy turned sharply. 'You know I can't say anything.'

'No, but… this is my daughter, Livvy. What did she tell you? I need to know how she is.'

'She's a lovely, well-balanced, young woman. You should be proud of her.'

'That's not what I meant.'

'It's all I'm going to say… apart from suggesting you listen to what she has to say. Now, if you'll excuse me, I need to make a cup of tea before my next client arrives.'

Giving a groan of what might have been acceptance, Dan left, and Livvy made the cup of peppermint tea she craved.

To Livvy's relief, the rest of the day passed smoothly, and tonight was the monthly meeting of the book club. She'd missed it while she was in England and, now she was back, had offered to host this month's meeting. She'd finished the book last night, so caught up in the investigation of a series of murders in early twentieth century Singapore in A M Stuart's *Agony in Amethyst* that she'd read well into the early hours and was looking forward to a lively discussion about it. It would be good to have company tonight. She still hadn't spoken to Erica or Liz again, afraid they might have a list of eligible men to suggest she meet. She might envy their good fortune in finding a partner, but she wasn't sure she was ready to start dating at her age.

*

As Livvy had expected, the evening went well. Perhaps female company would ease her loneliness and there was no need for a man in her life?

But she knew this wasn't the case when she remembered how Gill and Joe, Liz and Finn and Erica and Jamie looked at each other. And they weren't the only ones. Liz and Gill's friends, Poppy and Rachel had also found love a second time around and seemed blissfully happy. If she could only achieve that without having to go through the messy process of meeting and getting to know a stranger.

Livvy feared the worst when both Gill and Erica stayed behind after the others left, ostensibly to help clear up, and Gill said, 'Now, what are we going to do about you, Livvy?'

'What do you mean?' Livvy closed the door of the dishwasher and set the cycle. As the machine began to rumble, Erica said, 'Why don't we go back through to the living room. Is there any wine left?'

Livvy sighed. While the members of the book club had restricted themselves to one glass each, both Gill and Erica lived within walking distance. She took a fresh bottle from the fridge, Erica picked three glasses out of the cupboard, and the three made their way through the cottage to the large room facing the ocean. It was Livvy's favourite part of her home. The original small rooms had been opened up to make one large living/dining area with floor-to-ceiling windows which during the day let in lots of light. Although it was now dark outside, the light from the moon and the stars shone through the glass giving the room an ethereal atmosphere.

Livvy switched on a tall lamp, and they all sat down, Livvy in her favourite armchair and the others on the sofa. 'Well?' she said, afraid she knew what was coming.

'We're worried about you,' Erica said, glancing at Gill who nodded.

'There's no need. My new practice is going well. I have more clients than I hoped for,' she said, wilfully misunderstanding them.

'You know that's not what we mean,' Gill said. 'You need more in your life than work, and now Dylan is settled with Rory, and we have both found our happy ever after, it's your turn.'

'I don't think so.' But Livvy couldn't help wishing they were right.

'I know Liz thought that Dan Parker…'

Livvy flinched.

'… but Erica and I realise that, however attractive he is, it may be awkward for you to become involved with someone at the wellness centre, so…' she glanced at Erica, 'we've put our heads together and…'

*It was what she'd been afraid of.* Livvy closed her eyes, hoping she could will them away, but when she opened them again, they were still there.

'I think you should go,' she said. 'I don't want to be involved in whatever it is you're planning. Is Liz behind it?'

Both women looked guilty.

'You're practically the only one of us still single,' Erica said. 'Except for Rhana, and she's always been the odd one out.'

'She's happy as she is… as I am,' Livvy lied. 'And you can tell Liz that from me.'

'Okay, but we tried,' Gill said. 'And don't dismiss Dan too readily. He's not only attractive, he…'

'Just go, before I throw something at you.' But Livvy was laughing. She knew her friends only wanted the best for her, but the fact they'd found happiness didn't mean she could too.

But once they'd gone, with promises never to mention it again, Livvy was beset with the same sense of loneliness she'd experienced before. *What was wrong with her? Why couldn't she feel satisfied with her life? And why couldn't she find her own special someone like Gill and Erica had?*

# Twenty-two

Kim had been quiet in the two days since her first session with Livvy, and it took all Dan's willpower to avoid asking her about it. Livvy had told him to listen to what his daughter had to say, but she didn't seem to want to talk about it.

By the time Saturday came around, he'd had enough. 'Why don't we go out for breakfast?' he said, when Kim appeared in the kitchen, bleary-eyed from another late night out with friends. He'd heard her come home in the early hours and it had taken him ages to get back to sleep, telling himself that he was young once too. *Had he caused his parents the same degree of concern or was it different with a daughter?*

'Sounds good,' Kim yawned. 'Where?'

'I've heard *The Blue Dolphin Café* puts on a good spread. What do you think?'

'Mmm. Maybe. I need to shower and dress. Can I have a coffee first?'

'Sure.' Dan poured her one, and one for himself, then went outside to let Kim become fully awake without his presence to distract her. Perhaps he could persuade her to open up to him over breakfast.

It was over an hour later, and Dan was beginning to feel really hungry, when Kim reappeared wearing a pair of tight, black, three-quarter-length pants topped with a loose white shirt, her auburn hair lying in waves on her shoulders. For a moment he stared in awe at the beautiful young woman his daughter had become. It didn't seem that long since she'd been a small girl pulling at his arm for attention.

'I'm ready, Dad,' she said, snapping him back to the present.

'Sure. Let's go.'

The café was busy at this time on a Saturday morning, and Dan nodded to several of his clients on the way in, before settling at a table by the window, from which they could see the harbour and marina.

'Good time last night?' Dan asked.

'Mmm.' Kim didn't raise her eyes from the menu.

*So much for that. Maybe this wasn't going to produce the result he was hoping for.*

'Can I have the buttermilk pancakes with grilled banana, bacon, maple syrup and cinnamon?' Kim asked, proving she might not be so grown-up after all. As a child, she'd always loved pancakes for breakfast. It made Dan realise he'd never cooked them since Cheryl's death. Perhaps he needed to change too.

'Of course you can, sweetie,' he said, ordering bacon and eggs for himself, along with more coffees.

It was while they were waiting for their meals to arrive, that Kim said, 'Livvy said I should talk to you.'

Dan felt a wave of relief. At last! 'Go ahead. I'm listening.'

Kim didn't start immediately, instead spooning up the chocolate from her cappuccino which had already been served. Then, 'You don't always, Dad. Listen, I mean.'

A surge of guilt flooded Dan. *Had he been too caught up in his own emotions to pay attention to his daughter?* That was going to change, he vowed. 'I will now. I promise.'

'It's about Mum.' Kim picked up the stick of sugar and emptied it into her coffee.

Dan shifted around in his seat, wishing she'd get on with it.

'When she died, everything changed. I couldn't sleep, couldn't eat. I couldn't speak to you about it because you were caught up in making a move, moving us away from everything I'd always known, from everything that reminded me of Mum. It was as if you didn't care, as if you couldn't wait to get away. I couldn't talk to my friends about it, either. They didn't understand.'

'But you like it here.'

'I do now, but it was hard, having to change schools, make new friends…'

Dan's guilt grew stronger. It was all true. He hadn't considered how Kim was feeling, only thinking that it would do her good to make a fresh start.

'It was too many changes all at once.'

'I'm sorry, sweetheart. I should have realised. I thought… It doesn't matter what I thought. It seems I was wrong. What can I do to make things better?' Kim didn't need to know how his relationship with Cheryl had deteriorated, how he had been about to leave before she became sick.

'Well…' she fixed him with her gaze, '… Aunt Sharon and Haley are the only links I have left with Mum. I want to go to Haley's party, to spend Easter with them in Sydney. I know what you said, but it would make me happy.'

Dan exhaled. While he hated the thought of her going there, of spending Easter without her, it was a small thing for her to ask. And if it would make her happy… 'Of course. I know what I said earlier. Sharon and I have never seen eye-to-eye, and Darryl… Least said about your uncle the better. But I know they love you, and you and Haley have always been close, so…'

'Thanks, Dad!' Kim leapt up and hugged him, her eyes brimming with tears, just as their meals arrived. 'Love you.'

'I love you too, sweetheart, more than you'll ever know. Now, we should eat this before it gets cold,' he said brusquely, hiding his own tears. It wasn't often he felt so overcome with emotion, especially in public.

'There's Tilly,' Kim said, pointing to a group who were taking their places at a table outside the café. It comprised five adults, two small children, one little dog and Kim's friend.

Dan smiled at the sight of his friend, Finn, who was accompanied by his partner, Liz, his daughter, Adele, and grandson, Sandy, with Sandy's dog. He also recognised Kim's friend, Tilly and her mother, but not the other man and the little girl. He assumed it was Adele's new partner and his daughter who he'd heard about.

They were still there when Dan and Kim left some time later, the two children playing with the dog while the others finished breakfast.

'Finn,' Dan said as they passed the table.

'Dan… and your daughter. I didn't notice you in there. As you can see, we're quite a crowd. Join us for another coffee?' He looked around for another couple of chairs.

'I don't…' Dan began, before noticing Kim and Tilly whispering together, then. 'Okay if Tilly and I head off, Dad?' Kim said, while Tilly was clearly asking the same of her mother. 'Okay,' he said to Finn, taking the seat Tilly had vacated, between Finn and Liz. He was introduced to Alexander, the only member of the group he hadn't met before, then joined in the conversation about the growth of the number of cabanas which had appeared on Main Beach that summer.

'You should write an opinion piece about it, Finn,' Liz said, poking him in the chest with a finger. 'It's not on, not in Pelican Crossing.'

'It's the same everywhere now, Liz,' Finn's daughter said. 'When Alexander and I…' she blushed, '… when we took the children down to Bellbird Bay, it was the same there. There was hardly a bare spot on the beach.'

Dan relaxed. After the emotions stirred by the conversation with Kim, it was good to be part of this family group where the only issue was the proliferation of beach cabanas. He started with a jolt at the sound of his name.

'So, Dan, you have Livvy Grace working with you at the wellness centre now?'

He wasn't sure if it was a question. Liz was a friend of Livvy's. 'That's right,' he said, unwilling to expand on her comment. He looked around, but no one else was listening. They were all still debating the cabana issue.

Liz dropped her voice. 'I shouldn't say this, as I know what happened when I tried to introduce you to women before, but Livvy's a friend of mine and…'

Dan could feel himself redden. Liz hadn't only tried to introduce him to a series of women, she'd made it impossible for him to refuse a date with them. Was she intending to do the same with Livvy? If so, she didn't know her friend very well. He could tell her it was no use trying to set anything up between them.

Just as he was about to reply, Finn turned towards them, the other conversation appearing to have stalled. 'Liz!' he said, warningly.

A flush crept across Liz's cheeks. 'I was just… Sorry, Dan. It's none of my business. I only want what's best for Livvy. She deserves to find happiness.' She glanced at Finn.

'We all do, honey,' Finn said, 'but I'm sure Livvy can work things out for herself. Dan too.'

Dan nodded, feeling he'd just been rescued from another of Liz's attempts to matchmake. He wondered if Livvy was aware of what her friend was up to.

# Twenty-three

Livvy loved the weekend. After much deliberation, she'd decided not to book clients on Saturdays, giving her two whole days to herself. Today, she had persuaded Rhana to come into town and have lunch with her and Erica. It would be like old times, when they'd bunked off school to buy pizzas and eat them on the beach. The difference was that today, she'd be cooking lunch for them in her cottage.

Livvy sang along to the local radio as she made the feta and spinach potato crust quiche, a recipe she'd found on Facebook. It was a tad more exotic than pizza and she smiled as she scattered the feta and wilted spinach onto the cooked potato base before adding the egg mix and popping it into the oven. There was just time to prepare the green salad she planned to accompany it before her friends arrived.

Rhana arrived first, giving Livvy a warm hug and sniffing as she walked into the kitchen. 'Something smells good,' she said. 'I hope you haven't gone to too much trouble. Pizza would have been fine.'

They both chuckled.

'It's nice to have someone to cook for. You'd understand that.'

Rhana nodded. 'But sometimes it's nice not to have to bother. You sound as if you're lonely.'

'Not exactly, but…' Livvy shrugged, 'sometimes it gets to me. Apart from you, everyone I know is part of a couple… even Dylan.'

'How is he? I hear he's shacked up with Rory Whittaker. Shame about his accident.'

'Yes, to both. They seem happy together. I'm glad for them, and glad he's decided to stay in Pelican Crossing. Don't you ever…' She was about to ask Rhana if she ever got lonely when there was a knock at the door, and Erica appeared carrying a bottle of wine and followed by a small, black spaniel.

'I hope you don't mind me bringing Bandit along,' she said. 'I thought you'd like to see how he's grown, Rhana.'

'Not at all.'

As Rhana made a fuss of the little dog, who seemed to recognise her, and commented on how much he'd grown, Livvy was struck again by the glow of happiness which seemed to surround Erica.

'Wine, anyone?' Livvy asked, when the dog, having had enough petting, found his way to the bowl of water Livvy had provided for him.

Checking all was well with the oven, Livvy poured three glasses of the chilled Mateus Rosé Erica had brought along.

'Remember?' she asked, holding up her glass. It had been the first wine the three of them had tasted, a bottle sneaked out of Erica's parents' wine collection. That first bottle hadn't been chilled, and they hadn't been sure they liked the taste, but had felt very grown-up and sophisticated as they drank it out of paper cups on the beach.

They all smiled, Livvy feeling more relaxed than she had all week and buoyed up with the prospect of spending the next few hours reminiscing about their teenage years.

The quiche turned out well and was praised by Rhana and Erica, both asking for the recipe, and Bandit was happy with the dog biscuits Erica had brought along for him. Livvy was about to launch into one more anecdote when Erica said, 'A little bird told me you had dinner at the yacht club with a certain physiotherapist, Livvy.'

There was a sudden silence, broken only by the sound of a car driving past in the street outside and Bandit snuffling from his spot at Erica's feet.

'How do you know?' Aware of Rhana staring at her wide-eyed, Livvy couldn't deny it, but she hadn't expected anyone she knew to find out.

'One of the nurses at the hospital saw you. She recognised Dan and knew you were a friend of mine. So, it's true?'

'We… I… It didn't mean anything. We were working late. Got to chatting about a client. He suggested dinner.' There was no reason to mention the client had been Dan's daughter, and their discussion had been personal rather than professional.

'You're a dark horse,' Rhana said. 'I've heard about the new physio in town. So, you found more than a location for your practice in the wellness centre?' She raised one eyebrow.

'No, I said it's not like that. We're just two health professionals who work together.'

'But…?' Erica asked. 'There's always a *but.*'

Rhana nodded sagely. 'You can tell us, Livvy, the three musketeers.' It was what they'd called themselves back in primary school when they got up to mischief together. Livvy hadn't heard the term for years.

'There's nothing to tell.' Livvy was getting angry. This wasn't what she'd expected when she'd invited her two best friends to lunch.

'Sorry, Livvy. I didn't mean to upset you. When Ginny told me she'd seen you in the club, I was pleased for you. I'd hoped…' She bit her lip. 'I'm sorry.'

Livvy stared at her friend. Was she sorry she'd mentioned it, or sorry there was nothing to it, that she and Dan weren't in any sort of relationship other than a professional one? For a fraction of a second Livvy was sorry too.

'Bandit seems to be doing well,' Rhana said, adroitly changing the subject.

'He's a dear,' Erica said, taking her lead, but giving Livvy a glance which told her she hadn't heard the end of it yet, as the conversation turned to focus on Rhana's next litter and how busy her breeding program kept her.

Livvy felt the tension leave her. She wasn't sure why the mention of her and Dan made her chest tighten and her stomach churn. She listened with half an ear to Rhana and Erica's talk of dogs and took a series of deep breaths.

She was glad when they left, for once relieved to be alone. But as soon as she'd finished tidying away the lunch dishes, Erica's words came back to her. *Why was everyone trying to see her and Dan Parker as a couple? And why did the idea bother her so much?*

# Twenty-four

Dan rose early on Sunday morning with a sense of purpose. Kim had wakened him again when she returned home in the early hours, and he'd lain awake planning what he was going to do. He knew Livvy was one of the band of wild swimmers who greeted the dawn each morning on the stretch of beach referred to as the dog beach because it was where dogs were allowed off leash. It was where there had been a spate of poisonings the previous year, but thankfully the perpetrator had confessed and there was no more danger to their furry friends.

It was still dark when he pulled on a pair of track pants and tee-shirt, sluiced his face in cold water, and called to Cooper, who was loath to leave his bed so early. But, as always, the promise of a walk was all the incentive the dog needed to join his master at this ungodly hour on a Sunday morning and hop into the car.

Once at the beach, Dan could make out a number of figures running towards the water, but it was too dark to be able to identify anyone. He sat in the car for several minutes wondering if he was making a mistake, till Cooper's low whine forced him to make a move.

Although he considered this a crazy time to swim, Dan had to admit that it was glorious here at this time in the morning, with the sun gradually peeping above the horizon and the sky changing colour from pink to gold as the golden orb moved higher in the sky.

With Cooper running ahead and stopping from time to time to sniff at a tiny sea creature or a strand of seaweed, Dan made his way from one end of the beach to the other, trying to work out what he was going to say to Livvy when he met her, as he was determined to do. He was tired of her avoiding him, of her insistence that their relationship remain professional, and he intended to use an encounter on the beach to change things.

When he turned to walk back along the beach, the sky had lightened, and the swimmers were making their way back to the shore. From this distance they all looked the same, a group of women – larger than he had anticipated – wearing dark swimsuits, towelling themselves dry, their voices breaking into the silence of the morning.

*What had he expected? How was he going to find and approach Livvy here – one man amongst a gaggle of women?*

But he had calculated without Cooper. The dog unerringly went up to one of the women and sniffed at her. Dan followed slowly. As he drew nearer, he recognised Gill Dickson. And standing beside her was… Livvy.

*

Livvy was towelling her hair dry, feeling refreshed as usual after her early morning swim. The water was still relatively warm despite the cooler air temperature, but she knew it would soon be cold enough to take her breath away. Gill had been telling her about the latest call from her daughter, who taught in a university in Sydney and was in the throes of her first love affair when she suddenly went silent.

Livvy paused her hand holding the towel to check what had happened. A large labrador was sniffing at Gill's ankles, and its owner was hurrying towards them.

'Sorry,' he said. 'Cooper, heel.'

Livvy stared at Dan Parker who was the last person she expected to see here on the beach at the crack of dawn on a Sunday morning.

'Good morning, Dan. Your dog seems to recognise me,' Gill said with a laugh. 'Pity Coco's not with me today.'

Now, Livvy stared at her friend. *What did Joe's dog have to do with it?*

'Joe and I met Dan and his dog when we were walking Coco,' Gill said. 'The dogs seemed to hit it off.'

'Oh!' But that didn't explain why Dan was here on the beach. No one came to the beach at this time apart from the group of swimmers, and it didn't look as if he intended to join them. *Why was he here?*

'Morning,' he said in reply to Gill, before turning to face Livvy. 'Good morning, Livvy. Good swim?'

'I...' Livvy suddenly realised she was standing there in her old swimsuit, the towel, which she'd dropped from her head, barely covering her. She blushed, feeling uncomfortable at Dan seeing her like this and wishing the beach would open up and swallow her. 'Yes, thanks,' she managed to mutter.

'I wakened early, and Cooper wanted a walk.' He gestured to the dog who was now digging in the sand. 'I hadn't realised how beautiful it would be here at this time. I should do this more often.'

*Please don't!*

Livvy just wished he would go away, but Gill seemed to have no such desire, and began to chat to him about how wonderful it was to be able to use the dog beach again. It seemed there had been some problem with it while Livvy was away, not one which affected the swimmers, though it had been closed for some time. She closed her ears to their conversation, pulling on her clothes quickly and heading to the car park.

She had just reached her car, when Gill caught up with her. 'What's the rush? You dashed off as if the hounds of hell were at your heels.'

'I need to get back.'

'Nothing to do with meeting Dan down there?' She nodded towards the beach. Following her gaze, Livvy could see Dan and his dog were still there. He was gazing up at them. 'What's your problem with him?'

Livvy shrugged. She was beginning to wonder that herself. At first, it had been his arrogance, then her reluctance to become involved in anything other than a professional relationship with him, now... she had no idea. She only knew that she became so annoyed in his presence, that she couldn't wait to get away.

'Don't forget you're having breakfast with Joe and me,' Gill called as Livvy started to drive away.

'I won't,' she called back. At least Gill wasn't likely to say anything more about Dan. She'd promised.

# Twenty-five

'Well, that didn't go how I expected,' Dan said to a puzzled Cooper, dragging a hand through his hair as he watched Livvy's car pull away. Bumping into Gill too hadn't been part of the plan, but there was no way he could have avoided her, and she was the mayor's partner. One plus was that she'd suggested he join her and Joe for breakfast at *The Blue Dolphin Café*. He'd enjoyed meeting Joe at the dinner with Finn and Liz and looked forward to getting to know him better. The council elections were coming up and an endorsement from the mayor would be a bonus.

'You were up early, Dad.'

To Dan's surprise, Kim was already up and dressed and was sipping one of her favourite smoothies when he and Cooper arrived back home. 'I might say the same about you,' he said. For someone who'd arrived home at around three, she looked remarkably wide-awake.

Seeing how quickly she'd managed to bounce back made Dan feel his age. He wasn't eighteen anymore, nowhere near it.

'We're going surfing, then plan to hire kayaks and...'

'Who's we?'

'Me, Clover, Tilly, Jay and some others. What does it matter?'

'I just like to know who you're with.' So, Jay was still in the picture. He wondered if she'd been with him till three in the morning, but didn't dare ask lest he was accused of not trusting her. It was Jay he didn't trust, but he had to trust his daughter. 'It sounds like a fun day.'

'What about you? Are you just going to mooch around here all day?'

'No. I'm going to breakfast with the local mayor and his partner. Cooper and I bumped into Gill at the beach this morning – we went out for an early morning walk – and she invited me to join them.'

'Oh, I suppose you want to talk about standing for the council. I don't know why you want to bother. Don't you have enough to do?'

Dan sighed. Now wasn't the time to explain how being on the council could enhance his business prospects, increase his standing in the community. She'd probably never be able to understand, regardless how or when he tried to explain.

Kim didn't wait for a response. At the sound of a car horn outside, she said, 'I need to go. Bye, Dad,' and giving him a quick peck on the cheek, she was off.

Dan sighed again, his stomach churning as he heard the car engine rev up and race off. He knew there was no sense in worrying but he couldn't help himself. He remembered what Livvy had said. He needed to trust her… and listen to her. Well, he was trying to do that, but she didn't share much and asking about her life was like getting blood out of a stone. *Were all teenagers so secretive?* He tried to remember what he had been like at that age, but it had been so long ago. All he could remember was that his parents were old, too old to understand how he felt about things. He guessed that was how Kim felt about him.

By the time he had showered and changed into a pair of smart jeans and a green and white striped linen shirt, Dan had almost forgotten his worries about Kim. He was looking forward to meeting Joe Harris again and to what he knew would be an excellent breakfast at *The Blue Dolphin*.

Reckoning that Joe would have his dog with him, Dan had Cooper on his leash. He was whistling as he walked along, Cooper straining in an attempt to reach the pelicans strutting along the path. As he neared the café, he could see the group sitting at one of the outside tables. As he'd predicted, Joe's dog was there along with her master, Gill and… Livvy. Dan's heart raced at the sight of the blonde woman who hadn't noticed him approach.

*

Livvy was debating with Gill the merits of gas versus electricity for cooking in Gill and Joe's renovated kitchen, when she became aware of Joe greeting someone and Coco giving a friendly bark. Pausing mid-flow, she looked up to see Dan standing there along with the dog which had been with him on the beach. Surely Gill hadn't…?

But sure enough, both Joe and Gill were greeting Dan warmly, Joe pulling out a chair to allow him to join them. Livvy glared at her friend who only smiled smugly.

'I thought it might be nice if Dan joined us so he and Joe could talk council business,' Gill said, making Livvy recall hearing something about Dan planning to stand for the council. But if that was the case, why was *she* here?

Wanting to leave but realising she couldn't do so without being rude to Joe – she didn't care about Gill who she'd speak with later – Livvy gave a tight smile. 'Good morning again Dan,' she said, in response to his greeting.

'I didn't expect to see you here,' he said, taking the empty seat beside her.

So, he'd been taken by surprise too. Livvy glanced at her friend who was making a fuss of Dan's dog, then at Joe who was studying the menu. There was going to be no help there.

To Livvy's relief, the conversation during breakfast revolved around Dan's attempt to stand for the council, and she learned a little more about the man who, much to her annoyance, was disturbing her sleep. It wasn't something she was willing to admit, especially not to any of her friends, those so-called friends who seemed determined to see them as a couple, but… She glanced at him out of the side of her eye. He and Joe were discussing the argument about shark nets which had been raging in the community since before Rory Whittaker had been attacked. Wearing a smart green and white striped shirt, which matched his eyes and with his thatch of dark-blond hair, Dan looked younger than the fifty-four she knew him to be, and far too attractive for his own good. Maybe she was being too harsh on him.

Livvy was pulled out of her thoughts by Gill asking, 'You're going, aren't you, Livvy?'

'What? Sorry, I must have been daydreaming.'

'The annual sports award night. It's in two weeks' time. We've always gone together, and this year Joe and I are getting together a party to have dinner beforehand.'

'I guess so.' Livvy had forgotten all about it. It was one of the major events on the Pelican Crossing social calendar, a night when local sportsmen and women and their friends, families and supporters got together in a massive event. She stared at Dan who was looking at her in a way that… *Damn, what had she just agreed to? Was he going to be included in the party?*

# Twenty-six

'How could you?' Livvy hissed at Gill while Joe and Dan were busy chatting. 'You promised.'

'Calm down, Livvy. I promised not to mention Dan. I didn't promise not to invite you both to breakfast… or dinner. I think it was pretty clever of me.' She smiled smugly again, making Livvy want to slap her. She might even have given in to the urge if Joe hadn't turned to them at that point saying, 'Dan and I are going to take the dogs for a walk on the beach. Do you two want to join us?'

Livvy shook her head, eager to be rid of Dan's company, while trying to subdue the annoying flutter in her stomach which his presence now seemed to trigger. *When did that start happening?*

When the two men had left, along with their dogs, Livvy and Gill ordered another round of coffee. 'You have to admit he's rather attractive,' Gill said with a grin.

'I suppose so, but…'

'But?'

'Oh, I don't know. I think we got off on the wrong foot, and since then…'

'It's not like you to take against someone based on first impressions.'

'I know. But he owns the wellness centre where I work, and his daughter is one of my clients. It's all too complicated.'

'It doesn't have to be. And as far as I know, you haven't made a vow to avoid men, not like I had.'

'No.' It was true. Livvy remembered hearing how Gill's divorce had made her decide she never wanted to get involved with another man… until she met Joe. Whereas she had been feeling envious of her friends' good fortune.

'Then why not give the man a chance?'

'Listen to you. I don't even know if he's interested in me… in that way.'

'Of course he is. Why do you think he was walking his dog on the beach so early this morning? I'm betting he knew you'd be there.'

Livvy's eyes widened as she stared at her friend. Could she be right? It had seemed odd to see him there, but… She winced at the memory of how she must have looked in the old black swimsuit that showed all her curves, the towel she was holding barely hiding her modesty. She was glad she'd left as soon as she could. Then she thought of all the times she'd managed to avoid him at the wellness centre and flinched. How could he possibly be interested in her? But he had invited her to dinner, a dinner she'd enjoyed until… And he'd suggested they do it again, while she had insisted they keep things on a professional footing. 'It's too late,' she said, a note of regret in her voice. 'I've made it clear to him how I feel.'

'You have? What did you say?'

'That we should keep things on a professional level, with his daughter being my client.'

Gill rolled her eyes. 'That's not exactly telling him how you feel though, is it? So, how do you feel?'

Livvy hesitated. How did she really feel?

'You agreed that he's attractive,' Gill went on.

Livvy sighed. 'Maybe so. But like I already said, I need to keep things on a professional level, for his daughter's sake. When I said as much to Dan, he agreed. So, it's too late to even contemplate…'

'It's never too late, Livvy,' Gill cut in. 'There's the awards night coming up. It's the perfect opportunity for the two of you to get together. We just need to…' Gill's eyes sparkled, and it occurred to Livvy that instead of a divorce solicitor Gill would have made a good matchmaker. And while she doubted her friend's ability to work miracles, for once she was willing to go along with whatever Gill had in mind.

*

Dan and Joe had almost exhausted their talk about the forthcoming council elections and Dan's chances of being elected. While he was grateful for the mayor's support, Dan knew it wouldn't be easy to gain sufficient votes, given he was still regarded by many as a newcomer to the town.

They had paused to allow the dogs to have a swim, when old Agnes appeared, her long skirt trailing in the water as usual, her white hair blowing in the breeze. Her spaniel jumped into the water to join Cooper and Coco.

'What are you two plotting?' she asked.

'Nothing much, Agnes,' Joe said, looking faintly embarrassed.

Dan remembered his last encounter with the woman when she'd made some comment about a lonely old age. It had been before he'd met Livvy.

Now, she shook a finger at him. 'I know what's what,' she said. 'You only need to ask the mayor. That counsellor woman's the right one for you. I've seen the way you look at each other.' She nodded then strode off, her dog following after shaking itself all over Dan and Joe.

'What was that about?' Dan asked, trying to figure out when old Agnes could have seen him and Livvy together, as well as what she might have noticed about them.

Joe chuckled. 'I think she was referring to you and Livvy.'

'I gathered that much,' Dan said, 'but why did she say I should ask you?'

'Ah,' Joe said, 'Agnes is a wise old bird. When she saw Gill and me holding hands, she told us it had taken us long enough and that she'd known we'd get together. She was right with us, maybe with you too. It doesn't pay to ignore old Agnes. Is there something going on between you and Livvy?'

Dan grimaced. 'Chance would be a fine thing. She's a great woman, attractive, intelligent with a mind of her own.' He rubbed his chin. 'I guess that's the problem. Every time I feel I'm getting close to her, she freezes me out, and now she's counselling Kim, I can appreciate how she sees a conflict of interest.'

'Your daughter?'

'Yeah, she… she has a few issues, partly grief about her mother. Livvy's helping her come to terms with it all. She's good at what she does.'

'So Gill's told me. It was a pity what happened to her business.'

'But a plus for me and the wellness centre.'

'Mmm. Wish I could be of some help, but the way women's minds work has always been a mystery to me. I was married to Barb for over twenty years and now I'm with Gill who continues to surprise and confound me.' He shook his head, but Dan had the impression he had loved his late wife, and now Gill, without reservation.

They continued their walk in silence, each contemplating the mysteries of the female mind, only breaking the silence again to bid each other farewell and go in opposite directions. As he walked home with Cooper padding happily by his side, tired from his exertions in the ocean with Coco, Dan considered what they had spoken about, both the discussion about the elections and the later one about Livvy. He wasn't sure what to think. It had been a surprise to see her at breakfast, a pleasant one, though he wasn't sure she'd been pleased to see him. Then there had been old Agnes's comment about how they looked at each other – he still wasn't sure where she'd seen them together. But Joe seemed to put great store in the old woman's words. What if she was right? What did that mean for him and Livvy, for any possibility of them forming a relationship in the future? Because he knew now that it was what he wanted more than anything else. Livvy Grace had managed to get under his skin, and he knew he wouldn't rest until he could hold her in his arms and tell her how he felt.

# Twenty-seven

The day of the sports awards had arrived, and Livvy swung between excitement and regret that she'd agreed to attend the dinner Joe and Gill were hosting. Gill had made no secret of the fact that Dan would be there, and Livvy couldn't decide whether to feel pleased or annoyed at the prospect of spending an evening in his company.

She twirled in front of the full-length mirror, examining the dress she'd bought especially for the event the previous Saturday on a trip to Bellbird Bay. The boutique there, *Birds of a Feather*, had recently expanded its stock to include evening wear, and Erica had persuaded Livvy to accompany her, insisting they both needed new outfits. Livvy had been dubious, but as soon as she saw this dress, black shot with silver threads with a v-neckline and low back, she'd been unable to resist it, knowing it would complement her blonde hair perfectly. Looking at her image in the mirror now, she knew she'd been right. It made her feel like a celebrity. For a moment, she wondered what Dan would think of it, then she dismissed the thought. She didn't care what he thought... *or did she?*

Stepping into the high-heeled black sandals she hadn't worn for years, Livvy checked her newly styled hair – she and Erica had spent the afternoon in their local hair salon – examined her makeup and decided she was ready.

Since there would be alcohol both at dinner and at the sports event, she had arranged to share a taxi with Erica and Jamie and meet the others at *Crossings* where they were to have dinner. She hadn't eaten there since she got back, but the restaurant held fond memories of special occasions with friends and family and, of course, its signature Melbourne Cup Luncheons. The food and service were always excellent.

Tonight was no exception. Even the fact she'd been seated next to Dan failed to dim her pleasure, and she even managed a rueful smile in response to his whispered, 'Have we been set up?' when he joined her.

The meal of seafood chowder followed by macadamia crusted barramundi served with roasted pumpkin, fetta and rocket, and finishing with gooey date pudding with butterscotch sauce and ice-cream was delicious. It was all washed down with an Italian pinot grigio of which Livvy was careful to only accept one glass, as she knew from experience that the wine would be flowing later and wanted to keep her wits about her. She was pleased to notice Dan did the same. One point in his favour, as was his conversation during dinner which proved innocuous, and during which she learned that he'd taken her advice to listen to his daughter and had agreed to her going to Sydney at Easter to visit his in-laws.

By the time they arrived at the sports hall where the main event was to be held, several of their party were very merry, and it was easy to fall into the prevailing mood of high spirits as they pushed their way through the noisy crowd of happy revellers, accepting complimentary glasses of champagne on the way. It was such a crush, Livvy was glad Dan kept close to her side, protecting her from being bumped or spilling her wine.

The group of six finally found a space where they could enjoy their drinks without any danger of interruption. They had a good view, applauding when first one, then another local hero mounted the stage to accept their trophies.

Finally, the main part of the evening was over. The music started up – a local band which was making a name for itself up and down the coast – and Livvy's feet began to tap. She wasn't alone and soon the hall was a mass of whirling colour as one couple after another took to the floor. As the only two singles in their party, Dan and Livvy soon found themselves standing alone.

'Shall we?' Dan asked, taking Livvy's now empty glass and placing it with his on a nearby table.

Reluctantly, Livvy allowed herself to be led onto the floor, unable to subdue the shiver of excitement as he clasped her hand, and his arm reached around her waist to hold her in a firm grip. She was glad the music was loud, making conversation impossible. Whatever she had imagined might happen tonight, it wasn't this. It was a long time since a man had had this effect on her, and she was torn between wishing she could stay in his arms all night, and hoping the music would end soon.

'Thanks,' she muttered, when the music did finally come to an end, and they made their way back to where the others had managed to procure a bottle of wine and glasses.

'Thank you,' Dan said. 'You're looking very lovely tonight, Livvy.'

'Thanks,' she said again, blushing furiously. *When had a man last paid her a compliment?* Had Gill been right when she said Dan was interested in her, or was he just being polite? Confused, she grabbed the glass Joe offered her and took a gulp. Maybe getting tipsy wasn't such a bad idea.

As the evening wore on, Livvy danced again, with Joe, Jamie and a few other guys she'd known for years. It wasn't until towards the end of the evening that Dan claimed her for another dance, just as she was thinking she'd imagined the spark between them, or that she'd been the only one to sense it.

'I've been wanting to do this all night, but didn't want to monopolise you,' he murmured into her hair, 'and I know what these things are like. It's easy for rumours to start, and I imagine you don't want us to be on the front page of *The Echo* next week.'

He was exaggerating, but Livvy knew what he meant. The gossip mill was alive and well in Pelican Crossing and rumours abounded. The regency balls in the novels she'd devoured as a teenager were nothing compared to this event when it came to rumours starting about who was seen with whom. She was grateful for his consideration, while surprised at the tinge of disappointment that they hadn't spent more time together. She had to remind herself that this was Dan Parker, the man whose friendship she'd vowed to keep on a professional footing. But the music and the wine were having their effect, and her head was spinning as she abandoned herself to the whirl of sensation.

'I can drive Livvy home,' Dan said, when they were standing outside the hall waiting for taxies. Livvy was about to refuse when she realised that, unlike her and the others, Dan was still remarkably sober.

'Thanks, mate,' Joe said, as the others piled into a taxi, leaving Livvy and Dan alone. While they had been inside, a cool breeze had blown up, and Livvy began to shiver, unsure if it was from the temperature of the air or Dan's closeness.

'My car's not far,' he said, throwing an arm around her shoulders and making her shiver even more.

Before she knew it, Livvy was bundled into Dan's car and on her way home. 'You didn't need to do this,' she said.

'It's not a problem. I could see it was going to be crowded in the taxi, and it's an opportunity to have some time with you. I never seem to be able to get you alone at the wellness centre, and we weren't able to talk on the dance floor.'

'No.' Livvy was reminded of how it had felt to have his arms around her. She was glad it was too dark in the car for him to see her blushes. What did he want to talk about? They had spoken during dinner, and at breakfast two weeks earlier, which seemed so long ago. But both times, they had been part of a group.

The car drew to a halt and Livvy realised they weren't outside her cottage but in a car park overlooking the ocean. Glancing around, she recognised the spot. It was one favoured by courting couples, or had been when she was younger. Tonight, it was deserted apart from her and Dan.

They sat in a silence only broken by the sound through the open window of the waves crashing on the shore. There were no stars, only the faint light from the moon relieving the darkness of the night sky.

'It's beautiful here,' Dan said at last, 'so different from the city.'

'You're glad you made the move?'

'Yeah. It was time. I sometimes wish…'

Livvy turned towards him, but his face was shrouded in darkness. 'You wanted to talk to me,' she prompted.

'It's… difficult,' he said. 'I know what you said… about keeping things on a professional footing. But I'd like to get to know you better, Livvy, on a more personal basis. I've been on my own for a while now. Even before Cheryl died, before she became sick, we were living separate lives, and… well, I've always avoided any sort of relationship.

I did date a little when I first came to Pelican Crossing, with a bit of… encouragement… from your friend, Liz,' he said with a chuckle.

Livvy chuckled too, having experience of being the focus of Liz's *encouragement*. She wondered who Liz had tried to set him up with, feeling an unwarranted niggle of jealousy.

'Anyway, nothing came of it, and I decided I was destined to spend the rest of my life alone. I had Kim, my pet project, the wellness centre. It would be enough. But that was before a blonde firebrand walked into my office. I know we got off on the wrong foot. I apologise for that, for my suspicions. I tend to be over cautious where people or things I care about are concerned. I realised pretty soon that I was wrong about you, that you were squeaky clean, and your former partner was at best a fool, and at worst a criminal. You've been a brilliant addition to the centre. Heck, I'm putting this badly, aren't I? I'm out of practice at this sort of thing. What I'm trying to say, Livvy, is… I like you. I like you a lot. I'd like us to start spending time together… outside of work. I know last time didn't go too well, but will you have dinner with me again?'

# Twenty-eight

The next few moments seemed like for ever as Dan waited for Livvy's reply, and when she turned towards him and said, 'Okay. Why not?' he felt like punching the air. Instead, he settled for saying, 'Good. Why don't we make it tomorrow?' He was afraid that if he allowed her too much time to think, she'd change her mind.

Livvy chuckled. 'I won't change my mind if that's what you're afraid of, but… can we keep it to ourselves? I feel enough people have had a hand in this already. Some of my best friends.'

'If that's what you want. I'll find somewhere.' He wasn't sure he could, especially if he wasn't able to ask any of the guys he knew. But he understood Livvy's concern. He'd figure something out.

In the end, he asked Kim at breakfast next morning, aware she was more knowledgeable about the local scene than he was.

'Somewhere you won't meet anyone you know? What are you up to, Dad?'

But Dan could see she wasn't really interested, more intent on finishing her smoothie quickly so she could go out to meet her friends – and no doubt Jay would be one of them. He'd given up worrying, or was trying to.

'I've heard there's this posh place in the hinterland,' she said after a long pause, during which Dan had almost given up hope of getting a reply. 'It's where Clover's mum celebrated her fiftieth birthday. I think it's called *Addison's*.'

*Addison's*. It rang a bell. Dan had heard about it somewhere. 'Thanks, honey.'

'No prob. So, I guess you'll be out tonight. Can I have some friends round?'

Dan winced, wondering if by friends, Kim meant Jay, but he was grateful for her help so decided not to object. 'Sure, just remember…'

'I know.' Kim heaved a sigh. 'No drugs, no sex, don't drink all your alcohol.'

Dan winced again, but just nodded. 'You know the rules.' He wasn't sure when the *no alcohol* rule had been dropped and *no sex* had been added to the list, but remembered what Livvy had said.

When Kim had left, Dan checked out *Addison's* on his iPad, to discover it was a high-end restaurant situated in the hinterland as Kim had said, its website claiming it specialised in seafood and provided *perfect views of the sun setting over the ocean.* Even better from Dan's point of view was that it was at least twenty-five minutes' drive from Pelican Crossing. Using the website's app, he made a booking.

Feeling a nudge at his ankles, Dan looked down to see Cooper gazing up at him pleadingly. 'You'd like a walk, wouldn't you?' he said to the dog who immediately went to stand below where his leash hung beside the old hat Dan wore when walking. 'Okay, boy. Give me a minute.' He packed the breakfast dishes into the dishwasher, then popped on his hat and attached the leash to his excited pet.

Then they were off, heading to the dog beach which was Cooper's favourite spot.

This morning, the beach was busy with other dog owners, and it wasn't long before Dan met up with Joe and Coco, and Finn with his grandson and his spaniel. The adults stopped to chat while the dogs and the boy played in the shallow water.

'A successful evening,' Finn said to Joe, who nodded.

'And the sales of raffle tickets for the new cancer centre went well too.' This was Joe's latest pet project, a building for cancer treatment and a centre for palliative care located here in Pelican Crossing. It would be a boon to cancer patients, providing care close to home and eliminating the need to travel to a larger town for treatment.

'I hear there are moves to call the palliative care centre *Barbara Harris House,*' Finn said.

Joe gave a slow nod. 'It would be an honour to have her remembered in that way, though I think she'd have laughed at the idea.'

Dan nodded. He seemed to recall hearing that Joe's late wife had died of cancer after a long illness. She'd been lady mayoress at the time, so it seemed a fitting tribute.

The three men chatted for a few minutes longer, then Sandy, Finn's grandson, joined them with a request for ice cream, and Finn said, 'Sorry, guys. Sounds like it's time for us to go. See you soon, and look out for the announcement in *The Echo*, Joe.'

'It was a good day for Pelican Crossing when Finn Hunter decided to move here,' Joe said with a smile. 'You heard how he saved the paper?'

'I heard you had a hand in it too.' Dan tried to recall what he'd heard about how the mayor and newspaper editor had refused to allow the paper to become part of a takeover.

'Maybe, but we couldn't have done it without Finn's help.'

The two dogs returned to shake water over them, and Joe and Dan headed in different directions with Dan vowing to make sure he heard the whole story at some point. It had been interesting to meet the two men again, and he was glad there had been no mention of him driving Livvy home. He chuckled. He was becoming as paranoid as she was.

*

Livvy couldn't decide what to wear to dinner with Dan, and she couldn't ask anyone's advice as she didn't want her friends to know. She could just hear them saying, 'I told you so'. She contemplated the array of outfits lying on the bed and berated herself for being so indecisive. It was only dinner, after all, with Dan Parker who she saw every day. Well, not every day, she admitted, remembering how she'd successfully avoided him at work in recent weeks, and anyway, at work she was always dressed in her pale green uniform.

Making an impulsive decision, she picked up a dress she'd bought in England, in the English summer. It would be perfect for the sort of balmy evening the Bureau of Meteorology promised, and she could take along a wrap in case there was a cool breeze. Livvy had no idea where Dan planned to take her. She only hoped it would be well away from her usual haunts, and those of her friends.

When the knock came on the door, Livvy took one last glance in the mirror, satisfied with what she saw. Yesterday's trip to the hairdresser had paid off and her hair was still looking good. She gave it a final pat and opened the door, her heart skipping a beat at the sight of Dan wearing a smart, navy, linen jacket over a white shirt and a pair of cream pants.

'Where are we going?' After their initial greeting, neither had spoken as Dan drove out of town, but now it seemed they were driving into the hinterland.

'A restaurant called *Addison's*. Kim told me about it, and it had good reviews. Do you know it?' Dan glanced at her.

'I know of it, but I've never been.' Livvy tried to remember what she'd heard. She seemed to recall Liz mentioning it when she and Finn first dated and didn't want the entire town to know. It appeared to be the place Pelican Crossing couples went to when they wanted to remain undetected. She smiled to herself. It would be amusing to meet another couple who wanted to get away from *their* friends. 'Your daughter recommended it?'

'Not from personal experience. It seems the mother of one of her friends had a birthday party there.'

'Right.' Livvy remembered now. Liz had said it was very upmarket, which meant expensive, and that the view was amazing, as was the food. She settled back in her seat. If nothing else, she should be able to enjoy a good meal.

The sun had already set, but the sky was still light when Dan parked the car outside the restaurant.

'Pity we missed the sunset. It's supposed to be spectacular,' Dan said as they stood gazing out at the distant ocean.

'It's still special. I can't believe I've never been here before. Thanks for bringing me.'

'Better wait till we've eaten,' Dan laughed. 'But the food's supposed to be good too.'

The food *was* good. The seafood platter they shared matched anything Livvy had eaten at *Crossings*, which was her standard of comparison, and the vanilla crème brûlée melted in her mouth. 'That was delicious, thanks,' she said as Dan poured the last drop of wine into her glass.

'And no sign of anyone we know.'

'No, thanks for that too.'

'They will find out, you know,' he said with a grin. 'And now you've decided I'm not such an ogre as you first thought, maybe we can do this more often?'

Livvy put her head to one side considering. Dan had proved to be surprisingly good company, their conversation over dinner ranging from the trials of being a single parent to a shared love of books and music… and her passion for wild swimming. Then there was this fluttering in the pit of her stomach she experienced in his presence. 'Perhaps,' she said with a smile.

# Twenty-nine

To her surprise, Livvy slept soundly after dinner at *Addison's*, feeling refreshed when she wakened at her usual time, pulled on her swimsuit in the dark and headed to the beach. The feelings of the previous evening were still with her, causing her to feel confused and to question her earlier impression of Dan. Perhaps the routine of her morning swim would help clear her thinking.

As she did every morning, Livvy ran into the water and struck out rapidly, her arms windmilling as she raced across the bay, only stopping to float on her back when she ran out of breath. The sea was becoming cooler but was still warm by most standards at around twenty-four degrees Celsius. Livvy floated spreadeagled, gazing up at the changing colours of the sky, a spectacle that never failed to both amaze and delight her, and pondered the feelings Dan had prompted. She wasn't a foolish teenager or twenty-year-old to be swayed by a handsome face and ripped body, though Liz had been right when she said he was attractive, and Livvy had now revised her opinion of him. He was a good guy. But none of that explained the way she felt when they were close, in his car or seated opposite him, their knees almost touching. It was as if she had no control over her body, as if his presence was like a drug lulling her into a sense of euphoria. Livvy almost laughed out loud at how ridiculous this seemed. She turned over and swam back to the beach.

'Good morning,' Erica and Gill chorused when Livvy reached her towel. 'You were out there for a long time this morning,' Erica added.

'We nearly sent out a team to rescue you,' Gill joked.

'I was thinking.'

'I often do that out there too,' Gill said.

'Me too,' Erica agreed. 'What was so pressing this morning that it took you so long?'

'Just the usual.' Livvy busied herself with her towel, unwilling to provide any more information. Gill and Erica were good friends, Erica her best friend, but she wasn't ready to share her thoughts about Dan with them.

Thankfully, neither asked anything more, and Livvy managed to escape to her car without having to try to explain herself. But once she was back home, her thoughts returned to Dan and to the prospect of seeing him in the wellness centre. How would she feel, seeing him there after spending the evening with him? Last time they'd had dinner together, she'd managed to avoid him at work, but she had a feeling this time it would be different. This time, she'd enjoyed his company, had agreed to see him again – they had both known her *perhaps* was tantamount to saying *yes*.

Livvy's breakfast of muesli, topped with fruit and yoghurt and accompanied by a cup of lemon and ginger tea, was interrupted by a Facetime call from Nancy. They tried to connect a few times each week, but it was difficult with the time difference combined with Livvy's work commitments and Nancy's routines which centred around the children. Mornings for her were busy, while she was often too exhausted to talk in the evening.

'Hope I'm not calling at a bad time, Mum. Your three granddaughters are all asleep and I wanted to try to catch you before you went to work,' she said.

'Perfect timing, honey. I'm just back from my morning swim and enjoying my breakfast, sitting in the courtyard in the sun.'

'Half your luck. It's been snowing here again.'

Livvy shivered, remembering why she had been so eager to leave England. 'You haven't thought any more about returning to Australia?'

'We've talked about it a lot. Since I'm Australian and all three of the girls have dual citizenship, Aiden is the only one who needs a visa. He's putting together all the documentation for a partner visa – it's not cheap – and it could take anything from ten to twenty-one months to process. Then he'll need to find a job. Sometimes it all seems too hard.'

Livvy closed her eyes and sighed. 'I'll keep hoping, sweetie. How are the girls?' She listened avidly as Nancy recounted the latest exploits of Livvy's granddaughters, finishing with, 'I'll try to call when they're awake next time so you can see them for yourself. They're growing so fast you'd hardly recognise them.'

'I'd like that.' It was the one thing Livvy regretted, missing out on so much of her granddaughters' lives. It was a few weeks since she'd seen them on Facetime and as Nancy said, they grew so quickly.

The call ended all too soon and Livvy was left staring at the blank screen and wishing for what must have been the hundredth time that they didn't live half a world away. But at least Dylan was here, she consoled herself, and she was seeing Rory and him tonight.

*

Livvy took a deep breath as she pushed open the door to the wellness centre trying to pretend this was just like any other morning.

'Good morning, Livvy. Good weekend?'

Livvy whirled round at the sound of Katrina's voice. She couldn't know, could she? But the other woman's expression was as genuine as usual. 'Yes, thanks. You?'

'Pretty good. We took the kids sailing yesterday. It was a perfect day for it.'

'How lovely.' Livvy couldn't remember the last time she went sailing. It must have been when Nancy and Dylan were little, before she and their dad parted, she realised. The life of a single mother didn't lend itself to taking two children out in a small boat, and later, there hadn't been the opportunity. For a brief moment, she wondered what it would be like to go sailing with Dan, before dismissing it as an idle thought. The man probably didn't know one end of a boat from the other, unlike Dylan and most of the guys she'd grown up with.

Leaving Katrina, Livvy made her way to the office in her suite where she had made herself at home, opening her computer to check her schedule. She was reading the notes for her first client when there was a gentle knock at the door and Dan's face appeared.

'Oh!' Livvy tried to hide her confusion. She hadn't expected to see him so soon, before she had worked out what to say to him.

'Sorry to take you by surprise. I thought we should get this meeting over before…' He gestured to the corridor where the others were arriving for work.

'Oh, right. Yes.' Livvy didn't know whether to stand up or stay seated. She decided to stay where she was, the trembling in her legs making her afraid to move.

'I just wanted to say how much I enjoyed last night and to reassure you that I don't intend to bother you here. I'm sure that, like me, you'd prefer to keep our relationship to outside of work hours.'

'I… of course.'

'Great. I'll call you.'

Livvy stared after him, *Relationship? It had been one dinner. Since when did that count as a relationship?* But she smiled as a warm glow flooded her. Maybe she wasn't the only one who was feeling this sense of something momentous about to happen.

# Thirty

It was Easter, and three weeks since Dan had dinner with Livvy. The day before, he'd driven Kim to the airport to send her off to Sydney for her cousin's birthday party and to spend the holidays with her aunt and uncle. While he was still unhappy about her trip, he reasoned that they couldn't do much harm in the ten days she was to spend with them, and his agreement had made her happy. He'd do almost anything to keep his daughter happy, even agreeing to her spending time with Sharon and Darryl.

And, as it happened, he wasn't going to be as lonely over the weekend as he'd anticipated. The past three weeks had passed in a flash. Dan had been busy at work, but he and Livvy had managed to spend several evenings together, plus one spectacular day when he'd hired a yacht and taken her sailing, amused at her surprise he was an experienced sailor. Those days as a member of the Middle Harbour Yacht Club in Sydney hadn't been wasted. His regular participation in the Friday Twilight Spinnaker Racing had been a feature of his life for many years.

He and Livvy planned to spend most of the weekend together and, as a huge step forward, she had agreed to their joining some of her friends for a barbecue on Good Friday, which was today. They were going sailing again on Saturday and there had been some mention of him being introduced to her son at some stage. Dan also entertained hopes of their relationship moving to the next level during the weekend but was conscious of Livvy still being reluctant to do anything that smacked of commitment. However, with Kim gone, they were both free agents, so he could dream.

He grinned when his phone beeped with a text from Kim. As promised, she'd called him last night when she arrived in Sydney to tell him all was well and to stop worrying. As if he could. She had no idea how much he worried about her, had done all her life. He couldn't imagine a time would come when he wouldn't worry about her, where she was, who she was meeting and what she was doing. But for now, he had to trust her aunt and uncle to take care of her. He knew they loved her, and Sharon was Cheryl's sister, but… He checked out the text to see it was a Happy Easter gif. He grinned again and sent one back. This would be their first Easter apart, the first when he hadn't presented her with a chocolate treat at breakfast. He'd given her one before she left, one of the Lindt dark chocolate Easter bunnies she loved and had preferred ever since she decided she'd outgrown standard Easter eggs. But it hadn't been the same as sitting it at her place on the kitchen table along with the special boiled egg they always ate for breakfast that day.

Dan had made himself a boiled egg and tried to pretend nothing had changed. He'd found a Ferrero collection of hazelnut eggs in the fridge, tied with a large ribbon and a sign which said, *Do Not Eat Before Easter*. Kim knew his weakness. He hoped Livvy liked chocolates too as he'd bought her a heart-shaped box of Ferrero Rocher chocolates which he intended to give her when he picked her up for the barbecue.

The barbecue wasn't till lunchtime, so breakfast over, Dan took Cooper for a walk. The beach was busy this morning, but he didn't meet anyone he knew, only catching sight of old Agnes in the distance and glad she wasn't any closer. He wasn't in the mood for any of her homespun homilies today. For once, there was no pleasure in the walk. The sand had been churned up by the groups of children, and there was a bunch of teenagers playing beach cricket. It was a challenge to prevent Cooper from chasing their ball and a relief to leave the beach behind. Their only encounter on the way home was a confrontation with a posse of pelicans wandering across their path, from which Cooper retired, his tail between his legs after straining on his leash to chase them. He'd never learn he was no match for those birds.

Back home, Dan filled Cooper's water bowl, showered and changed into an outfit more suited to a barbecue than the beach. Then he took the chocolates and a bottle of chardonnay he'd purchased especially for the occasion from the fridge, gave Cooper two of his favourite gravy bone treats, ruffled the dog's ears and told him to guard the house, before making his way to the car.

*

Livvy hadn't stopped all morning. She felt like the Energizer bunny as she rushed around the cottage, unable to sit still. Today was to be a first. She was taking Dan to the Easter barbecue Erica and Jamie were hosting and, although they were already aware she was seeing him, for her it was a big deal, not least because of the way both Erica and Gill had tried to persuade her it would be a good idea to hook up with him. But she hadn't – not in the way people used the term *hook up* these days – though she supposed it was only a matter of time. She shivered at the prospect of becoming intimate with Dan. Already they felt like a couple. It was why she'd agreed to invite him. Also, she was tired of being the only single when her friends got together.

The morning had begun with a Facetime call from Nancy even before she headed to the beach. She had still been half-asleep, but it had been lovely to see her three granddaughters and to wish them Happy Easter, even though their Easter hadn't yet started. She'd sent Nancy money to buy the older two Easter eggs and the littlest one a cuddly toy, and they were excited at the prospect of a visit from the Easter bunny. She remembered fondly their enthusiasm the previous year as they searched for Easter eggs in the garden, carrying their little baskets. There was still no news about their coming to Australia, but Nancy said Aiden had submitted his application for a partner visa and was checking out suitable job opportunities. Livvy had her fingers crossed.

Then, when she returned from her swim, there had been a call from Dylan to say that both he and Rory planned to be at the barbecue. Jamie, Rory's dad, had invited them but it had been dependent on how Rory was feeling that morning. Dylan reported that his partner was raring to go. So, Livvy would be able to kill two birds with one stone, so to speak, and Dan already knew Rory.

127

Livvy had vacuumed, cleaned the kitchen and bathroom until they sparkled and put on a wash, but there were still hours to get through before Dan arrived. She picked up her book club book for the month but even the latest Jack Hawksworth novel by Fiona McIntosh failed to hold her attention. Finally, she pulled her hat off the hook and headed across the road to the beach, hoping a walk on the sand would help calm her.

Stepping down from the path, Livvy took off her sandals and made her way down to the edge of the ocean. She was glad she was wearing the beige linen capris and the navy shirt she'd donned for the barbecue as she dipped her feet into the shallow water and gazed out to the horizon. It was glorious out here and as always, Livvy experienced a sense of being at peace with herself and the world. She closed her eyes for a moment and lifted her face to the sun. The only sound was the crying of the seagulls wheeling overhead.

When she opened them again, she saw a figure coming towards her. As the woman drew closer, she could see it was Lou. Of course, *Books and Coffee* would be closed today, one of the few days in the year when it was. Suddenly, Livvy was beset with guilt. She hadn't seen Lou since she was so kind to her, when she was in tears after Ingrid's betrayal and again just before her massage with Katrina. She'd promised to let her know how it went, but had forgotten, and she hadn't visited *Books and Coffee* since. *What sort of friend was she?*

'Happy Easter, Lou. I owe you an apology. After you were so kind to me, I didn't come back to thank you. Let me do it now. You were right. Katrina is wonderful.'

'No worries. I know you've been busy. I hear you joined the crew at the wellness centre. Are you liking it there? I believe Dan Parker can be a bit difficult to get along with.'

'Oh!' Livvy blushed. 'I'm really enjoying it there. Dan has collected a great bunch of people. We're all dedicated to our work. And I don't find him difficult to get along with, quite the reverse. Though I may have had some reservations to start with.'

'Well, I'm glad for you. And I'm glad I bumped into you. I was intending to drop in to see you.'

Livvy raised her eyebrows.

'It's about the beach gatherings. You always organised them before you went away, and with you gone, they fell apart. I did arrange one to welcome your friend, Erica, when she moved into your cottage. But now you're back, and we have the mayor and his partner living in the end cottage, I wondered if you were willing to start them up again.'

Livvy was flooded with even more guilt. Since returning to Pelican Crossing and her cottage, she hadn't given a thought to the beach gatherings she'd regularly arranged where the owners of the line of cottages got together for drinks and nibbles and caught up on the local gossip. 'Of course. I'm seeing Joe and Gill today… and Erica and Jamie. I'll talk with them about it and maybe we can arrange something for next month?'

'Sounds good. So, I can leave it with you?'

'Why don't you drop round one evening next week? We can discuss it, and I can fill you in on what I've been up to.'

'I'd like that. We haven't seen you in *Books and Coffee* either.'

'I know.' Livvy bit her lip. 'I'm sorry. I have been busy. I know that's no excuse, but now I'm working at the wellness centre, it's not so easy for me to nip in for a coffee and one of Ron's delicious offerings.' It was the one disadvantage of being located on the outskirts of town. When she had been in the medical centre, it had been easy for Livvy to drop into *Books and Coffee* for a quick caffeine fix, or lunch with Liz. Now she had to make do with the wellness centre kitchen and a packed lunch from home.

By the time Lou and Livvy parted, and Livvy made her way back home, it was almost time for Dan to arrive. She had just pulled a brush through her hair and refreshed her lipstick when she heard him at the door.

'Happy Easter,' Dan said, handing Livvy a heart-shaped box of her favourite brand of chocolates and holding up a bottle of wine in the other hand. 'Let me get rid of these and I'll greet you properly.'

Livvy laughed nervously, took the chocolates and led him into the kitchen, where, putting the bottle down on the benchtop, Dan took her into his arms and crushing her to him, pressed his lips to hers. Livvy felt transported on a soft and wispy cloud, only coming back down to earth when his lips moved to brush her forehead, before he gently released her.

'I guess we'd better go, or I won't be able to leave you alone,' he whispered, his breath warm in her ear.

'Yes,' she murmured, as her heartbeat settled down to a more even rate. Livvy couldn't believe the effect Dan had on her. To think this was the man she'd once considered arrogant and uncaring. How wrong she'd been.

When they arrived at Jamie's cottage, there was a flurry of greetings as everyone hugged each other, and Livvy introduced Dan to Dylan, Rory's brother, Gary, and his wife, Mandy, who were the only people he didn't already know. Even though Livvy had already told Erica and Gill about her and Dan, she noticed their raised eyebrows and wished she could check if her hair had become disarranged during Dan's hug. She hadn't taken time to check it again before they left, but she surreptitiously checked him for any sign of lipstick, relieved when there was none.

The barbecue proceeded as most others Livvy had attended, with the menfolk gravitating to the barbecue while the women chatted over glasses of wine and set out the salads. It was good to see Rory joining in with the other guys, despite his wheelchair. For once, Livvy didn't feel the odd one out, and each time Dan looked across at her she felt enveloped in a warm glow.

It was well into the afternoon before Dylan said, 'Time we were getting back. It's been a long day for you, Rory,' and Livvy noticed the young man was flagging.

That was the sign for the others to leave too, and Livvy and Dan were soon walking hand-in-hand back along the way to Livvy's cottage.

'Are you going to invite me in?' Dan asked when they reached the gate, his hand tightening around hers.

Too overcome for words, her heart racing madly in anticipation of what she knew would happen once they were inside, Livvy nodded.

# Thirty-one

Livvy could barely contain the sense of ecstasy which filled her when she wakened next morning with a smile on her face. The sun had already risen, so she'd missed her morning swim, but she had no regrets. It had been late when Dan left, citing the need to get home for Cooper, but before then they had spent hours curled up together in Livvy's bed, reminding her of what she'd been missing for so long. Dan was a gentle lover, who had brought her to heights of delight she could only have dreamt about. She lay there for several minutes remembering… then leapt up and into the shower, mindful they were going sailing again today, and Dan would be back in – she checked the time – less than an hour.

After a quick breakfast of toast spread with peanut butter and mashed banana and a cup of her favourite lemon and ginger tea, Livvy pulled on a fresh pair of capris and a pink tee-shirt. Blushing, she picked up her clothes from the day before from the floor where she – or Dan – had thrown them in their haste and dropped them in the laundry basket. Then, pulling her hair back into a band to prevent it from blowing into her eyes on the water, she applied the requisite amount of sunscreen and added a smidgeon of lipstick. She was ready.

Livvy was glad Dan had suggested he pick up a picnic basket from *The Blue Dolphin* on his way as it saved her thinking of what to take. Next time, she promised herself, sure there would be a next time, given Dan's love of sailing, which had been a pleasant surprise. It seemed he'd been involved in competition sailing before he came to Pelican

Crossing and, delighted to get involved again, was thinking of buying his own yacht. She'd heard him chatting to Rory and Dylan about it at the barbecue and they'd encouraged him to visit *Pelican Marine*, confident he'd find something suitable there. Meantime, he was hiring one from Jamie.

They weren't the only ones with plans to spend the day sailing, and it took them longer than they anticipated to make it out of the harbour. But eventually they were out in the bay and heading for the open sea. It was a perfect day to be on the water, the sun shining down on them and making the waves glisten like diamonds, with a light breeze, just enough to keep them on course.

As they sailed up the coast, they were joined by a pair of dolphins who kept them company for a time before veering off in a direction of their own, and of course, there were the inevitable seabirds whirling overhead in search of food.

'Hungry?' Dan asked as he steered into a small bay where the water was still, and so glassy Livvy could see down to the seabed.

'Mmm.' It was hours since she'd had breakfast, and the fresh air had whetted her appetite.

'Good.' Dan smiled. He'd been doing a lot of that today. She had too, still wrapped in the glow of their lovemaking.

Livvy relaxed next to Dan, revelling in his closeness as they demolished the dainty morsels the café had provided – tiny sausage rolls, miniature quiches and slices of ham and cheese – washed down with cans of low-alcohol beer. All too soon, it was time to make the return trip.

'Cooper has been on his own all day,' Dan said when they had moored the yacht and handed back the keys. 'He'll be ready for a walk. Join me?'

'Of course.' It had been such a lovely day, Livvy didn't want it to end, and Cooper was an old dog and had been friendly to her on the few occasions they'd met. She knew how fond Dan was of him, though she'd never owned a dog herself.

Dan helped her into his car, and they drove off, one of his hands on the steering wheel and the other on her thigh, sending shivers of desire through her.

*

Dan felt Livvy tremble at the touch of his hand. He felt like pinching himself, unable to believe this amazing woman had not only agreed to spend time with him, but… Last night had been a dream come true. It had been so long since he'd been with a woman, since he'd allowed himself to feel, to give way to his emotions. But it had been worth the wait. Livvy Grace was something else. And to think of his suspicions of her when they first met. It proved that first impressions could be wrong, so very wrong.

He hadn't been looking for companionship, for love. Even though he had anticipated being alone when Kim went to university, he'd been content to focus on his work and Cooper. But now… He glanced at Livvy out of the corner of his eye and his heart turned over as her gaze met his. He quickly returned his eyes to the road ahead. This was no time to take his mind off the road. They would soon be home.

'Come here.' As soon as they were inside, Dan pulled Livvy into his arms. He pressed his lips to hers, caressing her mouth more than kissing it, encouraged to hear her moan gently in response. He was about to take things further when he became aware of something damp on his ankle. He'd completely forgotten about Cooper.

Livvy was laughing when they pulled apart and the dog began nuzzling her ankles too. 'We were going to take Cooper for a walk.'

'So we were. You distracted me.'

'Don't blame me.' She was still laughing, and Dan joined in. 'Okay,' he said, 'It might have been my fault, but you are difficult to resist, and I've been patient all day.' He grinned, feeling like a little boy who'd been denied a special treat.

'And you need to be patient for a bit longer.' She tapped Dan on the nose, and he grasped her hand and kissed it, enjoying the banter and what amounted to foreplay for what they both knew was to happen later.

'Okay.' Dan feigned a sigh, but he was smiling. Cooper gave a small bark. 'Sorry, Cooper. Yes, it's walk time.' He took the dog's leash from its hook as the dog jumped up in an attempt to grab it. 'Ready, Livvy?'

It was quiet on the dog beach, most of the other dog owners having already left, so they had it almost to themselves. Dan took Livvy's hand, a thrill coursing through him as her fingers wound around his, while Cooper wandered along the edge of the water, stopping from time to time to sniff at a small crab or jellyfish on the sand.

'Have you heard from Kim?' Livvy asked, looking up at him. 'Her cousin's party is this weekend, isn't it?'

Dan frowned. He had been trying to forget the image of his daughter with her mother's family, the tagged photo of her and Haley which Cheryl's sister had put on Facebook with the post *Back together again*. 'Yes,' he said. 'Party's tonight. I suppose she told you all about it?' Kim was still seeing Livvy for counselling and as far as he could tell it was working. He hadn't heard his daughter crying in the night for some time.

'You know I can't tell you what we discuss,' she said.

'Of course not.' But he had hoped, with their new closeness, that she might be willing to relinquish her professional persona for him. Kim was his daughter, and he was… if not her boss… a close colleague and, as of last night, her lover.

By the time they'd walked to the end of the beach and back, even Cooper was ready to go home. On the way, by mutual agreement, they stopped at the Italian restaurant for a takeaway, and the bottle shop for a bottle of prosecco, both feeling they needed to celebrate the new stage in their relationship.

They were enjoying the spinach and feta cannelloni when Livvy's phone rang. At first, she ignored it, but as the ringing continued, she gave him an apologetic look. 'I should take this,' she said, rising from the table and going out into the yard, closing the door behind her. *What was that about? Who was calling her, whose conversation she didn't want Dan to hear?* Stifling his concern, Dan took a gulp of wine and stared at the closed door. Cooper, sensing his master's mood, rose from where he'd been lying under the table to put a paw on Dan's knee.

'It's all right, old fellow,' Dan said, fondling the dog's ears and hoping it was true.

Livvy was outside for over ten minutes, and when she came back in her face was drained of colour and etched with worry.

'What's the matter?' Dan rose and went to take her in his arms, but she shrugged him off.

'It was Dylan,' she said. 'Rory's had a fall, and Dylan thinks he's damaged his leg, the bad one. He can't move him by himself and can't rouse Jamie or Gary, so he called me. I need to get over there. I'm sorry. I know we had other plans.'

Dan was tempted to ask why her son hadn't called an ambulance but remained silent. It was Easter weekend, and he knew from experience how overworked the ambulance service was, especially on holiday weekends when the town was filled with tourists.

'Just as he was making such good progress too.' It was almost as if Livvy had forgotten Dan was there.

'I'm coming with you,' he said. 'It sounds as if you're going to need someone with more strength than you, someone who knows how to lift an injured patient.'

'Thanks.' Livvy gave a rueful smile. 'Sorry to spoil your evening.'

'It's your evening too, and we have all the time in the world. Let's see what we can do to help Rory and put your son's mind at rest.'

'Thanks,' Livvy said again, and gave him a hug, before they hurried out to the car.

# Thirty-two

Livvy was glad Dan had offered to come with her. While she wanted to respond to Dylan, she hadn't been sure how much help she'd be on her own. Selfishly, she wished either Jamie or Gary had been available. Then her evening with Dan wouldn't have been spoiled. But Dylan's need was greater than her desire to spend another evening in bed with Dan, and as he said, they had all the time in the world. The way he'd said that had sent shivers down her spine. It was as if he was saying he wanted to spend the rest of his life with her. But she couldn't think of that now. Dylan was in trouble. Rory needed them. She could only hope his leg wasn't badly damaged and that, if necessary, they could get him to the hospital.

When they arrived at Rory's apartment, Dylan let them in immediately, his eyes brightening at the sight of Dan. 'Good to see you, Dan,' he said, leading them inside. 'Rory's in the bathroom. He slipped when I was helping him shower and seems to be wedged. His leg… I'm worried he might have damaged it.'

'Let's see, shall we,' Dan said, instantly taking charge. 'Why don't you make us all a cup of tea, Livvy?'

'Sure.' Livvy's eyes followed them, hearing Dylan say, 'I called for an ambulance but seems there was a bad accident in the hinterland between a tourist bus and a truck…' His voice died away as they moved out of range. Livvy took a deep breath, feeling she'd been sidelined. But Dan was right. There wasn't anything else she could do to help, and Rory would most likely be embarrassed for her to see him naked.

She went into the kitchen, filled the kettle and turned it on. Making tea was something she could do.

The kettle had boiled, Livvy had drunk her tea and was staring out of the window when she heard some movement, and Dan appeared in the kitchen doorway.

'We have Rory back in his wheelchair. The wound hasn't opened but he's in a lot of pain so I'm going to help Dylan take him to the hospital. You can…' He dragged a hand through his hair, his forehead creasing.

'It's okay. I'll go home. I can make my own way from here. Call me later and let me know how Rory is going.'

'Thanks, sweetheart.' Dan pulled her in for a quick kiss, but Livvy could tell his mind was elsewhere.

'Go,' she said, aware how important it might prove for Rory to be seen by a doctor as soon as possible. 'I can lock up here.'

'Thanks, Mum.' Dylan gave her a hug and a peck on the cheek. 'Love you.'

'Love you too. Take care of Rory.'

'Of course.'

*

When she was back home again, Livvy felt drained. So much had happened that day. It was difficult to believe that, only a few hours earlier she and Dan had been lazing on the deck of a yacht with no thought further than where they'd choose to spend the night. With the call from Dylan, Dan had been thrown into Livvy's family troubles, and he'd risen to the challenge. It had no doubt helped that in his role as a physiotherapist, he was already treating Rory so the guy wasn't a stranger to him, but he'd only met Dylan for the first time the day before.

Now the pressure to help Rory was over and he was on his way to hospital, Livvy realised she was hungry. She and Dan had barely touched their Italian meal when Dylan called. They'd left the food lying on the table. She should have gone back and put it in the fridge, but she didn't have a key to Dan's house. She pulled a frozen meal out of the fridge, one of several she kept there for times like this and poured herself a glass of wine. She knew it could be some time before she heard from Dan but wouldn't be able to sleep till she did. She turned on the television, surfing the channels but found nothing to interest her, so leant back on the sofa, reliving the events of the past two days.

She must have fallen asleep, because the next thing she was aware of was a loud hammering on the door and a dog barking. Pushing herself up, Livvy made her way to the door to be greeted by Dan and Cooper.

'I thought it best to bring him along. I hope you don't mind,' he said, as the dog sniffed at the strange scents in Livvy's hallway.

'Not at all.' Livvy, still half-asleep, was pulled into Dan's arms. 'How is Rory… and Dylan?' She glanced behind Dan, but there was no sign of her son.

'They're keeping Rory in overnight, to make sure everything is okay, and Dylan is staying with him. Jamie and Gary arrived, and it was becoming a bit crowded, so I thought it better to leave, and I called in at home to pick up this one,' he gestured to where Cooper was padding through the house, 'and to throw out the food. It wasn't worth keeping it.'

'Sorry.' By this time, they had reached the living room and Cooper had found a spot in front of the sofa and settled down, head on his paws, looking quite at home, while Livvy and Dan were seated on the sofa. 'It's good to see you… and Cooper. Thanks for your help with Rory.'

'No problem. And there's nothing to apologise for. You didn't have a key so couldn't do anything about the food.'

'True.' Livvy snuggled up to Dan, secure in the knowledge that Dan would look out for Rory and Dylan. It was as if they were already a family. As he pulled her into a warm hug, she couldn't disguise the shiver of anticipation at the knowledge that with Cooper here, there would be no need for Dan to leave before morning, and she could look forward to waking up beside him.

# Thirty-three

After the drama of the dash to help Dylan and take Rory to hospital, the rest of the Easter weekend passed relatively peacefully. Waking to see Livvy's head on the pillow beside him on Easter Sunday had sent Dan's heart racing, and it had been some time before they rose. It was only when they could no longer suffer the sound of Cooper whimpering, and Livvy said, 'You need to take care of your poor dog,' that Dan swung his legs out of bed to feed him, glad he'd taken time to pack the dog's food and bowl the previous evening.

Cooper greeted him with a welcome bark, immediately forgiving Dan for seemingly abandoning him in a strange house.

'You didn't go for your swim this morning,' Dan said to Livvy, when they were walking Cooper along the stretch of beach opposite her cottage, having enjoyed a breakfast of avocado and poached egg on toasted muffins with coffee for Dan and a herbal tea mix for Livvy.

'I'm taking the weekend off,' Livvy replied with a smile, her eyes meeting his and reminding him of how her body had melted against his, how their legs had entwined, how his world had spun and careered on its axis. He swallowed hard and pulled her close, delighting in the feel of her body next to his.

'We have two more days,' he said. 'What would you like to do?' He'd be happy to spend them in bed with her, but knew it was a forlorn hope.

Livvy glanced at him. 'I had planned to visit my friend, Rhana, before...' she blushed. 'I could cancel or... you could come too. She lives out of town and breeds spaniels. We could probably take Cooper. She loves animals… more than humans, I often think.'

'If you're sure…' It wasn't how Dan had planned to spend the day, but he was willing to go along with whatever Livvy wanted to do.

'I am. I can call her first to check. Then…' she glanced at him again, '… a few of us were going to the yacht club for dinner tonight. I guess perhaps Jamie and Erica will pull out because of Rory, but…'

Dan sighed. He should have realised. Livvy had a full social life before he came along. He couldn't expect her to drop everything because of him. But he wished she would.

'You'd be welcome to come too,' she said, taking away some of his disappointment.

'Who will be there?'

'It'll be quite a crowd. You know most of them, I think. Joe and Gill, of course, and Liz and Finn. Then there will be Poppy and Rachel, friends of Liz and Gill's with their partners, Cam, who owns *Pelican Marine*, and Luke, who…'

'Isn't he the guy who was acting as vet before the regular one came back?'

'That's right. You've met him?'

Dan nodded. The group didn't sound too daunting. 'Is Poppy the owner of *Crossings*?' he asked, recognising another name.

'She is. I don't usually have such a full social calendar. It was all set up before you and I got together. I think Erica wanted to fill my lonely evenings.' She chuckled.

'Not so lonely now.' Dan pulled her into an embrace, lifting her feet off the sand and kissing the top of her head.

'No,' she agreed, snuggling into him.

*

Although Livvy had warned him, Dan couldn't hide his surprise when he stepped out of the car at her friend's property to find himself surrounded by a bevy of spaniels. Seemingly equally surprised, after his first indignant bark, Cooper lay down in a prone position allowing the pups to swarm all over him, before Rhana called them away.

'So, this is the guy I've heard so much about? Welcome!' Rhana said with a smile.

Dan glanced at Livvy who was blushing. *What had she been saying about him?*

'All good things,' Rhana assured him. 'Your wellness centre is the talk of the town, and I read the article in *The Echo*. It's good to finally meet you. I don't get into town much, as you can see.' She gestured to the pups who were now crawling over each other, pretending to fight. 'This lot will be going to their forever homes soon, but there's another litter on the way.'

*Livvy had been right when she said her friend cared more about her animals than people.*

The visit proved to be more fun than Dan had expected. In addition to her love of spaniels, it appeared Rhana grew all her own vegetables and loved to cook. She secured the dogs in a fenced play area and the three humans enjoyed home-made bread with a delicious quiche, followed by apple tart served with thickened cream – a richer meal than Dan was accustomed to.

During lunch, Dan learned that Livvy, Rhana and Erica had been best friends all through school and he listened with interest as Livvy and Rhana reminisced about some of their exploits as teenagers. It appeared Rhana had never married, though she was somewhat reticent when he rashly asked if she had ever come close. Livvy later told him that neither she nor Erica had ever been able to find out either, which surprised him as they had been such good friends. But what did he know about female friendships, other than that they were very different from men's?

Overall, it was a pleasant visit, and he was looking forward to the evening, to meeting more of Livvy's friends, surprised by how quickly he'd been thrown into her close circle and accepted by its members. It made him realise how limited his own circle of friends in Pelican Crossing was, even after living here for four years.

'Thanks for coming.' Livvy covered Dan's hand with hers when they got back into the car.

'Not a problem. It was fun. I like your friend, and if ever I want another dog, I know where to come.' Rhana had made Cooper welcome, providing him with a special treat while they ate and making a big fuss of him before they left.

Livvy laughed. 'She always seems to have a litter on the way and appears to enjoy the solitude out here.' She stared around at the empty landscape, the rolling hills in the distance and no other house in sight and shuddered. 'It's beautiful, but I don't think I'd like it. I prefer to be closer to other people.'

Dan chuckled, leant in and kissed her on the cheek 'You and me both.'

*

When Dan and Livvy arrived at the yacht club that evening, the others were already there, and the wine was flowing. After greeting those of the group he'd already met, Livvy introduced him to the others as Liz took charge of the seating arrangements, Dan found himself seated between Cam, the owner of *Pelican Marine*, and Luke, the vet he'd met when Cooper had his shots. It seemed that, unlike many other groups Dan had known over the years, these people didn't make a fuss about sitting men and women alternately. He would have preferred to be seated next to Livvy, and her rueful glance from across the table told him she'd have preferred it too.

However, as the meal progressed, Dan discovered that both Cam and Luke were good company. Cam was a mine of information about yachts for sale both here and farther up the coast, and before the main course was over, he'd arranged to visit him to check out what he had available.

When he turned to his other side to reacquaint himself with Luke, he was pleased the vet remembered both him and Cooper. After a brief chat about the dog, Luke's stint as a locum for Bob Reed and the wellness centre, the mention of Dan's previous practice led them to the realisation they both came from Sydney and from that to the discovery of several mutual acquaintances. Dan felt quite at home, secure in the knowledge he'd made two new friends.

'Sorry about that,' Livvy said when the evening was over and they were walking back to her cottage where they'd left Cooper, 'Liz is a law unto herself, and it seems she decided to split up all the couples tonight.'

'No worries,' Dan threw an arm around her shoulders and pulled her towards him. 'It was a good evening. I enjoyed it. I like your friends.'

'You do?' Livvy pulled away and peered at him as if to make sure he wasn't lying.

'I do. They're a great bunch. Cam told me about a yacht that might be of interest to me, and I've arranged to see it tomorrow. You can come along if you like.' He smiled as she cuddled into him and nodded her agreement. 'And Luke and I found we had a lot in common. Although we both came here from Sydney, we lived a fair way apart, but he knew a few of the guys I sailed with, took care of their animals. It's a small world.'

'Mmm.'

They reached Livvy's cottage before any more could be said and Cooper's enthusiastic greeting put paid to anything further until he was petted and fed

. Dan's heart was filled with a sense of unfiltered joy that he had found this woman, a woman he could see himself spending the rest of his life with, a woman who seemed to like him too. His only worry was what Kim might think about it.

# Thirty-four

It seemed so natural to see Dan sitting across from her at breakfast next morning that Livvy had to remind herself this was a holiday weekend, and everything would go back to normal next day. But meantime, she intended to enjoy every minute of it. She was even growing accustomed to Cooper's presence in her kitchen, where the dog had made himself at home.

'You mentioned looking at a yacht,' she said when Dan was on his second cup of coffee, and she had almost finished her lemon and ginger tea.

'Mmm.' Dan nodded. 'Cam said he'd be at the marina after ten. He has a bit of work to do there, despite it being a holiday. Still want to come with me?'

'Of course.' Livvy wanted to spend as much time with Dan as she could before the working week began. His daughter would be returning home too – she wasn't sure how long Kim was in Sydney for – and spending time like this would become more complicated.

'We should take Cooper for a walk first, then drop him off at home – my home. Okay with you?'

'Sure.' Livvy tried to hide her disappointment that he wanted to take Cooper back to his home. It meant he wouldn't be staying here overnight. But what had she expected? Tomorrow was a workday. She'd be back to her morning routine, her early morning swim. Dan would have a routine too for the working week. Life wasn't one long holiday.

Livvy was mollified when Dan took her hand as they crossed the road to the beach. 'I wish every day could be like this,' he said, 'but life gets in the way. Back to work tomorrow, back to old clothes and porridge as my Scottish grandmother used to say.'

'I didn't know you had Scottish connections,' Livvy said, interested to learn more about him.

'She emigrated in her twenties, met an Australian soldier during the war and came here afterwards. I went over for a visit when I was at uni, met some of the relatives. Could barely understand them.' He chuckled. 'What about you? No foreign connections?'

'I come from convict stock,' Livvy said. 'Mum researched the family tree at one stage and managed to trace it back to a young girl who was sent here for stealing a handkerchief from her mistress.'

'You've come a long way.' Dan laughed. 'And now your daughter's living back there. You weren't tempted to stay?'

'No! I couldn't stand the weather. It was so cold.' Livvy shivered at the memory of the snow lying on the ground, the need to pile on layers of clothes before venturing out. 'I'm hoping Nancy and her family will come here. Aiden has applied for a partner visa. But it'll take time.'

'You must miss them.'

'Terribly. We talk on Facetime a lot, but it's not the same.'

'Mmm. I know how I'd feel if Kim chose to move overseas. Even with her in Sydney, I miss her a lot. I'm not looking forward to her starting uni next year.'

'When does she get back?'

'The end of next week.' He paused and gazed at Livvy. 'I plan to tell her about us.'

Livvy shivered again as a ripple of excitement shot through her. If Dan intended to tell Kim about her, it must mean that he intended their relationship to continue. Kim already knew her, but as far as she was concerned, Livvy was her counsellor, someone who worked with her dad in the wellness centre. She swallowed. 'How do you think she'll react?'

Dan sighed and dragged a hand through his hair. 'I have no idea. She still misses her mother. You know that. You might have a better idea of how she'd react than I do.'

Livvy experienced a sudden feeling of heaviness in her limbs. How could she have forgotten? She was counselling the girl. Kim was still consumed with grief, still coming to terms with her mother's death. How could Livvy hope she'd accept her as what she'd see as a replacement for the mother she'd lost? 'I don't think this is a good idea,' she said, pulling her hand from his.

*

'What?' Dan stared at Livvy in amazement. *What did she mean? That he shouldn't tell Kim, or…*

'You and me. All of this.'

'I don't understand.' Dan continued to stare at Livvy in disbelief. Was this the same woman to whom he'd made love, whose lips had met his with such passion who…

'There's nothing to understand. Kim's your daughter. Her feelings are more important than ours. She lost her mother. I'm her counsellor. I should have known better. Instead, I conveniently decided it didn't matter, I was wrong. I'm sorry, Dan.' She raised her face to him, tears trickling down her cheeks.

All Dan wanted to do was to take her in his arms and comfort her, tell her it didn't matter how Kim would react, what she might think. But it did. 'I'm sorry too,' he said, his heart breaking at the realisation Livvy was right. It probably didn't matter whether it was Livvy or some other woman. Kim was still grieving for Cheryl, and while *he* was ready to fall in love again, Kim wouldn't be prepared to let anyone else take her mother's place. 'You wouldn't be…' he began, but he knew it was no use. Livvy had made up her mind.

'I'm sorry,' she said again through her tears. 'I need to go now.' Turning, she stumbled up the beach, Dan staring after her, feeling as if he'd been dealt a blow from which he might never recover.

'Come, Cooper,' he said to the dog who was happily playing at the edge of the water, unaware of how Dan's life had suddenly changed, how his plans for the future had taken a dive. He cursed inwardly as the dog ran towards him, tongue hanging out with the joy of being alive. It was how Dan had been feeling only an hour earlier. How quickly life could change.

Dan checked the time. It was already ten o'clock. Cam would

be expecting him and, while the last thing he felt like doing was examining a yacht, he'd made a promise and he had nothing else to do with his day.

Leaving Cooper at home, Dan drove back to the marina and parked outside *Pelican Marine*. Despite the hollowness in his chest at the thought of never seeing Livvy again outside the wellness centre, the layout impressed him. Cam must be doing well.

Cam greeted him with a firm handshake. 'Good to see you. Livvy not with you today?' Cam's eyes travelled to the empty space behind Dan.

'No, not today.' Remembering Livvy's son worked here, Dan was glad it was a holiday and he wasn't likely to see Dylan here today. Cam was a friend of hers too. He wondered how soon people would find out they were no longer a couple. They wouldn't hear it from him, but in Pelican Crossing news travelled fast.

Dan perked up a little when he saw the yacht Cam had for sale. It was a beauty. The twenty-five and a half foot Catalina 750 Sport was exactly what Dan had been looking for, and this one had myriad upgrades making it even more attractive. The asking price of $95,000 was a bit steep but not beyond Dan's budget. He could imagine Livvy sitting in the cockpit, her hair blowing in the breeze, the sail billowing in the wind. He pulled himself back to earth. Livvy would never be on this yacht.

'Want to take it out?' Cam asked.

'Sure.'

The trial sail went smoothly, the yacht handling as well as Dan had expected. He was impressed, too, by the cosy and modern feel below and the dining table which could fold down to convert into a double bed. *If only…*

'Well, what did you think?' Cam asked, when he pulled into the marina again.

'It's pretty much what you said, what I've been looking for. I'll need to talk to the bank when it opens tomorrow, but you've got yourself a sale.'

'Good man. You won't regret it. How about we seal the deal with a beer?'

'Sounds good to me.' Alcohol might help staunch the ache in his gut.

As Dan and Cam crossed the road to *The Grand*, a pair of pelicans strutted across in front of them forcing them to swerve out of their way. At any other time, Dan would have laughed at the two ungainly birds, but today he was not amused.

By the time he and Cam were seated in a booth with glasses of beer, Dan was feeling a little better, but his face must have given him away. 'What's the matter, mate? Woman trouble?' Cam asked.

Dan grimaced. He'd only met Cam the previous evening, and he was a friend of Livvy's, or his partner was. There was no way he could confide in him. It wasn't something men did anyway, not like women who shared their feelings at the drop of a hat. Though he sensed Livvy wasn't like that. She tended to keep things to herself. It was one of the things that had attracted him to her.

Dan was on his third beer to Cam's one, even though he knew trying to drown his sorrows wouldn't help. He was considering it was time to go, to get back to Cooper, when Cam said, 'Sometimes it helps to talk about it. I don't know you very well, but I can tell something's bothering you. And you don't need to worry. Anything you say stays here. My lips are sealed.'

Dan gazed into his glass as if the beer held the answer, then he said, 'As you guessed, it's Livvy. She…' He proceeded to give Cam a potted version of their conversation on the beach finishing with, '… and the trouble is, I know she's right. Kim's not ready for me to move on, despite it being four years since we lost Cheryl.'

'Hell of a mess, Dan. I know what kids can be like. Poppy and I were fortunate in that regard, but I know others who weren't as lucky. I know it doesn't help, but I'd suggest you give it time. Before you know it, your daughter will have her own life and…'

Dan sighed. That was part of the problem. He was dreading Kim leaving home, and it had been such a solace to imagine Livvy would be there with her warmth and support, that he wouldn't be alone. Now, he didn't even have that to comfort him. 'Thanks, mate,' he said.

When he left the hotel, Dan, conscious of the three beers he'd consumed decided to walk home, but it seemed that everywhere he passed held memories of Livvy – the yacht club, *The Blue Dolphin*, the dog beach.

Cooper's enthusiastic greeting when he arrived home went some way to cheering Dan up, as did the text he received from Kim with a photo of her at Haley's party. Seeing her looking so happy reinforced Livvy's decision. It was the right thing for them, for Kim. Her happiness was what was most important to him.

# Thirty-five

It was now almost two weeks since Livvy had walked away from Dan on the sand, and it had been one of the hardest things she'd ever done. She took consolation in knowing she'd acted in the best interests of Kim who was not only her client but Dan's daughter, though it didn't make it any easier, and she'd cried herself to sleep every night since.

At least she'd managed to avoid Dan at the wellness centre, though she suspected he was just as eager to keep out of her way too. She wasn't sure why that irritated her, since it had been her who had walked out on him.

It had helped to get back into a routine, though she was also at pains to avoid Erica and Gill at the beach in the early morning. Livvy knew she'd have to tell them sometime that she was no longer seeing Dan, but she wasn't yet ready for the recriminations she knew would follow. While she might believe she was doing the right thing, she doubted her friends would agree.

This morning, she was feeling slightly more cheerful when she walked into the wellness centre. It must have shown in her expression because when she bumped into Patrick in the kitchen he said, 'You're looking better. Have you been sick?'

Livvy shook her head, wondering exactly what she'd looked like for the previous two weeks. No one else had said anything, and her clients seemed comfortable with her. 'Thanks, I'm fine,' she said.

'In that case, how about coming for a drink after work? The wine bar isn't busy at that time.'

'With you?' As soon as she said it, Livvy realised how silly it sounded. Of course he meant with him. There was no one else in the kitchen. 'I don't…' she began, then paused. Why shouldn't she have a drink with him? He wasn't Dan, but he was pleasant enough. She had no intention of becoming involved with another work colleague, but one drink wouldn't hurt, and it would delay the time she returned to her cottage which now seemed emptier than ever without Dan and Cooper. Even though they'd only been there briefly, they'd left an impression that was difficult to erase. 'Okay,' she said.

*

Dan was about to enter the wellness centre kitchen when he heard voices, one of which was Livvy's. So far, he'd managed to avoid her at work for his own peace of mind as much as anything else, and it appeared she felt the same. He was about to turn away when he heard Patrick invite her for a drink after work and his blood boiled. Surely she wouldn't…? He stopped in his tracks. There were a few moments of silence, then he heard her agree.

Dan couldn't believe his ears. How could she? It was only two weeks since they'd been in bed together, and now she was going out with Patrick. Had she meant any of the things she'd said to him? Had she missed him at all?

The rest of his day passed in a blur, although he took care to treat his patients with his usual care and was sure they didn't notice how distracted he was. The only time he was drawn into a conversation was when Rory Whittaker rolled his wheelchair into his clinic, but if he'd hoped the young man might have some insight into the thinking of his partner's mother, he was wrong. All he wanted to discuss was how soon he'd be mobile again. Dan wasn't able to give him an answer but was aware he was also still attending therapy sessions at the hospital and was making good progress.

Against his better judgment, Dan made a detour on the way home to pass the wine bar where he knew Livvy and Patrick were meeting. Feeling like a stalker, he peered in through the window, not sure what he expected to see. He'd never visited this relatively new addition to the local drinking establishments. It was more Kim's scene than his. He preferred to do his drinking in the privacy of his own home or in *The Grand*. From what he could see through the tinted glass, the place looked like any other pub. There was a bar with tall stools, and a number of small tables, at one of which he could see Livvy and Patrick and… They weren't alone. Sitting with them were several of the other therapists from the wellness centre.

Dan heaved a sigh of relief. Livvy and Patrick weren't on a date. He should have remembered hearing about how many of what he liked to call *his* therapists enjoyed getting together for a drink once a month. He'd even been invited to join them once, but hadn't realised this was where they met. Feeling foolish, he left hurriedly before anyone spotted him. It would be embarrassing to be caught out spying on them.

*

Inside the wine bar, Livvy sipped her glass of chardonnay, relieved when she and Patrick were joined by a number of her other colleagues.

'Glad to see you joining us,' Katrina said as she slid into a chair next to Livvy, dropping her bag on the floor. 'We do this about once a month. It's good to get together away from the centre to let our hair down, catch up.'

'And gossip about the boss,' one of the others put in with a laugh.

Livvy felt herself blush, glad the lighting was dim. *What did she mean? Could they know that she and Dan…?*

'Not really,' Patrick said, as if sensing her discomfort. 'We've invited Dan to join us, but he refused. Probably just as well. It means we can grumble about things without being overheard.'

'What are you unhappy about? I know I haven't been there long, but I don't have any complaints.'

'Nothing really, and if we have, Dan is quick to fix things. It's just easier to talk when he's not around.'

Livvy was beginning to wish she hadn't come, but it would raise their suspicions if she left now. She took another sip of her drink and let the conversation flow over her as the discussion moved on from the wellness centre to other local issues. After she felt sufficient time had passed, Livvy drained her glass. 'Sorry, I need to get home. I'm expecting a call from my daughter.' It wasn't exactly a lie. Nancy could call, but it was unlikely as she'd spoken to her only that morning.

Livvy wasn't sure how she felt about the gathering she'd just left. The others in the group were younger than her and the wine bar seemed more suited to them. She expected it would become busy later with groups of other young people and suspected it was more Dylan's sort of place than hers, making her feel old. She could understand why Dan might have declined to join them.

Arriving home, Livvy slipped off her shoes and changed into a comfortable old pair of track pants and a tee shirt, before heating up some leftover pasta and taking it out into the courtyard. It was a lovely evening, the fragrance from the lemon-scented gum filling the air. She had just taken her empty bowl inside and was planning to make a cup of herbal tea and settle down with a book when she heard someone at the door.

Her heart racing in the faint hope it might be Dan, even though it was highly unlikely, she hurried to open it, quickly checking her hair in the hall mirror on the way, to see Lou standing there holding a tray on which were four pieces of the salted caramel brownies Livvy loved.

'I'm glad I caught you home,' Lou said with a smile, holding out the tray. 'I thought we could have these with tea or coffee.'

Livvy had forgotten inviting Lou to drop round one evening. Recovering from her surprise, she said, 'Of course, come on in. I was about to make tea, or would you prefer coffee?'

'Tea will be fine.'

A few minutes later, both women were seated at Livvy's kitchen table with cups of camomile tea, enjoying the brownies Lou had brought home from *Books and Coffee*. Livvy had quickly agreed to arranging a get together of neighbours in a week's time, on the Saturday evening. As on previous occasions, they'd meet on the beach around four, and Lou promised to provide nibbles from the café. The men would provide beer and soft drinks, and Livvy would take care of letting everyone know about it. 'And I promise to do the same each month from now on,' she said, laughing. 'I'm sorry you had to remind me. My head's been all over the place since I got back.'

'Not to worry. Is everything all right now?' Lou asked, her voice loaded with concern. 'You don't seem as happy as you were when we last spoke.'

'No.' Livvy closed her eyes for a moment, remembering. She'd last spoken to Lou when they met on the beach at Easter before the barbecue at Jamie's, before she and Dan… So much had happened since then. Her eyes moistened. 'Oh, Lou!'

'What is it? Is there something I can do to help?'

'There's nothing anyone can do.' Livvy burst into tears, unable to hold them at bay.

'If you want to talk…'

'Thanks.' Livvy sniffed and wiped her eyes with a tissue. She looked at her friend and wondered if talking about it would help. She'd been bottling everything up since that time on the beach.

'So that's it,' Livvy finished. 'I couldn't risk alienating Dan from his daughter, so…' she spread her hands in a gesture of defeat, hoping her friend might tell her she'd been wrong. 'I guess I'm destined to remain alone,' she said with a sigh,

To her surprise, Lou seemed to freeze, then she squeezed Livvy's hand gently before letting it go again. 'There's nothing wrong with being alone, and you're not really, are you? You have your daughter in England, planning to return to Australia, and your son right here in Pelican Crossing. You did the right thing,' she said. 'Family rifts can go on for years, cause an untold amount of damage.' She stared into space for a moment as if thinking of something else, of another time, then seemed to collect herself and patted Livvy's hand. 'I should go now. I've taken up enough of your time. Thanks for the tea and for agreeing to start up our neighbourhood gatherings again.'

It was as if the conversation about Dan had never happened. Livvy wondered if she'd been insensitive to talk about being alone with Lou who also lived alone. She wanted to ask her what she meant about family rifts, if she'd been speaking from experience, but Lou's face held a shuttered expression which told her any questioning would be fruitless. 'I'll see you out,' she said. 'Thanks for bringing the brownies. They're my favourite.' This elicited a small smile from Lou.

Once she had closed the door on Lou, Livvy walked back into the kitchen. She was puzzled about Lou's reaction and disappointed her friend had agreed with her decision. What had she expected, hoped?

Livvy knew that ending her relationship with Dan had been right, the only course of action. It had been foolish to get involved with him in the first place, but… she couldn't dismiss the memory of how she'd felt for that brief time when she'd thought she and Dan might have a future together.

# Thirty-six

Dan was saved from brooding over Livvy by the prospect of Kim's return home. The house had seemed so empty without her, even Cooper's usual snuffling failing to fill the void. He supposed it was a taste of what it would be like when she went off to uni, wincing at the thought of the lonely future that faced him.

Leaving Cooper at home, Dan drove to the airport. He was looking forward to seeing Kim again, to hearing her lively chatter, even to have his ears blasted with her music. He'd missed her more than he thought possible. Since Cheryl's death, it had just been the two of them and although Kim was changing, growing up, she was still his beloved daughter. That would never change.

As he made his way down the coast, Dan's mind went back to the previous two weeks. It was as if he and Livvy had engaged in a well-orchestrated dance, each determined to avoid the other, and it had worked. They had never been in the same part of the wellness centre at the same time. But their lack of contact at work hadn't eradicated her from his thoughts or erased the memory of their times together, making him wish things could be different.

Kim's face broke into a grin when she saw Dan waiting to greet her. She dropped her backpack and threw her arms around him. 'Did you miss me, Dad?' she yelled, her voice so loud the whole airport must have heard her. 'How's Cooper?'

'Of course I did, sweetheart. The house was very quiet without you. Cooper missed you too. How was Sydney… and your aunt and uncle?'

Even though she'd texted him almost every day while she was there, her brief comments and emojis didn't tell him much.

'They're good. I spent most of my time with Haley,' she said, quickly dismissing her mother's sister and her husband as being of little importance to her, 'and Sydney was amazing. I have so much to tell you. I can't wait to get home.'

Despite her initial enthusiasm, Kim's energy level dropped as soon as she got into the car, and she slept most of the way home, so Dan had to wait for all the things Kim had to tell him. With her eyes closed and her hair falling over her face, she looked so like the four-year-old Kim he remembered, it brought a tear to his eyes. She'd been so innocent back then. It was a pity she'd had to grow up.

Kim opened her eyes and stretched her arms above her head as they reached the outskirts of Pelican Crossing and were passing the wellness centre. Dan smiled, as he always did at the sight of the sign announcing it as *Pelican Crossing Wellness Centre,* his pride in it never diminishing. As long as he had it and Kim, life was good, he thought, despite part of him wishing he could have Livvy too.

'Are we nearly home?' Kim yawned.

'Almost there. Hungry?'

Kim sat up and stared out the window. 'Can we stop at McDonald's?'

'Of course.' Dan was so pleased to have her back he'd have agreed to almost anything. Then Kim's phone pinged. Dan was aware of her reading a text and laughing. 'Okay if I go out tonight, Dad? A few of the gang are having a drink on the beach to welcome me back.' Dan's heart dropped. He'd been looking forward to spending a lovely evening at home with Kim, hearing all about her trip, the *so much* she had to tell him. But he guessed he'd have to wait. It was only natural that seeing her friends took precedence over an evening with her dad. He'd have felt the same at her age. He sighed. 'Of course it is, sweetheart.'

*

Next morning Dan awoke to the sound of music. Kim was home, but what was she doing awake at this time? He checked on the bedside table for his phone, touched the screen and blinked at the display.

Eight o'clock already? How could she be up and about? He'd been wakened at around two with Kim coming home, the front door slamming behind her. It was as if she'd never been away.

Glad it wasn't a workday, Dan stumbled out of bed and into the shower, hoping a blast of cold water would help get him properly awake. Then, dressed in a pair of jeans and a cotton shirt, he made his way into the kitchen which was the source of the noise, and which was filled with the aroma of coffee. He sniffed appreciatively. 'Good morning. You're an early bird.'

'Hi, Dad. I thought I'd make up for going out last night by cooking breakfast for you.' Kim grinned up at him from the bowl in which she was beating eggs, and the disappointment of the previous evening disappeared.

'Lovely,' Dan said, dropping a kiss on his daughter's head and pouring himself a mug of coffee. Cooper was standing over his bowl, munching happily.

'I fed Cooper too,' she said.

'Thanks, honey.' Dan took a seat and sipped his coffee, prepared to enjoy this new version of Kim while it lasted. 'Not seeing your friends today?'

'Not till later. I wanted to spend some time with you.' She grinned again, and his heart went out to her.

'That was delicious, honey. Now, I want to hear all about your trip,' Dan said, when they had finished the scrambled eggs and bacon Kim had cooked and served with slightly burnt toast, and Cooper was enjoying the bacon rinds.

'It was amazing. The party… and the whole trip. Haley shares this house in Glebe with some other students and she took me on a tour of the university. It's so old, different to the ones up here. Aunt Sharon says it's where Mum and you went, where you met?'

'We did.' Dan's mind went back to those far off days when he and Cheryl had both been students at the university. They'd met on a double date – his mate was dating her best friend – and hit it off immediately. They were both in their final year. He was studying Physiotherapy, and she was planning to be a teacher. They'd become inseparable, spending every spare minute together, married as soon as they graduated. They'd been so young.

Dan had been so wrapped up in his thoughts, he'd stopped listening to his daughter and suddenly realised she'd stopped speaking.

'What do you think, Dad?' she asked.

'Sorry, sweetie. What did you say?'

'I said I'd decided to study there too, at Sydney University, like you and Mum. I can stay with Aunt Sharon till there's a room available in Haley's house and…'

'What?' Dan couldn't believe his ears. 'What did you say?' he repeated.

Patiently, Kim repeated what she had said, finishing with, 'I thought you'd be pleased.'

*Pleased? How could she imagine he'd be pleased to learn that not only did she plan to attend university interstate, but to stay with her mother's sister who'd no doubt fill her ears with derogatory comments about him?*

'Are you sure about this, sweetheart? It's a big step to go so far away from home, from your friends.'

'I have friends there too. I caught up with some of the old crowd while I was there. Holly and Laurie are planning to go to Sydney too. I want to study physio, like you did. I thought you'd be happy,' she said, her voice heavy with disappointment.

'I am happy you want to follow in my footsteps. It's a great profession, very rewarding, but…' he paused for a moment, '… you could study it closer to home.'

'Oh, Dad! Aunt Sharon said you'd be like this. It's because of them, isn't it? You don't want me to have anything to do with Mum's family.'

Dan swallowed hard. She was right, but he couldn't let her know. 'I'll miss you.'

'I'd have had to leave home anyway. I'll just be a bit farther away. I can still come home for holidays.'

'Hmm.' How long would that last once she gained her independence? 'Look, sweetie. It's still a long way away. You have till September to decide, don't you? Let's see if you still feel this way then.'

'I won't change my mind.' Kim pushed her chair back and left the kitchen, almost stumbling over Cooper on the way and causing the dog to emit a short howl of distress.

'It's okay, Cooper,' Dan said, as the dog came to rub himself against his legs. 'It's not you she's angry with.'

The front door slammed, and Dan heard Kim's car start up. He sighed and hoped she'd drive carefully. Refilling his mug with coffee, he took it outside, Cooper following him.

He slumped into his favourite cane chair and stared into space, the mug clasped in both hands, Cooper lying at his feet, Kim's words going round and round in his head.

She couldn't be doing this. After all they'd done together, to choose her mother's family over him. Of course, as soon as the thought crossed his mind, he knew how foolish it was. This wasn't a competition. This was Kim's future, and it was her decision about which university she'd attend. But he'd hoped she'd choose one closer to home, closer to him, somewhere which would allow her to come home regularly to continue to be part of his life. Surely that wasn't such a selfish thing to want?

Cooper whined, looked up at Dan with his head cocked to one side and put one paw on his knee. 'You're right, Cooper. It's not selfish at all. We need some fresh air to clear our heads.' He drained the mug, went inside and took Cooper's leash from its hook. A walk on the beach might not change Kim's mind, but it would make Dan feel better.

# Thirty-seven

Livvy was feeling at a loose end. It was a holiday, and all her friends were otherwise occupied. Even Rhana was caught up at home, waiting the birth of her next litter, and Livvy didn't want to disturb her… or her bitch. She'd had her early morning swim, spoken to Nancy on Facetime, and sent a text to Dylan. Now she was sitting in the courtyard of her cottage with a cup of lemon and ginger tea and the remnants of her breakfast, with the whole day ahead of her.

She missed Dan.

It was crazy. Livvy knew that. They'd only been seeing each other for a few weeks, but in that short time they'd grown closer than she'd thought possible. His daughter would be home now. School started next day, and Kim had an appointment with Livvy on Wednesday. It could have been awkward if she and Dan were still a couple, if he'd told Kim about them, as he'd planned. No, it was all for the best. But she couldn't help wondering if Dan had bought the yacht he went to see and how much she'd miss sailing on it with him. Those hours together on the ocean had been magical, a time she'd never forget It did feel as if she'd lost something precious.

Taking her dishes inside, Livvy put on her hat and headed for the beach, her go-to spot when she was feeling low. The salty air and the sand between her toes never failed to boost her spirits. But today, it didn't have its customary effect. All she could think of was the loneliness that stretched ahead, the years of living on her own. It was how she'd felt when she returned from England, before she'd met Dan, before she'd had a taste of what her life could be like with the right companion. Now it felt even worse.

She was so engrossed in her thoughts that she was startled when she heard a dog bark, then a voice call, 'Lady!' She knew that voice. But what was old Agnes doing here, on this beach? Didn't she normally take her dog to the dog beach? It was where Livvy had met her before, before she'd gone to England.

The spaniel ran up to Livvy, who leant down to fondle the dog's ears. She was an old dog, probably around the same age as Dan's. It seemed she couldn't get him out of her head.

'On your own today? Where's that nice man of yours, the one I've seen you with?'

It was as if Agnes had read Livvy's mind. She couldn't recall seeing Agnes when she and Dan were together, but the woman had a habit of turning up where she was least expected, like a bad penny, Liz used to say. It was a phrase Livvy's grandmother had often used too, to mean the recurrence of something unwelcome. It wasn't Agnes herself who was unwelcome. She did good work, caring for sick pelicans. But she did have a habit of telling you some home truths which weren't always comfortable to hear.

Livvy was tempted to tell the old woman that she didn't know who she was talking about but knew it would be foolish. One thing about Agnes was… she was always right. While you might not like what she had to say, she always hit the nail on the head. 'He's not mine, not any longer.' Livvy's voice broke. Apart from when she'd spoken to Lou, this was the first time she'd said it out loud and somehow saying it again made it more real. If she didn't say it, didn't tell people, then maybe she could pretend they were still… what? Friends? Lovers?

'He'll be back,' Agnes said with a wise nod of her head. 'Mark my words. I'm always right.' And, still nodding, she called to her dog and strolled off, leaving Livvy staring after her, the words, '*It was me who left him,*' still unsaid. *Well*, Livvy thought, *you're not right this time, Agnes*, while wishing with all her heart she was wrong.

*

Wednesday, and Livvy's next appointment with Kim came around before she was ready for it. She winced as she re-read her notes on the girl, wishing she wasn't so aware of what Dan had told her about his marriage and his relationship with his former in-laws, or were they former when your spouse had died, she wondered. At least she was saved from wondering about a possible conflict of interests, now she and Dan were no longer seeing each other – not even in a professional sense. She hadn't as much as caught a glimpse of him since she'd walked off on the beach and, while she was relieved, she was also a tad disappointed and wondered if he was missing her at all.

'Hi, Kim. Good to see you again. How have you been? What's been happening with you since we last met?' Livvy asked, prepared to listen while Kim filled her in, and pretending she didn't know she'd been to Sydney to stay with her mother's family.

'I've had the best time,' Kim began, and proceeded to list all the things she and her cousin had got up to, and the long chats she'd had with her aunt about her mother and how she missed her. 'I think it helped,' she said. 'I can't talk to Dad about her. It's like he freezes up whenever I mention her.'

'Perhaps it's too painful for him?'

'Maybe. I don't know. But Aunt Sharon was happy to talk about Mum, about when they were growing up together, what they got up to, and when she and Dad first met. It was at uni and she said they were inseparable.'

At her words, a flash of jealousy shot through Livvy, which she immediately suppressed. How could she feel jealous of a dead woman, one who Dan had told her he'd stopped caring for? But emotions knew no bounds. How she wished she'd known him back then, before his marriage, before Kim, when they were both young and free. She pulled herself back to the present and to what Kim was saying.

'Being back in Sydney, seeing the uni where both Mum and Dad went, where they met, I decided that's where I want to study. And I want to study Physiotherapy, like Dad did.'

Surprised both by Kim's decision and by the belligerent tone in her voice, Livvy asked, 'Is your dad happy about your decision?'

'Who knows?' Kim shrugged. 'He went all quiet, then told me I'd change my mind. But I won't, and he can't make me. You don't think it's the wrong decision, do you. Livvy?'

'As I told you at our first appointment, I'm not here to judge you, but to help you come to terms with what's worrying you. Does it worry you that your dad's not happy with your decision?'

'I suppose… but…' she grinned, '… I'll win him round. He just needs time.'

When their session was over, and Kim had left, Livvy gazed into space, suspecting she knew exactly how Dan must be feeling and wishing there was some way she could comfort him.

# Thirty-eight

The neighbourhood get-together had gone well. It had been good to catch up with those of the neighbours Livvy hadn't seen since she got back, and now Erica had moved in with Jamie and Gill and Joe were living in the end cottage, it had been more fun than usual. When it finished, her four friends had come back to Livvy's for coffee and cake, where she'd had to explain Dan's absence and suffer Erica and Gill's commiserations and their well-meaning advice. They didn't understand, and Livvy didn't try to dissuade them. She knew they were only trying to comfort her when they said it would all come right in the end.

Now it was Wednesday, and the meeting of her book club had come around again. She'd missed last month's meeting, upset with what had happened between her and Dan and not wanting to answer any questions. Tonight, they were meeting in Jamie's cottage. Even though Erica now lived there, it would always be Jamie's cottage in Livvy's mind. Livvy had enjoyed reading *The Seachangers* by Australian author, Meredith Appleyard, and was looking forward to a lively discussion. She hoped her friends wouldn't make any further mention of Dan. It was unlikely, given the presence of the other book club members.

She was right.

The meeting followed its customary pattern of discussing the book, before relaxing with a glass of wine, which had been a recent innovation. Before she went to England, they had made do with tea and coffee. It was when the wine had been served along with a selection of delicious nibbles that one of the group said, 'Terrible about these break-ins. I don't know what Pelican Crossing is coming to. It's always been such a safe place to live.'

There was a murmured agreement, with another member suggesting it was incomers, groups of teenagers from further along the coast, even all the way from Brisbane. It seemed no one actually knew anyone who'd been targeted, and Livvy wondered if it was a beat-up, based on stories in the media and the state government crackdown on youth crime. She was glad when Erica voiced her opinion that those living in this line of cottages felt very safe and out of the orbit of any criminals, teenager or otherwise.

This discussion led to one about the upcoming local council elections which were to take place in two months' time, and a question to Gill as to whether Joe intended to stand for mayor again.

'Probably,' she laughed. 'I'm still getting used to being the lady mayoress and I can't hold a candle to Barb.' There was a moment's silence as the group remembered Joe's late wife who had been an active member of the book club. Then Gill continued, 'I know Joe does a great job and has been a popular mayor, but he'd be happy to hand over the reins if someone else wanted to take up the role. I'm not so sure about some of the other council members.' She chuckled. They all knew to whom she was referring. There had been quite a bit of dissension on the council in recent years, and most people thought it was time for a shakeup.

As the discussion continued with suggestions of who the new council might consist of, Livvy heard Dan's name mentioned. She remembered that he did intend to stand for the council at the forthcoming election and wondered if he'd be successful and what it might mean for the wellness centre if he was.

*

Further along the row of cottages, a similar conversation was taking place. With Gill tied up with the book club, Joe had invited Dan for a drink, and to discuss his bid for the council. Jamie had escaped the houseful of women who comprised the book club to join them, and Finn had come along in his role as editor of the local paper.

'You need a focus,' Joe told a fascinated Dan, 'roadworks, transport, health, or youth crime. Something to grab people's attention.'

Dan dragged a hand through his hair. 'I hadn't thought of that,' he said with a wry grin. 'Maybe health, given the wellness centre.' He took a sip of beer. 'What do you think?' He looked at the other three men for help. He was beginning to wonder if this was such a good idea. He hadn't realised it would be so complicated.

'I think youth crime would be the thing,' Finn said. 'There have been a lot of reports on the news about it. It's got people worried, even though we don't have a lot of it in Pelican Crossing… yet.'

'You think it'll come here?' Jamie asked. 'All the reports seem to be of incidents in Brisbane.'

'There were a couple here over the summer,' Finn said. '*The Echo* didn't report them as the local police put it down to holidaymakers and school holidays. We've been pretty lucky here, apart from a few incidents with electric bikes and scooters.'

'Don't mention them,' Dan said. 'I've seen the result of some bad accidents where the youths involved took no notice of road rules, ending up in hospital and needing follow-up at my clinic.'

'These are bad enough,' Joe said, 'but I fear it's only a matter of time before the residents of Pelican Crossing become subject to the same sort of home invasions we hear about happening in the city.' His forehead creased. 'I wish I could believe otherwise, but we can't stick our heads in the sand. We're just as susceptible to youth crime as any other place.'

'So, youth crime?' Dan wasn't sure he felt comfortable taking on this mantle, but he respected Joe's opinion, and if he thought it was a vote winner… And, thinking about it, maybe he could draw a connection between wellbeing and crime, thus promoting the centre while tackling a possible link between youth mental health and youth crime. He'd need to do some research, maybe talk to the local police, to see exactly how widespread it was and what measures he could suggest to counter it.

'Don't worry, Dan. I'll support you in this. It looks like I may be the only one standing for mayor again, unless things change drastically before nominations close. I have to say I'd be sorry to give it up, though I suspect it would please Gill. She hasn't really taken to the role of lady mayoress. I think, somehow, it goes against her principles.' He chuckled.

Seeming to have settled Dan's election campaign, the conversation changed to a discussion of the prospects of the local Aussie Rules team, until Gill's return home signalled it was time for Dan and Finn to leave.

Dan farewelled his friends, conscious he had a lot to think about and quite a bit of work to do before the election took place. There was a light on in Livvy's cottage when he drove past and although tempted to stop, he carried on driving. But her image was still imprinted on his mind, along with the memory of her kisses and thoughts of what might have been.

# Thirty-nine

The next few weeks were busy for Dan, leaving him little time to mope over Livvy. Though his heart still leapt when he caught a glimpse of her in the distance or passed her in the corridor, she gave him no sign that she felt the same.

Following the discussion with Joe, Finn and to a lesser extent, Jamie, Dan had boned up on youth crime figures in Brisbane and elsewhere in Australia, shocked by the data and some of the stories he came across. He'd also managed to speak with the local police officer he knew. Gavin was happy to help but hadn't been very reassuring. He told Dan it was highly likely the scourge of house invasions would spread, and Pelican Crossing might not be immune. While Dan didn't want to frighten people into voting for him, he felt obligated to warn them of the threat, and decided to mention it in his election material.

The election was looming, and he'd agreed to speak on a panel of prospective council candidates which was being organised by Finn, who as editor of the local paper, was viewed as neutral. Dan wasn't looking forward to it. He had never considered himself to be a public speaker, which made him wonder yet again why he had chosen to stand for election. At least the preparations took his mind off Livvy who was still choosing to ignore him.

One bright spark on the horizon was Kim's unexpected interest in his bid for the council. She'd arranged for a group of her friends to distribute fliers in mailboxes, once he had them printed. To his surprise, it seemed that Jay was the force behind it. He was fast revising his opinion of the young man who was still a dominant presence in his daughter's life. Now, all he had to do was make a final decision on the focus of his campaign, design and print some fliers and write his speech.

Dan had spent the past few evenings drafting a flier he was reasonably happy with when, on Saturday morning, Kim popped her head into the study. 'What do you think, Kim?' he asked, turning his laptop to face her.

'Youth crime? You've got to be joking, Dad. There are much more important issues at stake here.'

Discouraged, after spending so much time on this, Dan asked, 'Such as?' and sat back waiting for her reply. He didn't have long to wait.

'Such as shark nets, endangered loggerhead turtles. Jay says people need to become more aware of what's happening to our wildlife. Then there's parking at Main Beach, funding for the surf livesavers. Do you want me to go on?'

'No.' Dan looked at what he had written. Kim was right. There were more pressing issues, things happening right now in Pelican Crossing about which the community was concerned. He should leave youth crime to the police and the state government and concentrate on local issues. 'Thanks, honey.' He rubbed his chin. Where to start?

'I'm meeting Jay this morning,' she said. 'If you like, we can put some ideas together, help you design a flier using Canva.'

'That would be great.' He had no idea what Canva was, but it must be some sort of design software. He suspected both Kim and her friend were more familiar with such things than he was and he'd welcome their help.

Realising it might be some time before the young pair would be available to help him – Kim mentioned she was meeting Jay at the beach to go surfing and they'd see him afterwards – Dan called to Cooper, and they set off for the beach themselves.

After spending an hour there, and seeing Kim and her friends were still out in the ocean, Dan was pleased to bump into Joe and his dog, and happy to agree when Joe suggested coffee at *The Blue Dolphin*.

When they were seated at an outside table with large mugs of coffee and the apple and cinnamon friands Joe had insisted on, and two bowls of water for the dogs, Joe asked, 'How's it going? Decided on the focus of your campaign yet, youth crime, wasn't it?'

Dan took a long drink of coffee before replying, 'It was, but after talking with my daughter, I'm having a rethink.'

'Oh?'

Dan repeated the issues Kim had mentioned, finishing with, 'What's your take on it? You know this community a lot better than I do.'

Joe thought for a moment, then rubbed his chin. 'She may be right. It's all very well for Finn and I to worry about the possibility of youth crime reaching Pelican Crossing, but it may never happen, and the issues you've mentioned are very real ones right now. I'd say, go for it.'

'Thanks.' Dan was relieved. Despite all the time he'd spent researching youth crime, he hadn't really been comfortable using it as the focus of his campaign. If Finn was still interested, he could do an article on it for *The Echo*. Dan felt much happier focusing on issues that were of more current local concern.

'Interesting you should mention surf lifesaving,' Joe said. 'I've been wanting to see funding for a new clubhouse for some time, but there's been a lot of opposition from some factions of the council. Maybe with some new blood…' He grinned.

'Steady on. I'm not elected yet.' But suddenly Dan felt more confident. Maybe he could do this.

They were about to leave when Finn strolled by, accompanied by his grandson and his dog. The young boy was licking an ice cream, and Finn looked ready to drop. 'Feel like I've just run a marathon on the dog beach,' he said. 'I'm not as young as I used to be, and Sandy and Bluey have tired me out. I hope you weren't about to leave,' he said, seeing their empty mugs. 'Can I buy you a refill?' he asked before slumping into a chair, while Bluey stuck his nose into one of the bowls of water to the indignation of Coco whose bowl it was.

Dan and Joe looked at each other and nodded, laughing when Sandy said, 'Can I have a chocolate milkshake, Grandy?'

Before long Sandy was happily slurping a large chocolate milkshake, the three men had been served coffee, and Bluey had his own bowl of water. Joe explained Dan's change of focus to Finn who, after a brief creasing of his forehead, smiled and said, 'It's a good plan. We may be able to do something with it in *The Echo*. I can't be seen to be partisan where the elections are concerned, but I can use your campaign to focus on those issues, especially the surf lifesaving one as being a much-needed reform.'

'Good man,' Joe said. 'Glad you came along when you did.'

Dan was glad too. He'd been a little worried about how Finn would feel at his abandonment of his idea.

Draining his coffee, Dan rose to go, leaving the others still discussing the possibility of a new surf clubhouse, where it might be located and how it would benefit the community. Hopefully, Kim would be home by now and they could make a start on some ideas for fliers.

*

To Dan's surprise when he arrived home, not only Kim and Jay were there. They were accompanied by a group of their friends. They were all gathered around his computer.

'It's looking good, Dad,' she said, glancing up at him as a sheet of paper shot out of the printer to be fielded by Jay, who handed it to Dan.

For a moment, Dan couldn't understand what he was looking at. The colourful page was far removed from anything he could have created. Across the top in large letters were the words, *Pelican Crossing – your town*. Below, in smaller print, *Dan Parker is the man to watch*, then lower still, *Make sure our sea creatures are protected and we have the new surf clubhouse our lifesavers deserve*. Around the edges were pictures of sharks, loggerhead turtles, plus a recent photograph of a group of local lifesavers and one of Dan which he didn't recall having taken and which made him look younger than the face he saw in the mirror each morning. 'How did you do that?' he asked, bewildered.

'Jay designed it,' Kim said proudly, 'and I found the pictures. I took that one of you when we were on holiday last year.'

Dan and Kim had spent a week in Tasmania the Christmas before last. He remembered her taking a lot of photos on her new phone but had no recollection of having seen this one. 'Thanks, it's amazing,' he said. '*You guys* are amazing. How can I repay you?' He fumbled in his pocket for his wallet.

'It was nothing, Mr Parker,' Jay said. 'Only took a few minutes. It was fun to do.'

'Jay plans to study graphic design, Dad,' Kim said, throwing the boy an affectionate glance.

For a moment, Dan wondered if he planned to study in Sydney too, if that was part of the attraction for Kim. 'Well, at least let me treat you all to a meal.' He saw them glance at each other. 'How about I book a table at *Crossings*, my treat?'

'Ooh, yes, please. We'd like that, wouldn't we?' she said to a now embarrassed Jay, who nodded. The others all grinned. 'Thanks, Mr Parker,' they chorused.

When the group had left, Dan sat and stared at what they had produced in less time than it would have taken him to drink a cup of coffee. He could have this resized for both fliers and posters. He knew *The Echo* offered a printing service. Dan Parker, local councillor, was on his way.

# Forty

It was impossible for Livvy to forget about Dan. Not only was she conscious of him at work – even though they rarely met – but with the council election only a few weeks away, posters with Dan's face on them seemed to be everywhere she went – a tanned and smiling face that appeared more handsome than ever.

There was still no news about Aiden's visa. Nancy had said it could take over a year and there was no guarantee he'd be able to find a job in Queensland, though as an IT professional, his skills would be in demand. It would be wonderful to have all of her family in Australia.

Meantime, Livvy tried to spend as much time as she could with Dylan without interfering with his new relationship. Rory was making good progress and full of praise for Dan's skills in helping him regain the use of his leg. He was already talking about getting back to surfing, even though he was still unable to walk unaided.

More worrying was the letter Livvy had received in the mail the day before from a legal firm in Brisbane. It seemed Ingrid was attempting to sue her for stealing her clients. While many of Livvy's former clients had followed her to her new practice, they had done so of their own accord, and she had done nothing to persuade them. How dare Ingrid try to blame her after what *she* had done?

Glad it was Saturday, and she had arranged to meet Gill and Erica for coffee, Livvy picked up the letter and slipped it into her bag. She'd show it to Gill and get her opinion before taking any action, but the thought of having to defend herself for something she hadn't done, plus the prospect of an expensive court case, had kept her awake most of the night. She was still struggling to replenish her savings after her year off work. Grimacing at herself in the mirror, she applied a brighter shade of lipstick than usual in the hope it would take attention off the dark shadows under her eyes.

Entering the café side of *Books and Coffee* to avoid seeing Lou – she didn't think she could face her today – Livvy ordered a large cappuccino with a ham and cheese croissant. She hadn't felt like breakfast when she returned from her swim and was now feeling hungry. There was no sign of her friends, so she took a seat at a table by the window where she could watch for their arrival.

Livvy had almost finished her coffee and croissant by the time Erica and Gill arrived. When they had all hugged, and Gill had gone to order coffee, Erica peered at Livvy. 'What's up? You don't look your usual self. You're not pining for Dan, are you?'

Livvy blushed. The lipstick hadn't worked. Erica knew her too well. 'Not really,' she lied. 'It's something else. Wait till Gill gets back, and I'll tell you.'

'Hmm.' Erica peered at her again, but didn't say anything more.

'You two are looking very serious,' Gill said when she returned carrying a plate with three of the café's special brownies. 'I thought you might want something sweet after your croissant,' she said to Livvy, pointing to the flakes of pastry on the table, 'and you can never have enough of Ron's brownies. Now, what's up?' she asked, unconsciously repeating Erica.

'Livvy?' Erica prompted.

'I received this.' Livvy took the letter out of her bag and handed it to Gill.

Livvy watched and twisted her hands while Gill read the letter, Erica looking over her shoulder.

'She can't do this,' Erica said. 'Can she?' She looked at Gill for confirmation.

'It seems she has,' Gill said.

Livvy's heart dropped. 'What should I do?' she asked, trembling. 'The clients she's referring to are old clients of mine. They came to me of their own accord when they heard I'd opened my practice in the wellness centre. She can't force me to close down, can she?' It was the thought which had troubled her in the early hours and had kept her awake.

'Of course not. This is a load of rubbish.' Gill flourished the letter. 'I know of this firm. They'd take on any sort of shonky case if they thought they could make money from it. But you do need to reply. I presume your clients would be willing to sign affidavits that you didn't coerce them to leave Ingrid to come to you?'

'I… I suppose so.' Livvy hated the idea of having to ask them to do this, but if it would help…

'It would be good to have that. This woman stole your practice, even if she did act within the law. But it's not like a case where you had an agreement with her that you wouldn't see your former clients, as you would have if you'd sold her the practice or been her employee. It's common practice in cases like that.'

'How do I reply?' Livvy was still thinking of what Gill had said earlier.

'*You* don't do it. You'll need a lawyer's letter.'

'Can you do that for Livvy?' Erica asked.

'I could, but it would be better if it came from one of my colleagues. My specialty is divorce and family law and it would look odd if I signed a letter in connection with this matter. Dave Byrne is your man. I'll talk to him. He shouldn't charge much,' she said when Livvy blanched.

'Thanks.' A wave of relief flowed over Livvy, though she knew she wouldn't rest until she knew the outcome.

'Coffee, ladies? You all look very serious today. I hope there's nothing wrong.' Danny placed three coffees on the table.

'Not now,' Gill said. 'I saw you'd almost finished so ordered you another, Livvy.'

'Thanks,' Livvy said again, glad she had such good friends.

'Now, let's enjoy our coffee and brownies, and talk about something else,' Gill said. 'The council election is coming up and it seems Joe is going to be the only candidate for mayor, so it looks as if I can't avoid the lady mayoress tag for another four years.'

The other two laughed but Gill's mention of the election made Livvy think of Dan again. She couldn't escape him. There was even one of his posters on the café window.

Clearly seeing the direction in which she was looking, Gill said, 'Joe believes he has a good chance. Dan,' she added when neither Erica nor Livvy reacted. 'Seems he has an army of teenage helpers.' She chuckled.

'His daughter and her friends,' Livvy confirmed. She might not have spoken to Dan, but she'd had her final appointment with Kim, and the girl had been excited about helping her dad. Now Kim was no longer a client, one obstacle to her seeing Dan had been removed. But although the teenager was gradually recovering from her grief over her mother's death, Livvy didn't want to do anything which might jeopardise all her good work.

# Forty-one

It had been a hectic few weeks, forcing Dan to reduce his schedule of client appointments at the wellness centre, but it was almost over. The town meeting the previous week had gone better than he could have hoped, and he'd been heartened to see Livvy in the audience, sitting with her group of friends, though he didn't imagine she was there to hear him.

Kim and her friends were there too, surprising him with their continued enthusiasm. They'd made good their promise to distribute fliers, and their support showed no sign of flagging. Most of them were eighteen, and this would be the first time they'd been eligible to vote. He was glad voting was compulsory in council elections here in Queensland.

Now the big day was here. Dan had an empty feeling in the pit of his stomach as he showered and dressed in a pair of smart chinos, the green and white striped shirt which was Kim's favourite, and a dark green tie as a special concession to the occasion. He wished he'd found the courage to approach Livvy after the town meeting, but she left while he was accepting Joe's congratulations. Maybe after this, and now Kim's series of appointments with her had concluded, they could come to some sort of understanding.

The aroma of coffee drove him into the kitchen where Kim was cooking breakfast. Dan wasn't hungry, but it would be a long day, and there was no saying when he'd have another opportunity to eat. Joe had emphasised to him the need to visit every polling booth. It would take him all day. Then it would be over, one way or another. There was a part of him that hoped he wouldn't be elected and life could go on as it had before. But another part didn't want to disappoint his many supporters of whom Kim's friends were only a small part. He'd been surprised to learn how popular he'd become in the short time he'd lived in Pelican Crossing. And Kim had been right about the focus of his campaign. It had touched a nerve with members of the community. Even old Agnes had come up to congratulate him after last week's meeting, despite her saying, 'Don't forget the pelicans.'

'Good luck for today, Dad.' Kim waved a spatula at him before turning back to serve the bacon and eggs she was cooking. Even Cooper seemed excited, though it was perhaps due to the aroma of bacon.

'Thanks, sweetie, but don't be too disappointed if I'm not elected. There are a lot of candidates, and many are supported by political parties.'

'You will be,' she said. 'I've heard a lot of people say they're going to vote for you… and your posters were the best.'

'Thanks to you and Jay.'

She smirked, and Cooper barked his agreement.

*

The day was as long and nerve-racking as Dan had envisaged. He was emotionally and physically exhausted when all the candidates gathered in the town hall after voting closed. Only Joe could be confident of his role in the new council. But they were a friendly bunch with no apparent animosity. Regardless of who was elected, they were united in wanting to do their best for the community.

A group of ladies belonging to the local branch of the Country Women's Association provided tea and handed around plates of sandwiches, which the others seized on as they hadn't eaten all day. Dan felt sick. He wished he was anywhere but here, in this crowd, waiting for the result which could determine his future. It reminded him of the wait for his university results to be posted, and the celebrations which followed. He and Cheryl. He hadn't thought about that day for years. There had been good times, before they grew apart.

The evening drew on. It was getting late. There were doubts there would be a result before the officials handling the counting had to call it quits and reconvene next day. People were milling around, unsure whether to leave or stay. The younger members of Dan's support group were talking about heading to the beach.

Suddenly there was a shout. Everyone went quiet. 'We have a result,' Joe announced over the microphone, as people crowded forward to hear what he had to say.

'Thanks for your patience,' Joe said. 'It's been a long day, and I know many of you are anxious to get home.' There were a few laughs. 'All the results aren't in yet, but from what has been counted so far, I can announce that two candidates have received a sufficient number of votes to be sure of their seat on the new council. I'd like you to welcome Dan Parker and Ellen Nolan as our two new council members. Dan and Ellen, please make your way to the stage.' There was an explosion of cheers, and Dan felt himself being urged forward. Suddenly, he was standing on stage beside Joe and a woman he only knew by sight, but who'd been one of the other candidates.

'I'm sure they'd both like to say a few words,' Joe said, handing the microphone to a bewildered Dan.

'I...' Dan looked out at the crowded hall unable to think what to say. He saw Kim grinning at him, giving him a thumbs up sign, then his eyes settled on a tall blonde figure standing to one side. Livvy was there, an encouraging smile on her face. 'I want to thank everyone who has made this possible,' he said. 'I'm a relative newcomer to Pelican Crossing, and this community has made me and my daughter very welcome. This result tonight is beyond my expectations and as a member of the Pelican Crossing Council, I aim to do all I can to continue the good work which it has accomplished in the past, under the able leadership of our mayor, Joe Harris.'

There were more cheers and whistles. Then it was Ellen's turn. Dan was so overcome with the result, he barely heard what she said. He really hadn't expected to be elected but now he was a member of the town council for the next four years.

Once he stepped down from the stage, Dan was surrounded by well-wishers, all of whom wanted to hug him. Kim gave him a big hug, grinned and said, 'We're off to celebrate on the beach, Dad. Don't wait up.' Before he could reply, Dan found himself being hugged by old Agnes, therapists from the wellness centre, people he didn't know and… Suddenly, he was enveloped in a fragrance with which he was familiar. He could feel her breath on his cheek. 'Congratulations, Dan. You deserve this. The town deserves you,' Livvy said.

# Forty-two

Livvy had only intended to congratulate Dan, but the impulse to hug him was so intense, and everyone else was doing it. However, as soon as she was close enough to inhale his familiar musky scent and his arms wrapped around her, she knew it had been a mistake. The scent and the feel of his body so close to hers triggered so many memories, memories she'd tried unsuccessfully to stifle. She was so aware of his masculinity, his strength, that a wave of longing overwhelmed her, and she was flooded with a torrent of desire.

'Thanks, Livvy,' Dan said, his warm breath tickling her ear.

Suddenly aware of where she was and of the others behind her waiting to congratulate Dan too, Livvy pulled away.

'Are you okay?'

Livvy turned to see Erica staring at her. She pulled herself together and exhaled sharply. 'I'm fine. Why?'

'For a moment there, you looked like you were going to faint. You and Dan…' Erica raised her eyebrows.

'There's nothing, not anymore.'

'It didn't look like nothing, the way you were hugging each other.'

'Everyone was hugging him.' *But did he hug everyone back?* Livvy hadn't imagined his automatic response to their closeness. It was what had aroused her emotions and made her… No, she couldn't allow herself to remember.

'Hmm.' Erica didn't sound convinced. 'Joe and Gill are having a few people back for drinks to celebrate. Join us?'

'I don't think so.' No doubt Dan would be there, and it would be difficult to act normally, to hide the feelings which had suddenly erupted as if they'd been lying dormant ever since Easter when she'd finished the relationship which had barely begun. Livvy needed time to digest what had happened in the town hall, to work out what it meant, and how she was going to manage her emotions when she saw Dan again. Pelican Crossing was a small town, they both worked in the wellness centre, and they had friends in common. She couldn't avoid him for ever.

Back in her cottage, Livvy poured herself a glass of wine, went into her living room and curled up in her favourite armchair. She didn't close the drapes or turn on the light. It was peaceful, sitting in the darkness, looking out across the road at the ocean lit only by the moon and the stars, but her mind was in a whirl. *What had happened to her back there when she hugged Dan?*

Livvy heard footsteps and voices on the road outside as her neighbours walked past, returning from the town hall. Dan was with them. She'd been right about that. Her heart fluttered at the sight of him, and she took another gulp of wine. His head turned to glance in through her window, and she shrank back in the chair even though she knew he wouldn't be able to see in.

As the footsteps and voices faded into the distance, Livvy drained her glass, then rose to close the drapes. While she was glad she hadn't joined them, she'd dearly love to know what they were talking about, and what Dan was thinking. Had he felt as she had when they hugged, or had she been only one more person congratulating him? Had she only imagined his response? She was still wondering when she lay in bed and closed her eyes, hoping sleep would come soon.

*

Dan was surprised Livvy wasn't part of the excited group which made its way back to Joe's cottage to continue the celebrations. Thinking that perhaps she'd gone home first, he glanced at her cottage on the way past, but it was in darkness. Perhaps she was still on her way.

Her hug had both surprised and thrilled him. His body had

quickened with an indescribable yearning, and he'd wanted her to stay in his arms for ever, feeling bereft when she drew away and a stranger took her place. Dan was sure she'd felt it too, that inexplicable connection you only feel once in a lifetime. It hadn't been there with Cheryl, no matter how much in love he'd imagined they were when they first met. He couldn't wait to see Livvy again, sure he'd know as soon as he saw her face. She might still be concerned about Kim's reaction to them as a couple, but hopefully his daughter wouldn't stand in the way of his happiness.

Inside Joe's cottage, Dan took a welcome gulp from the can of beer Joe handed him. He was thirsty after his speech and the emotional effort involved in being greeted and congratulated by so many people, many of whom were strangers. He'd barely touched the glass of bubbly he'd been handed when he stepped down from the stage, as he'd immediately been surrounded by well-wishers.

The cottage was crowded with people. All those he'd met with Livvy were there, plus many council officials and a number of people Joe introduced as his neighbours, among whom he recognised Lou, the woman who manned the desk in the bookshop at *Books and Coffee*. He scanned the room but couldn't see Livvy anywhere.

'Okay there?' Finn asked, joining Dan who, by this time, had taken up a position in one corner of the room from where he'd have a good view of anyone entering the cottage.

'Sure.' Dan took another sip of beer. 'Joe has collected a crowd of people. I'm not sure what I'm doing here. I don't know half of them.'

'You will. You're the man of the hour. Your fellow councillor is here too.' Finn gestured to where Ellen Nolan was standing, looking as out of place as Dan felt. He should go over to speak with her, but what would he say beyond offering his congratulations which he'd already done when they stood on the stage together. It would be the polite thing to do, but what if Livvy arrived when he was talking to her and thought…? Realising he was making too much of what would be a friendly gesture, he saw Gill go over to speak with her and breathed a sigh of relief.

The remainder of the evening passed in a blur for Dan as he made conversation about his expectations for the new council, what he hoped to achieve as councillor and how he planned to combine his role on the council with his physiotherapy practice, something he had yet to consider. He had never really expected to be elected, so the issue hadn't seemed important.

By the time everyone started to leave, there was no sign of Livvy. Dan couldn't understand why she wasn't there, unless… she couldn't still be avoiding him, could she… not after that hug?

# Forty-three

It was two weeks since the election and all the new positions on the council had been confirmed. Dan examined himself in the mirror as he prepared for the first meeting of the new council, and his first as councillor.

'How do I look?' he asked Kim, who was working on an assignment. It was only three months till her final exams, and he was glad to see her taking it seriously. It had been fortunate the election had been held during school holidays otherwise he'd have lost some of his most valued supporters.

'Looking sharp, Dad,' Kim said, before turning her attention back to her laptop. Cooper, who was lying at her feet, grunted his approval too.

'Thanks, sweetie.' He straightened the tie which felt as if it was strangling him but which he'd deemed appropriate for the occasion, and which he'd last worn on election day, only to remove it as soon as he left the town hall. 'I'm not sure how long this will last. You may be asleep when I get back.'

'No worries, Dad.' Kim raised her head to give him a smile before going back to her work.

'Right.'

On the way to the town hall, Dan couldn't help thinking of the last time he'd been there, when Livvy had hugged him in a way that had made him think she'd changed her mind and was willing to become involved with him. But he'd been wrong. In the past two weeks, there had been no indication anything had changed, and his fleeting glimpses of Livvy in the wellness centre had only confirmed her determination to avoid him.

As soon as Dan arrived, the meeting got underway with Joe welcoming everyone, several of whom, like Dan, were new to the council. He was surprised to see a number of community members in the audience, then recalled Joe telling him that all the council meetings were open to the public in addition to being livestreamed. It made him feel somewhat uncomfortable that there was no way of knowing how many people were watching and listening, but he appreciated Joe's desire for transparency. It was one of the traits that made him such a popular mayor.

Being the first meeting of the newly elected council, there were no contentious issues to discuss, apart from one of the re-elected members of the previous council who wanted to know Joe's position on the possibility of banning cabanas on Main Beach, which was shouted down by other members. Dan was delighted when Joe made reference to the push for funding for a new surf clubhouse and the hope that some monies might be forthcoming from the state government. All in all, it was a fairly gentle introduction to local council politics.

It was still early when the meeting drew to a close, and Dan was happy to accept Joe's invitation to join him for a beer at *The Grand*, and to loosen his tie. He'd noticed that most of the others, including Joe, had been more casually dressed. He'd know better next time.

They were on their first beer when Finn joined them. Dan had noticed him among the members of the public at the meeting and assumed he was there in his role as editor of *The Echo*. The paper normally published the agenda of council meetings and followed up with a recap of proceedings.

'Well, what did you think of your first council meeting? Not regretting your decision?' Finn asked.

'Not yet. It was interesting. I guess maybe I should have attended one before I decided to stand for the council, but I have watched a couple online.'

'Not quite the same as being there. They can become quite heated. Joe could tell you a few stories…'

'Don't let Finn frighten you off,' Joe chuckled, 'but we have had our moments.'

This led into a conversation about some hair-raising council meetings during which Dan could only listen amazed and hope he was never present at anything similar.

'Don't worry,' Joe said, seeing Dan's concerned expression. 'We've got rid of the two troublemakers. Coatts and Small are now gone.'

Dan nodded. He'd heard about the two councillors who'd caused so much trouble in the previous council.

As they were leaving Joe took Dan aside. 'Now you've got your first council meeting under your belt, you'll know what to expect in future. I look forward to you doing great things.'

'Thanks, Joe. It was quite an experience.' He wondered if he'd ever have the confidence to speak up in front of all those people… and the possibly hundreds of others watching and listening online. Speaking at the public meeting was nothing compared to that. But he guessed it was why he'd been elected, and he should follow up on the promises he'd made.

The two men shook hands when they parted, with Dan feeling determined to make an effort in future meetings. But it was Livvy he thought of all the way home and while he took Cooper for a late walk. Had she been right? Had he been right to agree with her that Kim wasn't ready to accept another woman into his life? What if they'd both been wrong?

# Forty-four

Livvy had been sleeping soundly – as soundly as she ever did these days – when she awoke with a start. She lay still, holding her breath. Silence. Then she heard it again. The shatter of glass breaking. It was coming from the front of the cottage. Livvy froze, as it was followed by the sound of footsteps. She reached for her phone, her hand shaking. It wasn't there. Then she remembered. She'd left it charging in the kitchen.

Livvy didn't know what to do. She'd read about the home invasions in Brisbane and Townsville, remembered the conversation at her book club. But this was Pelican Crossing. It couldn't be happening here, to her. From what she could recall, the thieves would be after her car, searching for the keys. They wouldn't have to look far. They were sitting where they always were, in the dish on the hall table, clearly visible to anyone entering the cottage. She hated the thought of anyone taking her precious Toyota Yaris, but it was better than being attacked by a machete as she'd read happened to one family.

Livvy lay still, holding her breath, her heart racing, waiting for the sound of the garage door opening and her car being driven away. But the only sounds were of bangs and crashes as if the place was being torn apart. Then, as suddenly as they'd started, the sounds died away. She heard footsteps running outside and what sounded like youthful voices yelling to each other.

Slowly and cautiously, Livvy slid out of bed and pulled on her robe. She opened the bedroom door and listened intently. Nothing. Greatly daring, she switched on the hall light to see the floor covered in broken glass. The beautiful stained glass in her front door had been shattered and was now in pieces on the tiled floor. Her hand went to her mouth and a tear trickled down her cheek.

Her stomach churning, Livvy made for the kitchen. Her phone. She needed to call someone. She turned on the kitchen light, unable to comprehend what she was looking at. The room, which had been clean and tidy when she went to bed, looked as if a storm had struck it. Packets of biscuits, bottles of soft drink, jars of jam, a carton of eggs, and other pantry items had been emptied and scattered across the floor, along with several plates and mugs, including the special one she'd brought back from England, which was now in pieces.

Stepping around the mess, Livvy reached for her phone to discover it was only two o'clock. In a daze, she moved through the house. Her car keys were still where she'd left them, but when she entered the living room, she saw two paintings which had been on the wall had been torn down, their frames smashed, the vase of flowers on the table in front of the window had been thrown to the floor and smashed, and the cover had been ripped off the book she had been reading, the pages torn out and scattered on the floor. She bent to pick them up, then collapsed into a chair, put her face in her hands and began to weep uncontrollably.

Livvy clutched her phone. She needed to call someone, but who could she call at this time in the morning? Even the police station wouldn't be manned till much later. Taking a deep breath, she pressed Dylan's name on speed dial.

'Mum?' Dylan's voice was thick with sleep, then became tense. 'What's wrong? Why are you calling? It's only…' In the background, Rory's voice called, 'Who's calling us at this time?'

'It's Mum,' Dylan said, then repeated, 'Mum, what's wrong?'

'Someone broke in and…' Livvy burst into tears again, '… the place is a mess.'

'Are you okay?'

'I think so, but… Oh, Dylan, I don't know what to do.'

'Don't do anything. Don't touch anything. I'll be there as soon as I can.'

'Thanks.' But she was talking to herself. Dylan had already hung up. Livvy sat, clutching her phone and staring at the destruction of her precious belongings till she heard Dylan at the door.

The next few hours passed in a blur. Livvy was vaguely aware of Dylan taking charge, making coffee, pouring her a glass of brandy, then calling the police station and leaving a message.

Finally, she pulled herself together sufficiently to take a shower and dress. It was Sunday morning so there was no need to worry about her clients… or about contacting Dan to let him know she wouldn't be at the wellness centre. It was two weeks since the election, two weeks since she'd hugged him, and they hadn't spoken since.

Dylan stayed until the police officer arrived to see the damage and take details. Gavin, who was a friend of Dylan's, expressed surprise that her car keys hadn't been touched, or her phone stolen and suggested it was a prank, the work of a group of bored teenagers out to make mischief. But why here? Why her? He didn't have an answer but instructed her and Dylan not to touch anything until they were able to check for fingerprints, adding that it was unlikely they'd find any and recommending she install more security.

By the time the police had finished, it was well into the morning, and Dylan had to leave to help Rory who had graduated from his wheelchair to crutches but still needed assistance with showering and dressing, promising they'd both return later. Before he left, he insisted Livvy call Erica as he didn't want her to be alone. Despite assuring him she'd be fine, the sight of the mess which needed to be cleaned up forced her to agree.

When Erica arrived, Jamie was with her. Both were shocked by what had happened, Erica immediately pulling Livvy into a warm hug. Livvy clung to her friend for a few moments, still traumatised by the shock of being awoken so suddenly and the terror of hearing strangers ransacking her home.

'What can we do to help?' Erica asked. 'Why don't I make some tea while Jamie clears the kitchen floor, and how about I ring Gill and Joe to come to help?'

'I don't know…' Livvy said, feeling helpless. She couldn't believe how her confidence had been sapped by the intrusion into her life by strangers. She'd thought herself safe in her little cottage.

By the time Dylan returned with Rory, who was still struggling with his crutches, the place was looking better, Erica had made camomile tea and forced Livvy to sit down and drink it while the others worked on clearing up the mess.

'The screen door was easy for them to cut through,' Dylan said, pointing to the ragged edges, 'and we need to board up where the glass panel was until you can have it replaced.'

'I have some pieces of wood,' Jamie said. 'They'll provide a temporary fix till you can have the panel replaced. I'll go get them now.'

'Thanks, Jamie.' People were so kind, but the front door would never be the same. Livvy wept at the loss of the beautiful stained-glass panel she'd had specially made for it.

'Are *you* okay?' Erica asked, putting an arm around Livvy.

'I think so.' Livvy realised she was still trembling. 'It's the shock, the fact someone could break in, do all this…'

'They didn't take your car?' Rory asked.

'No.'

'That's odd. From what I've read about what's happening elsewhere, it's the first thing they go for. What did the police say?'

'Gavin was puzzled too,' Dylan said. 'He thinks it was a gang of local youths who might have been drunk.'

'But why here?' Rory gazed around the room. 'Why choose this cottage?'

'Let's hope they can find out,' Joe said. 'Are you okay if I let Finn know, have him write a column on it for *The Echo*?'

'Oh, I don't know.' Livvy didn't want to become an object of pity for everyone in Pelican Crossing.

'He doesn't need to identify you, only that it happened to a resident of Pelican Crossing, and for anyone with information to contact the police.'

'Okay then.'

Jamie returned and soon had the wood cut to size and nailed in place, and once that was done, her friends left, reassuring her that they weren't far away. Only Dylan and Rory remained, and Livvy found herself dreading them leaving too. It was as if Dylan read her mind.

'We're not going anywhere, Mum. Rory and I packed a bag. We're staying with you for as long as it takes for you to feel safe again. I'll contact a security company tomorrow, arrange for a security system and one of those Crimsafe security screens. You probably want to arrange for the glass panel yourself and it may take some time.'

'Thanks, guys.' It was good of them, but they had their own lives. This cottage had always been her safe haven. Livvy wondered if she'd ever feel safe here again.

# Forty-five

Dan was shocked at the sight of Livvy when he walked into the wellness centre kitchen on Monday morning. For once, she hadn't left as soon as he arrived. She was pouring hot water over a teabag in a mug, and from the shadows under her eyes it looked as if she hadn't slept. 'Is everything okay?' he asked, stifling the desire to give her a hug, much like the one she'd given him on election night.

'Of course. Excuse me.' She finished what she was doing and walked past, taking care not to brush against him.

Dan stared after her, his forehead creased. She didn't look as if everything was okay. She looked as if… He shook his head.

'Morning, Dan. Good weekend?'

Dan turned to see Patrick behind him and pulled his thoughts away from Livvy. 'Morning, Patrick. Yes, thanks. You?' It was the usual sort of Monday morning chat, the chat which Livvy had never taken part in, much to his disappointment. He'd spent most of the weekend on his new boat. It had taken a few weeks to sort out the payment and take ownership. Then he'd been busy preparing for the election. This past weekend, he'd been able to enjoy his new purchase, sailing it out the bay and up the coast, all the time wishing Livvy could be there to enjoy it with him. He'd invited Kim, but she'd preferred to spend time with her friends, so he'd been alone with too much time to think. Bumping into Livvy this morning had been a bonus, but she obviously didn't think so, and whatever was the matter, she didn't intend to share it with him.

Dan sighed and took his coffee back to his office to prepare for his first client and the busy day ahead.

*

Work over, Dan prepared to take Cooper for his customary walk on the beach. As usual, the dog was delighted at his return home and greeted him by leaping up on him, his tongue hanging out. 'Down, boy,' he said, but in a half-hearted manner. He loved the dog and could never be annoyed with him.

It was good to walk along the deserted beach. At this time of day, most other dog owners were at home preparing or eating dinner. The only other person there was old Agnes and, to Dan's relief, she and her dog were only figures in the distance. He didn't feel in the mood for her homespun wisdom tonight.

After dinner, Kim disappeared to her room, ostensibly to study, and Dan retired to his study. After the last council meeting, he'd promised Joe to put together some relevant information about shark nets and loggerhead turtles which had been the basis of his campaign. There was also the refurbishment of the surf clubhouse, but that would depend on funding, so Joe advised him it could wait a few months.

Opening his computer, Dan started to read articles for and against the use of shark nets. There were a lot of them, providing views on both sides, and he knew opinions on the council were divided too. After an hour, his eyes started to blur. He needed a break and headed to the kitchen to make coffee, after popping his head into Kim's room on the way to find her engrossed in her chemistry textbook. He withdrew quietly, without disturbing her.

Back in his study, as he made an attempt to compose something which he could present to the council, he remembered a conversation he'd had with Rory Whittaker at the young man's first appointment with him. Rory had been keen to discuss the attack, telling Dan how he'd been flung from his surfboard into the water, seen the look in the shark's eyes and found the creature's skin rough to his touch. When Dan asked him if he was angry that there had been no shark net to protect him from the attack, Rory's response had been immediate.

'Absolutely not. It was a great white, a protected species, a beautiful creature. The ocean is his natural environment. He had more right to be there than I did. People surf and swim in the ocean all the time, and there are very few shark attacks. It was simply bad luck, though I was lucky. I survived. Many don't.'

They had both remained silent for a few moments before continuing the conversation.

Dan decided to use Rory's words and to cite him as an example of someone who'd experienced an attack and was still in favour of the permanent removal of the nets, though he knew he'd encounter opposition to this point of view.

After a few false starts, Dan finally produced a document he was happy with. He stretched his hands above his head. It had taken longer than he anticipated, so he decided to leave the loggerhead turtles for another time. He already knew his main thrust would be the importance of turning off all non-essential lighting during the summer turtle breeding season, and expected that to be contentious too. But he discovered he was enjoying putting the information together. And at least it took his mind off Livvy Grace, her troubled expression that morning, and the way she'd been so careful to avoid touching him when she walked past.

# Forty-six

Livvy was still reeling from the shock of the home invasion. It had been a busy week, both at work and at home where Dylan and Rory were still staying. Dylan had insisted, saying that Rory would be there all day while both he and Livvy were at work, and, though Livvy had visions of Rory fending off any would-be burglars with his crutches, she'd agreed.

It was more likely they'd come at night, as they had before, and Livvy was grateful to know she wouldn't be alone if that happened. The police had been in touch but had nothing to report. They hadn't discovered the culprits, but even though they tried to reassure her they were unlikely to strike in the same place a second time, the memory of what it had felt like to awaken to the sound of breaking glass and footsteps could still make Livvy tremble with fear.

She was grateful she had such good friends. Erica and Gill had dropped round several times using the excuse of wanting to ask if she had heard anything from the police, and, when she heard what had happened, Rhana had called and asked if there was anything she could do to help. Livvy was glad too, that Erica and Gill had persuaded her to continue to swim each morning whether she felt like it or not. As always, she'd found it refreshing to be out in the ocean, even if the memory of her intruders was waiting for her back on the shore.

Joe had fulfilled his promise to talk with Finn, resulting in a half-page article about youth crime, citing the home invasion of an unnamed resident in one of Pelican Crossing's old fishermen's cottages, and warning people to take care. Even though Livvy hadn't been identified as the victim, she felt exposed by the article, sure the boards which were still on her front door would give her away.

Now it was Saturday, the sun was shining, and Livvy had persuaded Dylan and Rory to go back to their apartment for the day. She knew they couldn't stay with her for ever and she wanted to find out how it would feel to be on her own again. While it was lovely to have their company, they had their own lives to live, and she needed to get *her* life back to normal.

Checking that the new Crimsafe security screen was locked, Livvy took her ginger and lemon tea out to the courtyard. She'd feel safer when the security system Dylan had ordered was installed and her front door had been repaired. She'd dithered about getting another glass panel but decided not to let the actions of a few youths prevent her from having the front door she wanted, so had placed an order with the local artist who'd made the original one for her. Luckily, she was still in business and had a record of the old design. When it was installed, the door would look like new.

She had just finished her morning Facetime call with Nancy, who was unaware of what had happened to her mother, and was smiling at a story Nancy had told her about taking the girls shopping, when she heard someone at the front door. Livvy's stomach churned and she began to tremble. She was still holding her phone, and her initial reaction was to call someone, anyone. Then she pulled herself together. It was nine o'clock on Saturday morning. The burglars were unlikely to come at this time, or to knock on the door. It was probably Erica or Gill. She slipped the phone into the pocket of her jeans and went to answer the door.

*

Dan was planning to spend another day on the boat. Kim was still asleep after another late night – or early morning. He'd invited her to join him again, but she preferred to sleep late and spend the day with her friends. Wearing an old pair of white knee-length shorts with a long-sleeved pink linen shirt, he was enjoying a second cup of coffee in the yard, Cooper lying at his feet in a pool of sunlight. It was a perfect day.

Dan opened the latest copy of *The Echo*. He hadn't had time to read it till now and wanted to catch up with the local news. Finn could always be relied on to keep the community up to date. The front page was filled with photos of the new council, and Dan quickly turned the page. He'd seen enough of his own face in the lead-up to the election.

*Home invasion in Pelican Crossing – a warning to all residents to be aware*, Dan read, his heart sinking. *Had he been wrong to listen to Kim? Should he have focused on youth crime, after all? Could he have prevented this if he had?* With these questions whirling around in his head, Dan's coffee grew cold as he read on. In Finn's usual style, he was careful to avoid giving details of exactly where the home invasion had taken place, only mentioning it had been in one of Pelican Crossing's old fishermen's cottages. There were lots of those scattered around the town, including the row where Livvy, Joe and Jamie lived.

Finn did say the incident had taken place in the early hours of the previous Sunday morning and requested anyone seeing anything suspicious to report to the police. Dan recalled Livvy's strained face in the wellness centre kitchen on Monday morning. He'd been sure something was wrong, although she'd denied it. He hadn't seen her for the rest of the week. What if it had been her cottage which had been invaded? Feeling sick at the thought, he took out his phone and called her number. It went to voicemail.

Leaping up so quickly that Cooper let out a yelp of surprise, and his coffee cup overturned, sending coffee all over the table, Dan headed inside. Telling Cooper he wouldn't be too long and giving the dog a consolation gravy bone treat, he picked up his keys. He needed to find out for himself if Livvy had been the victim.

As soon as he arrived outside Livvy's cottage, the sight of what was obviously a brand new Crimsafe security screen and boards covering what had been a beautiful stained-glass panel on the front door told its own story. Swamped with guilt, Dan knocked on the door.

A pale-faced Livvy opened it, clearly surprised to see him. 'Dan, what are you doing here?'

'I just read the article in *The Echo*, and I had to make sure you were okay, but you're not, are you? I'm so sorry. It's all my fault.'

'What? How is it your fault? You didn't break in in the middle of the night and…' To Dan's dismay, Livvy began to weep.

'I'm sorry,' she sniffed. 'I don't know what's happened to me. I'm not usually such a wimp. You'd better come in.'

As soon as the door closed behind him, Dan pulled Livvy into a warm hug. He couldn't help himself. She looked so forlorn, with tears streaming down her cheeks. For a moment, she clung to him. His heart skipped a beat as he felt her warm skin next to his.

'Sorry,' she said again, pulling out of his embrace. 'I don't…'

'It's okay,' Dan said, stifling his disappointment. 'You've had a shock. You're allowed to fall apart. Why don't I make some tea?'

'I've just had…' Livvy looked around in a daze. 'That would be lovely. Thanks.'

A few minutes later, Dan and Livvy were sitting side-by-side at her kitchen table with cups of what Dan liked to call builder's tea, laced with lots of sugar and brandy, none of the herbal stuff he knew Livvy preferred.

'Thanks,' Livvy said, after taking a sip and screwing up her face. 'What made you think it was me Finn was writing about?'

'I wasn't sure, but I remembered how you looked on Monday morning, and I had to check. It's all my fault,' he repeated.

'Don't be stupid. How could it be *your* fault?'

'My campaign. Finn and Joe wanted me to focus on youth crime, but Kim had other ideas, and I went along with her. If I hadn't. If I'd stuck to my first idea, maybe…' He dragged a hand through his hair.

His words brought the hint of a smile to Livvy's face. 'I don't think so. I doubt the louts who broke in here at an unearthly hour on Sunday morning were aware of your campaign or any others. According to the police it was a prank that got out of hand. A prank!' she repeated in disgust.

'Did they take much?'

'That's the strange thing. They didn't take anything, just made a huge mess. It wasn't like those home invasions you read about where they take the occupant's car keys and steal the car. And I'd left my phone on charge on the counter, they didn't even touch that.'

'How odd.' Dan pulled on his ear. It seemed as if the youths who'd broken in here had some other motive, but right now he couldn't imagine what it could be. 'You haven't pissed anyone off lately?'

'Not if you don't count Ingrid.'

'Ingrid? Your former partner? I thought *she* was the one who did the dirty on *you*?'

'She did, then she tried to sue me for stealing her clients – *my* former clients who followed me after seeing Finn's article on the wellness centre. A letter from my solicitor to hers soon put paid to that. I can't imagine her going to the trouble of breaking in to get her revenge. Anyway, there were footsteps of more than one person. And I heard voices, at the end when they left. They sounded like kids.'

'Right.' But it put a bug in Dan's ear, and he determined to have a word with Gavin. It couldn't do any harm.

Now Dan was sitting with Livvy in her kitchen, regardless of the reason, all the feelings he'd tried so hard to suppress came to the fore. *Was this the opportunity he'd been hoping for? Had fate played into his hands?*

'You shouldn't be alone at a time like this,' he said, hoping she'd turn to him and accept that a relationship with him would solve her problems. He'd work things out with Kim later.

'I'm not alone,' Livvy said. 'Dylan and Rory are staying with me until I have a new security system installed. I should be right then.'

'Oh!' Dan hadn't considered that her son lived nearby. 'But I'm here too, and I think… I'd like it if…' Hell, how could he be so tongue-tied?

Livvy put a hand on his, making his heart lurch. She smiled sadly. 'Nothing's changed, Dan. We still have to consider Kim. I'm not sure she's totally recovered from the grief over her mother's death, and this is an important time for her with her Year Twelve exams coming up. I can't be part of anything that would jeopardise that for her.'

# Forty-seven

Livvy watched Dan leave, his slumped shoulders an indication of how disappointed he'd been when she told him nothing had changed. She was tempted to call him back, tell him she'd been wrong, the urge to feel his arms around her again threatening to overwhelm her sense of what was right. But she stood with her arms wrapped around her and said nothing as he got into his car and drove away.

Back inside, Livvy put the cups in the dishwasher then deciding to do what she always did when she was upset, she put on her hat and, carefully locking the cottage door, made her way across the street and down to the beach.

Although it was a sunny day, there was a strong breeze whipping up the white-capped waves as they surged towards the shore. Livvy stood at the edge of the ocean and watched them tumble towards her, their turbulent progress mirroring the confusion in her mind. She thought about the last time she'd been here, when she'd met old Agnes, when Agnes had told her Dan would come back. Well, he had, and she'd turned him away again. She must be mad. Livvy wished old Agnes would appear again to tell her everything would work out, but she had the beach to herself. With a heavy heart, she turned to return home.

Livvy wasn't alone for long. Dylan and Rory arrived with the news that the security company planned to come that afternoon. The security system would be installed before the day was over, then… 'There will be no need for you two to stay,' she said, a sense of dread enveloping her at the thought of being here alone again.

'We'll stay for as long as you want, Mum,' Dylan said, giving her a hug. Rory nodded. 'It's pretty nice here, and Dad's just along the way.'

'Speaking of which. A few of us are going to the yacht club for dinner tonight. Why don't you two join us... unless you have other plans?'

Dylan and Rory glanced at each other, before Dylan said, 'That'd be cool, Mum. Two birds with one stone, eh, Rory?'

Rory grinned. 'Dad worries about me, but I'm getting along fine. It'll be a chance to show him.'

'Good.' Glad to have that settled, along with the news about the security company, Livvy felt a little more cheerful. If it wasn't for the niggle in the back of her mind about Dan, she might even say she was happy, even if she did feel the need for company when it turned dark. She knew she couldn't rely on Dylan and Rory's company for ever, but for the moment it was good to know they'd be there, just in case.

*

Dan stared out across the bay. It was a perfect day for sailing. His new yacht was everything he could have hoped for. He should be feeling on top of the world. But there was an emptiness inside him that he couldn't shift.

Livvy should be here with him, leaning against him, smiling, her hair blowing in the breeze. He cursed inwardly at the cruel fate that was keeping them apart, annoyed that he understood her reservations. He worried about Kim too. She was all he had in the world, and she meant everything to him. But she'd be off to university soon, and even if she chose to attend a local one, life would be different.

Pulling his mind back to focus on the route he'd chosen which would take him up the coast to a small bay he'd discovered on his last trip, Dan tried to forget about Livvy. But it wasn't easy. The image of the blonde woman kept appearing in his mind, reminding him of what might have been.

Reaching the bay, he dropped anchor and opened the esky he'd packed before leaving home. The can of beer and ham and cheese sandwich should have satisfied him, but there was no pleasure in being alone in this beautiful spot. Maybe he should have brought Cooper. The dog was always good company, an antidote to his loneliness. But Dan had been unsure how the dog would react to being on a boat, at sea. He couldn't have borne to lose him overboard in a wild attempt at swimming. Cooper loved the water.

As Dan made his way back to the marina, he vowed to ensure he had company next time. If he couldn't persuade Kim to join him, there was Cam, who had sold him the yacht, or even one of his new friends – Joe, Jamie or Finn. He conveniently ignored the fact that they all had partners who were friends with Livvy.

# Forty-eight

It was three weeks since her cottage had been ransacked by intruders, and Dylan and Rory had returned home. Now she had a security system, Livvy felt more confident in being alone, though she did sometimes awaken in the night imagining she could hear footsteps and sit bolt upright, only to fall back against the pillows with a sigh of relief. On those occasions she found it difficult to get back to sleep, resulting in her feeling too exhausted to go swimming when her alarm woke her again before dawn.

Both Erica and Gill had expressed their concern when she was missing from the group of wild swimmers. They knew how much those times out on the ocean at break of day meant to her. It was one more thing the miscreants who'd broken in had taken from her. She'd been able to replace what had been broken, clean up the mess, but it was more difficult to regain her peace of mind.

At least nothing had changed at work, and Livvy was able to forget her own concerns and focus on those of others, though she sometimes wondered if she could benefit from counselling herself. She had even managed to make polite conversation with Dan on the few occasions she'd bumped into him, despite her stomach lurching each time.

She had heard nothing from the police since immediately after the incident and, although Dylan had promised to keep on top of it by regularly contacting his friend Gavin, there had been nothing to report.

It had been a busy morning, and Livvy was taking a well-earned break in her office, sipping a cup of peppermint tea and eating a Ryvita topped with an egg salad she'd brought from home, when her phone rang.

Assuming it would be Dylan or Erica, both of whom checked in on her on a regular basis, Livvy answered without looking at the number.

'Mrs Grace… Olivia Grace?'

'Yes,' she said cautiously. The voice was one Livvy didn't recognise.

'This is Detective Sergeant Bruce Wilton from Pelican Crossing police station. I'm calling about the home invasion you reported recently. The investigation is ongoing, but there's something I need to ask you. Are you familiar with an…' there was a pause, and Livvy heard the rustling of paper, '… Ingrid Allen?'

Livvy gasped. She remembered Dan asking her who might want to harm her, or words to that effect. 'Yes, we used to be business partners,' she said.

'I see. Good. Thank you, Mrs Grace. That's all I need for now. We'll be in touch.'

'Is she…?'

'I'm sorry. I can't go into any detail at this point. Like I said, we'll be in touch.'

Livvy stared into space, her heart thumping. She picked up her phone again to call Dylan, but it went to voicemail. Of course, he was at work. She tried Erica with the same result.

Livvy didn't know how she got through the rest of the day. As soon as she got home, she showered and changed out of the uniform she was now accustomed to wearing, poured herself a glass of wine and tried to call Dylan again. This time he answered.

'Don't worry, Mum,' he said when she finished repeating her conversation with the detective. 'I'll see Gavin at footy practice tonight. I can ask him what's happening then. So, they think Ingrid is behind it?'

'He wouldn't say, but why else ask if I knew her? Dan…' she bit her lip. She hadn't intended to mention Dan.

'Dan Parker? You're still seeing him? I thought…'

'No. It was when he heard about the incident. He came round to make sure I was all right.' Livvy's voice softened as she remembered how he'd pulled her into his arms, how… She gave herself a shake.

'He asked me if I'd pissed anyone off. She was the only person I could think of. Her attempt to sue me went nowhere. But surely it can't have been her. She wouldn't…'

'I wonder…'

'What?'

'Gavin had a problem with his knee a while back. I'm pretty sure Dan treated him.'

'You don't think…?' It would be like Dan to mention Ingrid to Gavin, but for the police to take it from there, to act on a throwaway comment from someone who wasn't involved… it was inconceivable.

'I don't think anything. I'll talk with Gav and get back to you. Okay? I'll come round if it's not too late.'

'Would you?' Livvy gave a sigh of relief. 'It won't be too late. I'm not sleeping too well these days.'

'Oh! Would you like Rory and I to come back? It's not a problem.'

'Of course not. You guys have done enough for me. I'm fine.' *And I need to learn to stand on my own two feet, not rely on my son and his partner.*

When the call ended, Livvy made another call, this time to Nancy. It would be early morning there and she was aching to talk to her daughter and to see her granddaughters. Nancy's recent calls had been made when the girls were asleep, and Livvy had missed seeing their bright little faces.

It was such a delight to see them all, to hear their chatter and to learn that Nancy was hoping Aiden's visa would come through soon. It had only been a few months, but Nancy was optimistic they'd be in Australia, if not by Christmas, then by the following Easter. It was something positive to look forward to and helped relieve Livvy's despondency. By the time the call ended, she was feeling much better. Nancy knew nothing of the home invasion – Livvy hadn't wanted to worry her – and it was refreshing to talk with someone who was ignorant of the whole affair.

Although she didn't feel hungry, Livvy heated up a frozen meal and forced herself to eat it, knowing it was foolish to go without food and wouldn't help her to recover the confidence which had taken such a hit.

She had fielded calls from Erica and Gill, both of whom had

expressed surprise at the detective's question – although Gill reminded her that you could never tell the lengths some people might go to if they felt thwarted – and was in the middle of watching a crime drama set in Iceland on SBS when Dylan arrived.

'Do you have any wine, Mum?' he asked after greeting her with his customary hug. 'I think you're going to need it when you hear what I have to say.'

Puzzled, Livvy pointed him in the direction of the fridge while she took two glasses out of the cupboard. After her one glass when she returned home, she'd stuck to water, aware how easy and self-destructive it would be to drink herself into oblivion.

'You spoke to Gavin?' she asked, when they were settled in the living room, the light from the full moon sending its beam through the window.

'I did.' Dylan took a sip of wine and rolled the glass between his hands. 'He told me they'd arrested three youths who were robbing a service station. They were after cigarettes. When they questioned them, Ingrid's name came up.'

Livvy's eyes widened.

'It seems the call you received was a bit of a shot in the dark, but one which hit its mark. They plan to do a bit of digging before they bring her in for questioning.'

'But…' Livvy was trying to get her head around what Dylan was saying. 'You mean, they think Ingrid was behind the youths who broke in and trashed this place?' She could feel her anger rising. 'What did she hope to achieve?'

'Who knows?' Dylan shrugged. 'Maybe she just wanted to upset you as some sort of twisted revenge.'

'Well, she certainly succeeded in doing that.' Livvy thought of all the sleepless nights, of the morning swims she'd missed, of how she'd lost confidence in herself. Hadn't it been enough that Ingrid had stolen her practice? What had Livvy done to Ingrid to make her treat her so viciously? No, Livvy couldn't believe Ingrid was behind this.

# Forty-nine

'Done!' Kim glanced up from her laptop to see if Dan was watching.

'What?' He had just returned from taking Cooper for a walk and was in the process of hanging up the dog's leash before making his nightly coffee.

'My uni application. I just sent it off.'

Dan's heart thumped. He'd been meaning to have a talk with Kim about this, point out the benefits of studying close to home, but had thought there was plenty of time. Applications didn't close for another month at least. 'Where did you apply to?' he asked, hoping against hope she'd say the local university or at least one in Brisbane.

'UAC, of course. I told you I wanted to go to Sydney, when I came home after Easter.' She grinned. 'It'll be awesome.'

'But you applied to QTAC too… as a backup?'

'No. Given my results so far, I'm pretty confident of getting an offer from my first choice. Don't worry, Dad. It's not your problem,' she said as Dan's forehead creased. 'If I miss out, I can always apply again next year.'

'What about Jay? Is he planning to go to Sydney too?'

'No way. He can study graphic design at TAFE and stay home. He plans to do some freelance work too.'

'But I thought you and he…?' Dan shook his head. He might not have approved of the young man at first, but he'd grown on him, and he'd thought…

Kim laughed. 'No, Dad. Jay's okay, but I'm only eighteen. I'm not ready to settle down when there's a whole world out there.' She spread her arms. 'Maybe I'll meet someone at uni, like you and Mum.' She grinned again. 'Wouldn't that be something?'

Dan felt his heart shrivel. She was serious about this, and Dan knew that once Kim had made up her mind about something she rarely changed it. He forced a smile.

'Yes, sweetie. It really would.'

'I'm off to bed now. See you in the morning.' Kim gave him a peck on the cheek and disappeared.

Alone with Cooper, Dan no longer felt like making coffee. Instead, he poured himself a glass of whisky and, Cooper following, took it out to the yard. There, with the full moon shining down on him, he contemplated his future, a future in which Kim would be spending time with the aunt and uncle who despised Dan and all he had accomplished. For the first time he wondered if it had been a mistake to uproot Kim, to move to Pelican Crossing. If they'd stayed in Sydney, her decision to study at Sydney university wouldn't be a problem. Was he being selfish to wish she'd chosen to study closer to what was now their home?

Cooper chose that moment to let out a sigh.

Dan sighed, too. He ruffled the dog's ears and took a long slug of whisky, welcoming the burn. 'It's going to be just you and me, old boy.' He sighed again. 'Just you and me.'

*

Dan didn't sleep well. Waking early, he took a delighted Cooper to the beach and made an effort to get himself into a better frame of mind before facing Kim at breakfast. But the salty tang of the sea and the pounding of the waves on the beach failed to have their usual effect. He was still feeling irritable when he returned, and the sight of Kim's cheerful expression at breakfast did nothing to alleviate it.

'What's the matter, Dad? Are you still annoyed I've applied to Sydney?' she asked, between mouthfuls of toast spread with peanut butter and mashed banana, her latest fad.

Dan took a sip of coffee before replying, and pushed away the bowl of muesli he couldn't face. 'I'll miss you, honey.' There was no sense in him bad-mouthing Sharon and Darryl, even though he wanted to.

'I'll miss you too, but it's exciting.'

'Of course it is. University is exciting. It's a new world. I'm sure you'll love it. I did.'

'And it's where you and Mum met.'

'Mmm.' There it was again, that reminder. How he wished he'd never agreed to Kim going down to Sydney at Easter. If she hadn't, she might never have decided to study there.

'What you need, Dad, is someone to spend time with, to stop you from missing me, from feeling lonely.' She took a last bite of toast and swept the crumbs off the table for him to sweep up later. 'Someone your own age, someone like…' she thought for a moment, '… my counsellor, Livvy Grace. She's really lovely. Need to go now, Dad. I'm meeting Jay before school.' She dropped a kiss on the top of his head and was off, leaving Dan staring after her in shock.

*

Dan couldn't get Kim's words out of his head as he treated his patients. If she meant what she said, there was no barrier to him and Livvy forming a relationship. But how was he going to bring it up with Livvy again when she refused to speak with him and avoided him as much as she could?

He was still puzzling over it when he returned home to find Kim still in the exuberant mood she'd been at breakfast. Picking up Cooper's lead, he headed out with him for a walk, hoping that some quiet time on the beach might help him come up with a solution.

There were a few people on the dog beach when Dan unclipped Cooper's leash, and the dog raced off across the sand. Dan wandered after him, still thinking of Livvy, so lost in thought he didn't notice Joe's approach.

'Penny for them?'

Dan looked up. 'Joe! Sorry, I didn't see you. I don't know if they're worth that,' he sighed.

'Want to talk about it? I liked that piece you sent me about shark nets, by the way.'

'Thanks. It was interesting to work on. I'll do one on the loggerhead turtles next.' He was aware he hadn't answered Joe's question. He wasn't sure Joe could help him, if anyone could help him.

'Fancy a beer? Gill's caught up with her Zonta group tonight, so there's nothing to rush home for.'

'Thanks, that'd be good.' Dan had nothing to rush home for, either. These days, Kim was either busy studying or out with her friends. It was a foretaste of what life would be like when she went off to uni, though, he wouldn't even have her company at mealtimes when that happened.

They managed to snag a table outside *The Grand*, the dogs happy to be provided with a bowl of water each, plus one of the doggy treats the hotel kept for them. Once they'd been served with a couple of the craft beers the hotel was fast becoming renowned for, brewed at a local brewery run by a couple of young men, Joe said, 'Sure you don't want to talk? You look as if you have something on your mind. Is there something worrying you about the council?'

'No.' Dan shook his head and took a sip of beer. 'Not about the council.' He hesitated for a moment. Perhaps it would be good to unburden himself to Joe. He had the feeling anything he said to him wouldn't go any further… and he did know Livvy. Maybe he could offer some advice.

'It's Livvy Grace,' he said. 'We were seeing each other. She blew me off because of my daughter. Long story, but she was counselling Kim, helping her get over her grief at her mother's death, didn't think she'd be willing to accept me forming another relationship, even though it's been four years since Cheryl died.'

'Hmm. Has something changed?'

'Kim. She's planning to attend uni in Sydney – that's another story – but when I said how I'd miss her, she told me I needed to find someone my own age. She even suggested Livvy.'

Joe chuckled. 'So, what's your problem?'

'Livvy. She avoids me, refuses to talk to me. I'm at my wit's end trying to figure out how I can approach her.' Dan picked up his beer again and took a long swig.

'I'm probably not the right person to ask.' Joe rubbed his chin. 'As I think I might have told you, I've never been able to understand women, but for what it's worth, from what I've gathered from being married to Barb for many years, and now living with Gill, women like a man to be upfront. All I can suggest is that you drop round to see her and tell her what your daughter said. What's the worst that can happen?'

'Hmm.' Dan wasn't sure it would work but as Joe said, what was the worst that could happen? She could turn him away, tell him she wasn't interested. Either way, he'd be no worse off, and at least he'd have tried.

# Fifty

Livvy had returned home from work on Thursday evening and was preparing for a quiet night at home after a busy day. She had caught Dan glancing her way several times as she moved around the wellness centre but had managed to retain her customary distance, despite wishing things could be different. Perhaps the following year when Kim started university, if Dan was still of the same mind, but it was a long time to wait.

When Dylan called, she had just come out of the shower and was pulling on the old tracksuit pants and long-sleeved tee-shirt she liked to wear around the house.

'I've been speaking to Gav again, Mum,' Dylan said, without any preamble. 'There's news.'

'Oh!' Livvy dropped into the nearest chair. Since Dylan had last reported on what Gavin had told him, she'd been unable to get the idea of Ingrid somehow conspiring to harm her out of her head. 'Wh… what did he say this time?' Surely he'd been wrong? Ingrid wouldn't… She couldn't… They'd worked together for years, socialised. She'd left her practice in her hands. And look what she did with it, a little voice reminded her. But this was different. This was criminal, or incitement to commit a criminal act – she hadn't watched all those crime shows on television for nothing.

'They were right. The youths confessed. Ingrid was behind it. She'd given them your address, paid them to create havoc. If found guilty, she'll be up for the same penalty as them – a maximum of eighteen months imprisonment. You'll be hearing from the police soon, but I wanted to give you a heads up. Pretend to be shocked when they tell you. Gav shouldn't have said anything, but he's a mate and he wanted you to know.'

'Thanks… I think. I still can't believe it of her. I thought we were friends.' Livvy still couldn't understand how Ingrid could have done this to her… 'And to think of her going to prison…'

'Mum! She stole your business, then tried to sue you.'

'I know, I know, but this… It's a lot to take in.'

'It seems you didn't really know her, what she's capable of.'

'No, I guess you're right.'

'Sorry, Mum. I have to go. Rory and I are going out to dinner to celebrate. He's finally off his crutches and walking with a stick. Your mate, Dan, has been a miracle worker. Would you like us to drop round later. You sound…'

*Not my mate.* But Livvy felt a warm glow to know how Dan had helped with Rory's recovery. 'No, I'll be fine. You say the police will be contacting me?'

'Someone will probably call round.'

'And I won't have to pretend to be shocked.' Livvy knew it would take her a long time to get over this latest act of treachery.

*

When there was a knock at the door later that evening, Livvy hurried to answer it, assuming it would be the police, come to tell her about Ingrid. She wondered if she'd already been arrested and charged.

It was a shock to see Dan standing there.

'Oh!' Livvy took a step back. 'What are you doing here?'

'I need to talk to you. Can I come in?'

Livvy glanced behind him, hoping to see a police car, an excuse to say he had to leave. But the road was empty. 'I suppose so.'

Livvy led the way into the kitchen, wishing she wasn't wearing her oldest clothes, her face devoid of makeup, her hair uncombed. 'What do you have to say that can't wait till we see each other at work?' she asked, aware she sounded abrupt, but she was still reeling from the shock of hearing about Ingrid.

'It would be difficult, since you seem to be avoiding me.'

Livvy blushed. *Of course he'd noticed she was steering clear of him.* A wave of guilt washed over her. 'I'm sorry. It just seemed easier. And I'm sorry if I sounded rude just now. I've had some bad news. Why don't you take a seat? Tea? Or something stronger?' A glass of wine might take the edge off her thoughts and help her hear whatever he had to say. It couldn't be good, and one piece of bad news was enough to handle.

'Wine would be good if you have any.'

'White okay?'

'Sure.'

Livvy busied herself pouring two glasses of wine, then joined him at the table. 'Well?'

'I'm sorry you've had bad news.' Dan paused, and Livvy hoped he wasn't going to ask her what it was. She couldn't bear to share with him how badly she'd been deceived. He continued, 'I won't add to it. What I have to say is good news. At least, I hope you'll think so. When I was speaking with Kim recently, she suggested I needed someone to keep me company when she goes off to university. She suggested you.'

Livvy stared at Dan, unable to believe her ears. *Kim had said that?*

'So it means that there's no barrier to us seeing each other… if you still want to.'

Livvy couldn't speak. She felt as if her world was turning upside down, first Ingrid, then this. She grasped hold of her glass.

'What do you say? Can we start again?'

Before Livvy could reply there was a loud knock on the door. It must be the police this time. 'I need to get that,' she said.

When Livvy opened the door, a tall dark-haired man in his forties was standing there. He was smartly dressed in a suit and tie and was holding up a badge, just like she'd seen on television.

'Mrs Grace, Olivia Grace?'

Livvy nodded.

'I'm Detective Sergeant Bruce Wilton. We spoke on the phone. May I come in?'

For the second time that evening, Livvy nodded and led a man through to the kitchen.

Dan was already on his feet. 'I should go,' he said. He'd obviously heard the detective identify himself.

The timing of the detective's arrival couldn't have been worse, but perhaps it had saved her from replying to Dan. 'I'll see you out,' she said to Dan, adding, 'Won't be a moment,' to the detective who was standing awkwardly in the middle of her kitchen.

At the door, Dan gave a wry smile. 'I was going to suggest we have dinner again,' he said. 'Would you…?'

'Okay.' Livvy just wanted him to leave, so she could deal with what she knew the detective was about to tell her.

'Great. Saturday? I'll text you.' Dan smiled again and walked away. Livvy shut the door behind him, then stood leaning against it, her eyes closed, focusing on her need to appear shocked at what she was about to hear.

'Sorry about that,' she said when she returned to the kitchen. 'My friend was about to leave. Do you have more news for me? Have you caught the youths who broke in?'

'You might want to sit down, Mrs…'

'Livvy's fine.'

'Livvy.'

Livvy took the seat she had only recently vacated, picked up her wine and took a sip, noticing as she did that Dan's wine glass was untouched. 'Why don't you take a seat too?'

The detective sat down, clasping his hands on the table. 'The short answer is yes, we caught them. But that's not all. They were encouraged to commit the break-in. The woman I asked you about… Ingrid Allen.'

Livvy gave what she hoped was a credible gasp and put a hand up to her mouth. 'Ingrid,' she said in a shocked voice. 'Ingrid was behind it?'

She must have sounded believable because the detective said, 'I'm afraid so. I know this must come as a shock to you as I understand you were previously business partners. As yet, we've been unable to discover her motivation, but we have yet to question her. Be assured we will make every effort to ensure the culprits are appropriately punished, though, of course, it will be up to the court to determine their sentences, assuming they're found guilty.'

Livvy nodded. So, there was a slight hope that Ingrid might not go to prison. Much as she wanted to see her punished, she hated the thought of her being incarcerated. Perhaps the indignity of being arrested, having to appear in court, the subsequent loss of her reputation would be punishment enough.

It wasn't till the detective left, that Livvy had time to remember about agreeing to have dinner with Dan and wondered if she'd made another mistake, even as she felt a bubble of excitement at the prospect.

# Fifty-one

Dan was feeling elated when he left Livvy's cottage. He'd done it. Livvy had agreed to have dinner with him. But his elation was tempered by the knowledge that she might only have done so under duress, eager to have him leave. He wondered what had happened after he did, what the detective had to tell her, no doubt news about the intruders who'd ransacked her cottage. He hoped they'd caught the culprits. Pelican Crossing didn't need youths like that creating fear and havoc.

When Dan arrived home, Kim was in the kitchen snacking on a sandwich she'd made with some leftover ham. Cooper, who had been sitting patiently at her side, waiting for a morsel to drop, padded towards him in the hope of a treat, or maybe a walk.

'Hi, Dad,' Kim said, her mouth full of bread and ham. 'Where were you?'

'Taking your advice. I've invited Livvy Grace to dinner.' He watched her expression, hoping she wasn't about to regret her suggestion.

'About time.' She continued munching. 'If you want to impress her, you should take her to *Crossings*. It's the best.'

'I am aware of that, but thanks.' Dan chuckled to himself. Who would have imagined he'd be getting dating advice from his eighteen-year-old daughter? *Crossings* was a good idea. He'd book a table, and… He stopped there, afraid of getting carried away. Livvy had agreed to dinner, nothing more. It was going to be up to him to ensure this dinner wasn't a one-off like the last one.

'Just saying,' Kim said, finishing her sandwich and taking her plate over to the sink. She yawned. 'I'm off to bed. See you at breakfast.'

'Thanks, honey, and thanks for your suggestion about Livvy. I thought…maybe…you wouldn't want me to form another relationship, I know how you still miss Mum.' He gave Kim a hug.

'I do, Dad. I guess I always will. I know you must miss her too. But I know you'd hate to be on your own when I leave, and I think Livvy is right for you. I'm glad you and she…' She grinned. 'Just don't let her take Mum's place.'

'No one could do that,' Dan said honestly. Livvy was a completely different person from Cheryl. It was one of the reasons he was so attracted to her, but there was no reason to tell Kim that.

*

By the time Saturday arrived, Dan was buzzing with nervous excitement. He planned to spend the day at home catching up with paperwork for his physio practice. Cooper, sensing his unease, refused to settle at his feet as usual, instead pacing around until Dan gave in and decided to take him for a walk.

Once outside in the fresh air, he felt better. He strode along Main Street on his way to the beach, Cooper padding along at his side, distracted from time to time by the sight of the pelicans who treated it as their personal thoroughfare. Finally, they reached the dog beach, and Cooper was able to run free.

Dan was enjoying the sound of the waves lapping on the shore, and the feeling of being at one with nature, when he saw old Agnes coming towards him. His heart sank, as her dog joined Cooper to play in the surf.

'Isn't it a lovely day?' she said as she drew close, her long skirt trailing in the shallow water as always and her white hair blowing in the breeze.

'It is.' Hopefully, she'd walk on.

'How's your daughter? She'll be off to university soon.'

'Next year. Kim's good.'

'It's a difficult time, when the young leave the nest, for humans as well as other creatures. Did you make those changes I suggested? Don't leave it too long.' She nodded.

How did she know? Did the woman have some sixth sense? Then he remembered her telling him he needed to change, not stand still. 'I'll be fine,' he said. He could manage his life without her help. He was seeing Livvy tonight for what he hoped would be the beginning of a major change in his life.

'I hope so. Just be sure you don't mess things up. We women can be fragile creatures.' She chuckled. 'Lady!' she called, and her dog came running up, Cooper following.

Dan stared after the old woman and her dog as they made their way back along the beach. He had no idea what she was talking about. He'd waited so long for this date with Livvy. There was no way he'd do anything to spoil their evening together, the evening he hoped would be the first of many.

When Dan arrived home, there were textbooks strewn around the living room and Kim and Jay were in the kitchen making popcorn. 'Just taking a break, Dad,' Kim said. Both she and Jay were drinking from cans of Coke. 'We thought we might watch a movie for a while, before Jay goes home. We have been studying,' she added.

'Okay.' Dan ruffled her hair, and as she slid out of his reach, he reflected how he wouldn't be able to do that for much longer. It was a sobering thought. Giving Cooper a treat and filling the dog's bowl with water he made his way to the study, hoping to finish what he'd started earlier, before he took Cooper to the beach.

'Looking sharp, Dad. You'll blow her away,' Kim said when she popped her head into his bedroom to see him staring at his reflection in the mirror. He'd been wondering if he'd overdone it. He was wearing his green and white shirt again, this time with a pair of grey pants and had knotted a dark green sweater around his shoulders.

'You think?'

'Really, and…' She came closer and sniffed. 'Is that the cologne I gave you for Christmas, the one that's been sitting there unopened?'

'It may be.' Dan had caught sight of the bottle when he was brushing his hair and thought, *why not?* 'It's not too much?'

'It's perfect. Have a great evening.'

'What are *you* doing?' He noticed Kim was dressed up too, in the off-the-shoulder dress she'd worn when he took her to *Crossings* on her birthday, even though it was a cool evening.

'It's Clover's party. I did tell you. Her eighteenth. Her mum and dad have gone away for the weekend, so we'll have the house to ourselves.'

'Hmm.' He had a vague recollection of her mentioning the party but not that Clover's parents would be gone. Now he wished he'd paid more attention. But what difference would it have made? Kim would have been quick to remind him she was old enough to make her own decisions and could take care of herself. 'Enjoy yourself, sweetheart, and don't be too late home.'

Kim grimaced, then grinned. 'You too, Dad.'

'Cheeky!' Dan pretended to throw a punch at her, and she stepped away, laughing.

*

Over the past two days, Livvy had gradually come to grips with the fact that Ingrid had been behind the intruders who broke into her home. The police had been back in touch to inform her that the culprits had been charged and would appear in the magistrate's court in the following week, and it had made the front page of *The Echo* with the headline, *Local woman and youths charged with home invasion.*

Now, she felt able to put it all behind her. Despite her initial reservations, she was looking forward to seeing Dan this evening and to having dinner at *Crossings*. When she received his text to say he'd booked a table at her favourite restaurant, her heart had skipped a beat, and she determined that this time, she'd say nothing to spoil it. She hadn't told anyone about it but knew that by next day, half of Pelican Crossing would know, and she was okay with that, she told herself. There was no reason to keep it secret.

But as the time for Dan to arrive grew closer, the butterflies in Livvy's stomach seemed to be dancing the tango. There was a knock on the door. She took a deep breath, gave one last glance in the hall mirror to check her hair and makeup, and opened the door.

'Hi, Livvy.' Dan sounded more subdued than usual. 'You're looking lovely tonight.'

'Thanks.' She was glad she'd chosen to wear the blue dress, the one Erica said matched her eyes and in which she always felt good. Dan looked great too, in a green and white shirt that matched *his* eyes. 'You look good too.'

They smiled at each other, lost in mutual admiration, until Dan said, 'Ready to go?'

When they walked into the restaurant, they were met by the hum of voices and an enticing aroma of cooking. They were greeted by a smart woman wearing black, shown to a table at one side of the restaurant, and handed menus. Livvy glanced around, reminded of the last time she'd been here, at the dinner before the sports awards. It had been the evening when she had felt the first stirrings of warm feelings for Dan. Then she had spoiled everything. She didn't intend to do that again. This time, there was no need to worry about his daughter's feelings. It was Kim who'd suggested they get together. She had no need to worry what her children would think. She knew both Nancy and Dylan would be delighted if she found a special person to spend the rest of her life with.

But she was getting ahead of herself. This was only dinner, one dinner. But they weren't children. They both knew the implications of deciding to start seeing each other again. Livvy's heart raced at the possibility of recapturing those remembered moments of intimacy.

'Hmm,' Dan said, studying the menu. 'What to have? It all looks delicious.'

Livvy almost said, *You look delicious*. 'I don't care,' she said instead. 'Whatever we have, I know it'll be amazing.'

# Fifty-two

Livvy was enveloped in a warm glow. She felt she was walking on air. She couldn't believe it had only been four weeks ago that she and Dan had enjoyed dinner together at *Crossings*, a dinner that had changed her life.

Tonight, they were going to celebrate with dinner in her cottage, and Livvy had made up her bed with the new sheets and doona cover, white with a design of banksia leaves and blooms, and set a pair of fresh towels in the ensuite in anticipation of the evening ahead.

Over the past four weeks, she'd managed to put the home invasion and Ingrid's part in it to the back of her mind. She'd learned that while all four had been convicted, the three youths had been remanded in custody and Ingrid had been released on bail. The associated publicity had resulted in the collapse of her practice, which meant Livvy's had become busier. And, although the medical centre had begged her to return, she preferred to remain at the wellness centre, not least because she could see Dan every day.

For the past few days, she'd pored over her cookbooks, determined to impress Dan and had finally decided on a simple meal of garlic Dijon pork tenderloin with crispy potatoes and green beans which could all be cooked in the same dish. For the sweet, she planned a light three ingredient dessert with bananas, frozen berries and Greek yoghurt, which she'd found on Facebook.

Livvy hummed to herself as she mixed the ingredients for the dessert before popping the finished dish into the freezer. A couple of hours there, and it would have the consistency of ice cream, a perfect finish to the meal before… Her heart skipped a beat at the prospect of what would follow.

She and Dan had dined at the yacht club a few times, so their relationship was no longer a secret and both Erica and Gill had echoed 'About time!' which was exactly what Dan said had been Kim's comment. Even the other therapists in the wellness centre had approved, which was a relief to Livvy who hadn't been sure about what their reaction might be. Katrina's comment of, 'Dan's a good man and deserves someone like you,' had sealed Livvy's happiness.

The dessert safely in the freezer and the table set with a candle in the middle ready to be lit when they sat down, Livvy set about preparing the main course. When it was all ready to go into the oven, Livvy decided it was time to shower and change. The meal would take less than half an hour to cook, just enough time for her and Dan to enjoy a glass of wine and have a cuddle.

Dressed in what Livvy now considered to be her lucky blue dress, she carefully applied her makeup and brushed her hair, before spraying herself with the perfume Dan had told her he liked. Then she fixed the blue and gold earrings Nancy had given her for Christmas into her ears and checked her appearance in the full-length mirror, trying to see herself through Dan's eyes.

She was interrupted by a knock on the door and hurried to answer it.

'Happy anniversary, sweetheart,' Dan said, pulling Livvy into his arms and lifting her feet off the floor. 'You're looking even lovelier than usual, and you smell good enough to eat.'

'Put me down.' Livvy protested, but she enjoyed feeling his strong arms around her.

'Not before…' Dan allowed her feet to touch the floor again as, crushing her to him, his lips met hers in a searing kiss.

Livvy giggled like a schoolgirl when Dan finally released her. He picked up the bottle which he must have placed on the step earlier. I thought we deserved something special tonight,' he said, handing her the bottle of Moët and Chandon Imperial Brut.

'Wow!'

'Only the best for you.' Dan followed Livvy into the kitchen where she took a pair of champagne flutes from the cupboard. While he opened the bottle, she slipped their meal into the oven, setting the timer for fifteen minutes, at which time she'd add the green beans.

Livvy glanced across the kitchen to where Dan was still fussing with the champagne cork, He was looking particularly handsome tonight, Livvy thought, in a pink linen shirt with a pair of khaki cargo pants, and when she was in his arms, she'd detected the faint scent of the musky cologne he'd worn on their dinner date four weeks earlier.

Livvy counted her blessings and gave thanks to whatever fate had sent this man into her life, recognising the hand Ingrid had inadvertently played in it. She hoped her former partner would avoid prison time, though that seemed unlikely.

'To us.' Dan held up his glass to clink with Livvy's.

'To us,' she repeated, her heart bursting with happiness.

After the meal, which Dan praised effusively, they sat together on Livvy's sofa, Dan's arm around her shoulders. When they had finished the last dregs of champagne, Dan took Livvy's empty glass, placed it beside his on the coffee table and pulled her into an embrace so tight, it took her breath away.

'I think we've waited long enough, don't you?' he said, his lips grazing hers and sending ripples of desire through her.

Too overcome to speak, Livvy merely nodded. She took his hand and led him into her bedroom where the candle she'd lit there earlier had released its delicate fragrance, bathing the room in a romantic haze.

# Fifty-three

Dan opened his eyes and looked at the face on the pillow beside him. He still found it difficult to believe how his dreams had come true, the dreams he'd had ever since Livvy Grace walked into his wellness centre, even before he'd rid himself of his suspicions about her past. He stretched luxuriously and kissed her bare shoulder. The sun was shining through the shutters. It would be perfect out on the water, an ideal day to go sailing. He couldn't wait.

When Livvy finally opened her eyes and smiled at him, Dan had already made plans for their day. 'Good morning, beautiful,' he said, pulling her into his arms, his lips slowly descending to meet hers. It was some time before they spoke.

'How would you feel about going sailing today?' Dan asked, Livvy still in his arms.

'Mmm. Sounds wonderful.' Livvy snuggled closer. 'I guess we should get up. I can make breakfast.'

'Sounds like a plan.' Dan kissed her once more, before sliding out of bed and into the shower.

When Dan walked into the kitchen, he was met by the aromas of coffee and bacon. 'You sure know the way to a man's heart,' he said, wrapping his arms around Livvy who was standing at the stove, 'and I don't just mean your cooking.'

Livvy giggled and turned round to give him a kiss. 'Help yourself to coffee. I prefer herbal tea in the morning, but I know you're a coffee drinker.'

'Thanks.' Dan found a mug in the cupboard and poured himself a brew.

Over breakfast, they talked about how they'd spend their day. Livvy wanted to know more about Dan's yacht, and he was happy to share the details, thrilled that she'd be joining him on it at last.

They had almost finished eating when Livvy said, 'Kim's exams start soon, don't they? How does she feel about them?'

'Confident.'

'You don't sound happy.'

'No. She's so confident she's only applied for one university – Sydney.'

'And that doesn't please you?'

'How could it? It's so far away. She won't be able to come home for weekends. And to cap it all, she plans to stay with Cheryl's sister and her husband.'

'And that's bad?'

'The worst. We don't get on, never have. Cheryl's family never approved of me, and her husband... Darryl will do his best to turn Kim against me. It's a disaster.' Dan was becoming more and more enraged as he spoke, and Livvy's eyes widened. 'I'm sorry. You didn't need to hear all that.'

'You need to calm down, Dan. And remember, as I think I may have said before, that Kim is old enough to make her own decisions. I'm sure she loves you too much to be swayed by what anyone else might tell her. You should...'

A burst of anger shot up, forcing Dan to say, 'Don't tell me what to do, that's what...' He stopped short, suddenly realising what he was about to say – 'That's what Cheryl used to do.' It hadn't been until she became sick, when her demands, her criticisms, and insistence she get her way ceased, when she became weaker, grateful for his help and easier to live with. 'I'm sorry,' he said, pushing a hand through his hair. 'Brought back memories.'

'Want to talk about it?' Livvy asked gently, her expression creasing into one of concern.

'No.' Dan shook his head. He wasn't prepared for Livvy to put on her counselling hat. He tensed up, aware of distancing himself from Livvy. It was as if he'd pulled up an imaginary drawbridge to protect his emotions. It was something he used to do… when Cheryl annoyed him. He thought those days were long gone. He was a different person now. But Livvy's words had hit one of his hot buttons, making him see red and reminding him of a time he'd prefer to forget.

Livvy didn't say any more, but with Dan's outburst, the mood in the room had changed.

'I should get back and feed Cooper,' he said. Until now, he'd been so encased in a glow of happiness he hadn't considered Cooper, assuming Kim would make sure he had food and water. But what if she hadn't? And it was the excuse he needed to give him time to himself, time to…

'Are we still…' Livvy began, then clearly seeing his expression, fell silent again. 'I'll see you out.'

At the door, Dan kissed Livvy, but his mind was elsewhere, wondering how he could have managed to ruin an otherwise perfect morning.

*

Livvy's heart dropped, the bubble of happiness she'd wakened with suddenly burst. One minute they'd been planning a day's sailing, and the next… She'd only said… Dan was right when he accused her of telling him what to do, but she'd only said what any good friend would have. Kim was eighteen. It was her life. She was old enough to make her own decisions. If only Livvy had kept her mouth shut, but she'd thought she was helping. It was what she did.

Livvy turned back into the house, rinsed the breakfast dishes and put them in the dishwasher, then headed for the bedroom. Once there, where less than an hour ago, she and Dan had made passionate love, the sight of the rumpled bedclothes brought tears to her eyes.

Everything had been so perfect, too perfect. She should have known it wouldn't last, but everyone had been so pleased, had said they were an ideal couple. Well, they'd been wrong.

There was a knock on the door. Livvy brushed way her tears and rushed to answer it, sure it was Dan returning to take her sailing after all.

But when the door swung open, Livvy's face fell at the sight of Erica standing there with her little dog, Bandit.

'We've just been for a walk on the beach, and I thought I might bum a cup of tea. Jamie has gone down to the harbour for a couple of hours. You are alone?' She peered behind Livvy.

'Totally. Come in.'

'Are you okay?' Erica asked, as she followed Livvy inside. 'You don't sound as cheerful as you've been lately. Is everything okay between you and Dan?'

'No, not really.'

Over cups of Livvy's favourite lemon and ginger tea, Erica managed to persuade Livvy to reveal what had happened with Dan. 'You need to go and talk with him,' she said.

'I can't, Erica. You didn't see his expression. It was as if a shutter came down, as if he retreated to a dark place where I couldn't follow.'

'Men!' Erica said. 'You weren't here when Jamie and I got together, but there was a time when it looked as if we'd break up. He actually stormed off when we were spending a romantic evening on the beach, left me sitting there in the dark.'

'What did you do?'

'Well, eventually, I took back his blanket – the one we'd been sitting on – and we both apologised. It always helps to apologise, even if you're not the one in the wrong. Most men don't like to be wrong, something about the male ego.'

They both laughed. But Livvy didn't see how it could help her. She didn't have the excuse of returning a blanket to give her a reason to go round to Dan's. Kim would be there, and he'd probably have gone sailing. She shook her head. She'd have to wait till next day, when they'd both be at the wellness centre. Maybe she could make some excuse to go to his suite, but she never had before. And if it didn't work… perhaps she'd accept the offer to return to the medical centre after all. She didn't know if she could live with the risk of bumping into him every day, after all they'd been to each other.

After Erica had left, Livvy was restless. She had a whole day to fill, a day which she'd expected to spend with Dan. Taking her hat from its hook behind the door, and slipping her feet into her sandals, Livvy headed for the place to which she always took her troubles. She went across the road and down to the beach, where she slipped off her sandals and made her way to the edge of the ocean.

# Fifty-four

Dan was feeding Cooper when Kim walked into the kitchen, her hair tousled, her eyes still heavy with sleep.

'When did you get home, Dad? I didn't see your car when I got back.' She yawned.

Dan didn't reply. He had no intention of telling his daughter he'd spent the night at Livvy's, then messed up. He continued to pour food into Cooper's food bowl, then filled the other one with water. He knew if he stayed here, Kim would wheedle it out of him, and he didn't need one more female giving him advice. 'I plan to spend the day sailing. You?'

'Studying.' She grimaced. 'A few of us are going to go over some maths problems together. Not my favourite way to spend a Sunday.'

'You'll do well,' he said, reminded of Livvy's words. She was right. Kim was a sensible kid – not such a kid anymore. 'Don't overdo it. Take some time out too.'

'We plan to. There's going to be a bonfire on the beach tonight, cooking sausages and marshmallows. We'll be done studying by then.' She grinned.

Cooper finished his breakfast and padded over to put one paw on Dan's leg and looked up at him, begging for a walk.

'Okay, Cooper,' he said. Now Livvy wouldn't be going sailing with him, he was in no hurry. But as he made his way to the dog beach, he found himself wondering how he had managed to sabotage the relationship which had been going so well.

Dan was glad there was no one he knew on the beach today. He wasn't in the mood for conversation. He walked the length of the beach, with Cooper running back and forth with a stick he'd found for Dan to throw. Finally, even the dog had had enough, and they turned to make their way home.

They were walking past the harbour, Cooper pulling on his leash at the sight of a pair of pelicans when Jamie hailed Dan. 'Not out sailing on this beautiful day? I thought you and Livvy might be…' his voice trailed off as he took in Dan's closed expression. 'Something wrong?'

'I screwed up.' Dan didn't know where the words had come from. He hadn't intended to say anything.

'Want to talk about it?' Jamie asked, echoing Livvy's words earlier.

This time, Dan remained calm. 'Wouldn't do any good. I think I've managed to ruin what Livvy and I had together. I let my temper get the better of me and said things I shouldn't. She's never going to forgive me.' He shook his head and stared down to where Cooper was sniffing at a scrap of fish someone had dropped on the road.

'Never's a long time, mate. It couldn't have been that bad.'

'Maybe, maybe not. I let something Livvy said get to me, hit one of my hot buttons, then I walked out on her. We were going to spend the day sailing. Everything was going so well, and I had to go and ruin it.' He sighed.

'It happens. Happened to Erica and me too. Not exactly the same, but I did go off and leave her… on the beach.' Jamie gazed into space as if reliving the incident.

'What happened then? How did you get back together?'

'Took weeks. She went over to Perth. I thought I'd lost her. I wouldn't like to go through that again. It was lucky she still had a blanket belonging to me. She brought it back and I opened the door before she could run away. You need to talk to her, apologise, put things straight, before it's too late.'

Dan had no idea what Jamie was talking about with a trip to Perth and a blanket, but one thing hit home, the advice that he should talk to Livvy… maybe tomorrow, at the wellness centre?

When he and Cooper arrived home, it was to find a group of teenagers around the dining room table and music blaring out from Kim's iPad. He shook his head, amazed they could study in such a clamour.

'Thought you were going sailing, Dad,' Kim said.

'I am. Took Cooper for a walk first.'

Dan was still wearing the outfit he'd worn to dinner the previous evening. He'd intended to come home to change before heading to the marina. Now he'd lost the urge to go sailing, the prospect of being out on the ocean on his own again holding no appeal. He quickly changed into a pair of jeans and a tee-shirt, pulled on a woollen shirt, grabbed a banana, and headed out. He'd go back and talk with Livvy today, while Jamie's words were fresh in his mind.

On the way to Livvy's cottage, Dan prepared what he was going to say. He'd apologise for losing his temper, try to make amends, and hope she'd forgive him.

When he got out of his car outside Livvy's cottage, he took a deep breath and walked up to the door.

There was no one home. Dan stared around for a few moments, then crossed the road and gazed down towards the beach where a lone figure was standing by the edge of the water, the early afternoon sun forming a halo around her blonde hair. His heart leapt.

*

'I thought I'd find you here.'

Livvy turned, shocked to see Dan. She'd been thinking about him, trying to figure out how to approach him next day and what to say, what might make things better between them. For a moment she wasn't sure if he was really there or if he was a figment of her overactive imagination. Then he smiled, a tentative smile as if he didn't know how she was going to react, and she knew this wasn't a dream.

Mindful of Erica's advice, Livvy didn't wait for him to speak again. 'I didn't expect to see you again after this morning. I'm sorry if I came across too strong. I was only trying to help. Sometimes, I… it's a failing of mine.'

'*I'm* sorry. I over-reacted. Can you forgive me? I promise never to do anything like that again. I love you, Livvy, and I couldn't bear it if we fell out over my stupidly losing my temper because something you said reminded me of a time I'd rather forget.'

Livvy's heart missed a beat. Had Dan said he loved her? It was a dream come true. Nothing else mattered. 'I love you too,' she said.

Before Livvy knew what was happening, Dan swept her into his arms. She thought she was going to explode with happiness as a wave of passion and love flowed between them, an emotion greater than anything she'd experienced before.

Livvy clung to Dan as his lips found hers again and again till they finally parted, her heart still racing.

They stood together at the edge of the ocean staring out to sea, Dan behind Livvy, his arms locked around her waist, the musky scent of him assaulting her senses and sending shivers down her spine.

'I love watching the ocean,' Livvy murmured, 'how each new wave breaks on the shore, then ebbs. Sometimes I think life is like the ocean. It changes like the waves. Each wave bringing something different, some good, some not so good, storms then periods of calm. It's been a stormy year, for me, one thing after another. But it's ended well. She smiled up at Dan.

'It hasn't ended. This is just the beginning for us, a new wave of change. And who knows what it might bring.

'Might it bring a day of sailing?' Livvy asked.

Dan dropped a kiss on her head. 'I thought you'd never ask.'

The End

If you've enjoyed Livvy and Dan's story, I'd love if you could leave a review on Amazon and/or Goodreads. A few words will suffice, no need for a lengthy review. It will mean a lot to me and help other readers find my books.

I'm thrilled so many of my readers are enjoying this series set in Pelican Crossing and are making friends with my characters.

What's next?

Do you want to know about the family rift which Lou refers to? The next book in the series, **A Family for Christmas in Pelican Crossing,** is Lou's story.

For *Lou Chalmers, Books and Coffee* in Pelican Crossing isn't just a bookshop and café, it's the realisation of a dream. But with her sixty-fifth birthday approaching, she's beginning to feel the weight of time and harbours regrets over her estranged relationship with her sister. Facing yet another lonely Christmas, she wonders if it's time to try and reconnect.

When retired widower *Blair Stevens* leaves Tasmania to join his daughter in Pelican Crossing, he questions if he's made the right decision. But as he delves into the town's history and starts writing the novel he's always wanted to, he becomes engrossed in his new life.

When an event at Lou's bookshop brings the two together, they strike up an unlikely friendship. As Blair helps Lou search for her long-lost sister, their connection deepens in a way neither of them anticipated. But as fate pushes them towards each other, will their friendship blossom into something more?

A heartwarming story of two strangers who find unexpected companionship in this small town on the Queensland coast.

You can order here https://mybook.to/AFamilyinPC

# From the Author

Dear Reader,

First, I'd like to thank you for choosing to read *Waves of Change in Pelican Crossing*. I hope you've enjoyed visiting Pelican Crossing as much as I've enjoyed creating it.

Like all my other books, although it is part of a series, it can be read as a standalone.

If you'd like to stay up to date with my new releases and special offers you can sign up to my reader's group.

You can sign up here

https://maggiechristensenauthor.com/subscribe/

I'll never share your email address, and you can unsubscribe at any time. You can also contact me via Facebook, Twitter or by email. I love hearing from my readers and will always reply.

Thanks again.

# Acknowledgements

As always, this book could not have been written without the help and advice of a number of people.

Firstly, my husband Jim for listening to my plotlines without complaint, for his patience and insights as I discuss my characters and storyline with him, for his patience and help with difficult passages and advice on my male dialogue, and for being there when I need him.

John Hudspith, editor extraordinaire for his ideas, suggestions, encouragement and attention to detail, and for helping me make this book better.

Jane Dixon-Smith for her patience and for working her magic on my beautiful cover and interior.

My thanks also to early readers of this book –Maggie, Helen and Anne for their helpful comments and advice, and to fellow writer and vet, Bernadette Rowley, for ensuring I had accurate information about veterinary practice. Any mistakes are my own.

And to all of my readers, reviewers and bloggers. Your support and comments make it all worthwhile.

# About the Author

After a career in education, Maggie Christensen began writing contemporary women's fiction portraying mature women facing life-changing situations, and historical fiction set in her native Scotland. Her travels inspire her writing, be it her trips to visit family in Scotland, in Oregon, USA or her home on Queensland's beautiful Sunshine Coast. Maggie writes of mature heroines coming to terms with changes in their lives and the heroes worthy of them. Maggie has been called *the queen of mature age fiction* and her writing has been described by one reviewer as *like a nice warm cup of tea. It is warm, nourishing, comforting and embracing.*

From the small town in Scotland where she grew up, Maggie was lured to Australia by the call to 'Come and teach in the sun'. Once there, she worked as a primary school teacher, university lecturer and in educational management. Now living with her husband of over thirty years on Queensland's Sunshine Coast, she loves walking on the deserted beach in the early mornings and having coffee by the river on weekends. Her days are spent surrounded by books, either reading or writing them – her idea of heaven!

Maggie can be found on Facebook, Twitter, Bluesky,Goodreads, Instagram, Bookbub or on her website.

https://www.facebook.com/maggiechristensenauthor
https://twitter.com/MaggieChriste33
https://www.goodreads.com/author/show/8120020.Maggie_Christensen
https://www.instagram.com/maggiechriste33/
https://www.bookbub.com/profile/maggie-christensen
https://bsky.app/profile/maggiechriste33.bsky.social
https://maggiechristensenauthor.com/